THE HOUSE ON WOODY Creek Lane

CLAUDINE MARCIN

MMAD Tales

MMAD Tales
PO Box 267
Abingdon, MD 21017
mmadtales@gmail.com
https://mmad-tales.square.site/

Book Cover by Creative Paramita
Illustrations by Claudine Marcin
First Edition, August 2023

ISBN: 979-8-9887359-0-8 (paperback)
ISBN: 979-8-9887359-1-5 (hardcover)
ISBN: 979-8-9887359-2-2 (e-book)

Here's to haunted houses and all those that believe in them.

The light cried out, "It's him! It's him!"
And the shade howled back, "Let me in! Let me in!"

Prologue

There are no monsters under the bed.

There's no such thing as the boogeyman.

Bigfoot isn't real.

Mothers tell their frightened children all sorts of things to help them sleep at night. James Hobart's mother was no different. So, when she told him that nothing he saw in *the light* could harm him, he believed that too.

But mothers don't always know what's hiding in the shadows.

He would have to learn that lesson all on his own.

Chapter 1

O n an early summer morning in 2001, James Mason Hobart stood on the lawn outside his family's home, his nose tickling with each breath at the sulfuric perfume still lingering in the air. Singed strips of colorful paper and spent matches littered the street in a leftover display of patriotism.

The weather forecast for the day predicted 85 degrees with 35% humidity. On a day like this, he would spend a couple of hours playing sharks and minnows at the neighborhood pool, followed by nine innings at the ball field where he would scoop up grounders like a young Brooks Robinson. After dinner, he would hunch over his Xbox controller for some Madden football. Then at sunset, he and his friends would reconvene for hide-n-seek until their mothers called them home.

It would be the perfect day. But he wouldn't be here to enjoy it.

"Come on, Slugger," his father called out.

Jimmy smiled, grabbed the handle of his SpongeBob SquarePants suitcase, and started walking toward the silver Taurus parked in the driveway where his parents and sister were waiting. The back of the car was packed to the ceiling with pillows, snacks, and gifts, leaving just enough room for his younger sister to climb in behind the passenger seat. Then the elder Hobart leaned through the back door and buckled the belt across her lap.

He was the tallest of all the fathers on their block and the first to lend a hand when needed. Handsome in a rugged sort of way, Benjamin Hobart's skin was leathered from hours of long days spent outside—and his muscles hardened by the work that went with it. He brushed his daughter's auburn curls aside and kissed her on the cheek. "Mind your mother and brother, Peach. I don't want to hear anything different, understand?"

"Yes, Daddy," she said.

Then he took the suitcase from his son and touched his finger to the boy's chest. "Remember what I told you? Look out for your mother and sister."

"Yes, sir," Jimmy nodded.

"Now, give your old man a hug."

Jimmy was the mirror image of his father—or so he'd been told. Over his lifetime, he'd aspire to live up to what *he* saw in his dad rather than try to be the reflection others saw. He held his father around the waist until he felt a kiss on his head and a pat on his back. Then he hopped into the co-pilot's seat, pulled the safety belt across his chest, and fastened the metal latch into the buckle.

"I wish you were coming with us," his mother said to her husband.

"Next time."

As his parents embraced and kissed, enveloped in a halo of light like a scene from one of the old, colorized movies, Jimmy closed the car door and found the road atlas tucked under the seat. He flipped through the pages until he found Virginia then searched for the highway they would take south, like his father had taught him.

When he'd found the route, the driver's side door opened, and his mother got in. She was effortlessly beautiful, with her henna locks pulled back into a messy ponytail, no makeup, and smelling of Noxzema and baby lotion.

When the car engine started, he rolled the window down and leaned out as far as the seatbelt would allow. "Bye, Dad. See you in two weeks."

The car slipped into gear and they were on their way from the suburbs to a place called Moultrie, Georgia, where he would meet his mother's mother for the first time. He didn't know until recently that he had another grandmother outside of his Grandma Lou—that was short for Louise he learned when was older.

Once on the highway, Jimmy and his younger sister made faces at truck drivers and pumped their arms until the mustachioed men wearing grease-stained baseball caps blew their air horns. Then they cheered and laughed until the next 18-wheeler passed by, and they started their shenanigans all over again. Every couple of hours, the family stopped at places called Stucky's or South of the Boarder to eat or shop for souvenirs. Or they stretched their legs at highway rest stops and used the bathrooms.

Finally, 10 hours later, they arrived on a quiet street lined with willows and oaks, their branches so long and trunks so tall they may have been the first trees to ever grow in the South. After a few turns, the car approached a one-story house with white siding and black shutters. There was no driveway like at his home, so his mother stopped next to the curb and turned off the engine.

The door to the house opened and an older woman stepped out onto the concrete porch, shading the sun from her eyes with one hand as she stared across the lawn. She had short silver hair, wore cat eye-shaped glasses, and a pink dress that stopped just across her knees.

Jimmy felt butterflies in his stomach for the first time as he stared out the window at this stranger. Back home it was supper time. His friends were sitting at their dining room tables, smelling of sweat and chlorine, waiting for the sun to set so the neighborhood games could begin. From the other side of the car, the door opened.

His mother called out, "Hi, Mama," as she slammed the door closed and ran around the front of the car and toward the house.

The woman on the porch smiled, the skin on her arm flapping back and forth as she waved vigorously at her daughter.

A wiry man with short red hair stepped out of the house, followed by an even taller man with blonde hair and wearing a white T-shirt that was pulled tight around his round belly. Jimmy's mother met them on the lawn and gave them each a hug. Then she ran up to the porch and embraced her mother, rocking back and forth like two wise old trees in a windstorm.

In the middle of the reunion, Jimmy's view was suddenly blocked by the two men that were now approaching the car. He scooted away from the window as the red-haired man opened the passenger door.

"You must be Jimmy," he said, reaching out his hand. "I'm your Uncle Steve."

Jimmy had seen his father shake hands with other men more times than he could count so he knew what to do. "Please to meet you, sir."

"And who's this sweetheart?" he said, smiling as he ducked his head and peeked into the back seat. "You must be Elizabeth."

She giggled and hid her face in her hands.

Jimmy unbuckled his seatbelt, climbed out of the car, then opened the back door and helped his sister so she could run after their mother. By then, the blonde-haired man was at the car.

"Well look at you," he said, pushing his glasses up higher on the bridge of his nose. He didn't stick his hand out for a shake though. He just stood there with his hands on his hips. "I'm your Uncle Larry. Bet you don't remember me."

"No, sir," Jimmy answered.

"Well, we best get these bags into the house. You're one of the men so you can help—ain't that right?"

Jimmy nodded and followed him to the back of the car while Uncle Steve went around to the driver's side and popped the trunk. Uncle Larry gave him one of the smaller bags then he and Uncle Steve handled the rest.

Elizabeth was on the porch by then, squirming in the old woman's arms and enduring rapid-fire grandma kisses as Jimmy followed slowly behind his uncles. He'd never seen anything like it. And when he finally made it to the steps, he stood the rolling bag up and hoped she was out of ammo before it was his turn.

"Well, aren't you a handsome boy?" the silver-haired woman said as she put Elizabeth down. Then she licked her red-stained lips as if she were reloading and spread her arms. "Come up here and give your Grandma June a hug."

He let go of the suitcase handle and climbed the two steps, ready for his turn in front of the firing squad as she puckered up. He grimaced and hugged her plump middle. She smelled like the bakery back home after they'd just put out a fresh pallet of buttermilk biscuits. He closed his eyes and breathed her in, suddenly not minding the feel of her lips on his cheeks. He lost count of the exact number of kisses, but it was a lot.

She sighed and straightened her back. "Supper's ready." Then Grandma June gave him one final kiss on his forehead. "Let's go inside."

"I hope ya'll are hungry," Uncle Larry said.

Jimmy wiped his cheeks, retrieved his suitcase from the lawn, and pulled it up the steps. The front room of the three-bedroom rancher smelled like heaven—if angels cooked fried food. He parked his bag against the wall with the others then went into the dining room where the table held heaping mounds of fried chicken, mashed potatoes with gravy, green beans, fried okra, biscuits—

"Wash up first," his grandmother scolded.

He followed her into the kitchen, and she helped him reach the faucet. When his hands were clean, he returned to the dining room and waited for the others before starting. Uncle Steve was back first. He poured Jimmy a glass of the sweetest iced tea he'd ever had and then sat beside him.

One by one, the table filled up. Then they began passing the platters and bowls, scooping food onto their plates. While they ate, his uncles entertained them with stories of their childhood. That's when Jimmy learned his mother was somewhat of a tomboy when she was his age.

"She didn't take any guff off us boys," Uncle Steve said.

Jimmy had never heard that word before, but he had an idea what 'guff' meant. And if he was right, his mother still didn't take any 'guff'—not from anyone.

After dinner and more stories, Uncle Steve said goodnight but promised to return in the morning with his family. It was dark by then—time for hide-n-seek back home. Elizabeth had already fallen asleep on their mother's lap while Jimmy fought the urge to join her.

Uncle Larry helped them get settled in the guest bedroom, which was more of a sewing room than a place for sleeping—unless you counted the couch. Jimmy wondered how they would all fit until his uncle removed the cushions and pulled—

Suddenly the couch had converted into a bed, already made up with sheets and a colorful quilt.

"I hope ya'll don't mind sharing," Uncle Larry said with a wink as he tossed their pillows onto the mattress.

"Think of it as camping," his mother said as she laid Elizabeth on the bed.

"Uncle Larry," Jimmy said, feeling bolder now that they'd gotten to know each other. "Have we met before?"

"That's right. I was passing through Virginia."

"I'm sorry I don't remember you."

"Well, you were about this big at the time," he said, holding his hands about two feet apart. "I don't expect you remember much from back then."

"No, sir," Jimmy said with a laugh.

"I'll tell you more stories tomorrow. Now it's time for bed." Then to his sister, he said, "I'll be in the next room if you need anything."

"You live here too?" Jimmy asked.

"That's right. I'll be right here in the morning when you get up."

**

Later in the quiet, Jimmy lay on one edge of the lumpy hide-a-bed with his eyes closed, listening to the wind blowing through trees. The old rafters *cracked* and *popped*, boughs reached out their tentacle fingers and scraped the window glass, and the wood siding groaned. The old house sounded different than his ... It sounded alive. And no amount of exhaustion would allow sleep to come for an out-of-place child.

And then he heard something else ... Like one of his friends trying to get his attention in class without alerting their teacher.

He opened his eyes and turned toward his mother on the other side of the bed. She was asleep, her hands tucked under her pillow. In between them was Elizabeth, cuddled close to their mother and almost completely hidden beneath the blanket except for her red curls. Then he heard it again.

"Psst."

He lifted his head to look over his mother's shoulder and saw a man, leaning against the doorframe, backlit by the hallway light. He thought of everyone he had met that evening—Uncle Larry, Uncle Steve, Grandma June. But he didn't recognize this man—and Jimmy had a good memory.

This man was older than his uncles and shorter, with a belly that would make Santa Claus jealous. He wore gray Sunday slacks and a matching suit jacket. The tie around his neck was dark—hard to tell exactly what color—navy or black. The hat on his head reminded Jimmy of his father's favorite black-and-white movies. He always pretended he couldn't remember what the hat was called just so his father would have to say "pork pie" and then he would laugh. He'd never seen one in real life though.

The man smiled and waved at Jimmy.

Jimmy waved back.

Then he tipped his pork pie hat, turned, and disappeared around the corner.

Jimmy laid his head on the pillow and pulled the blanket over his head.

***

Grandma June made breakfast for her guests and Uncle Larry the next morning. The table was only set for five so Jimmy guessed Uncle Steve and his family wouldn't be joining them just yet. But he wondered where the man from the hallway was. So, after his tummy was full of eggs, sausage, and more biscuits, he decided to explore.

Down the hall from the guest bedroom/sewing room, his grandmother's bedroom door was open. He wasn't allowed to enter his parents' bedroom un-invited, and he figured this was no different. From the doorway, he investigated the small room.

The mattress lay upon an iron bedframe and was neatly covered with a floral quilt and frilly pillows. The cherry wood side table nearest the door had a bible resting on top, a half-full glass of water, a tall reading lamp, and a round brass-plated clock with two bells on top. The matching table on the opposite side of the bed was bare.

He held the door frame and leaned into the room as far as possible. On the far wall stood a dresser in the same style as the tables, covered with a cream-colored lace doily runner. Standing on his tiptoes, he saw a hairbrush and mirror, a small jewelry box, and a bottle of perfume lying on top.

What he didn't see had him puzzled. There was no sign of a man ... Not anywhere.

The door to the room across the hall—Uncle Larry's room—was closed so he couldn't look in there. But he had an idea who the man was and figured he wouldn't be in there anyway. On his way to the living room, he heard a chorus of voices and footsteps, and the metal storm door slammed closed two or three times.

As promised, Uncle Steve had returned with his wife and their three kids—two girls and a boy about Jimmy's age. The youngest girl, Trixie, clutched a naked baby doll with unbrushed hair under one arm while hiding behind her mother's leg.

Ten minutes later, Aunt Ruby stepped through the door with her two sons. Her husband was at work and would stop by later but even without him, the house was full and rambunctious. The adults shooed the children outside so they could do what adults do.

Jimmy got to know his five cousins in his grandmother's yard while playing tag. He swung on a tire that was tied to a rope and hanging from a tree. He dirtied his clothes while crawling through bushes to look for snakes, frogs, and other creepy crawly things with the other children—even the girls!

Well, except Elizabeth.

He was beginning to like Moultrie.

***

A few hours later, after working up an appetite, Jimmy was the first of the children to wander inside. Aunt Ruby set the dining room table for lunch while his mother made sandwiches in the kitchen. The other adults were who knows where, which left the front room empty.

A long cabinet under the side window displayed an array of family photos—some black and white, some in color, all begging to be studied. Jimmy made his way over and started with the images in the front row. He recognized his cousins and there were pictures of himself and Elizabeth. He kept looking further back until one photo in particular caught his eye. He stretched over the front row, careful not to touch anything that would knock over the whole lot like dominos.

Once he had the frame in his hand, he lifted it over the others and carried it into the kitchen. Holding the photo behind his back, he walked up behind his mother and tugged at her apron.

She looked over her shoulder and smiled then returned to her work. "Lunch is almost ready, Honey. Wash your hands then go sit down."

"Momma," he said, tugging again.

"What is it, Jimmy?"

"Is your father having lunch with us?"

The knife slipped from her hand and *clanged* against one of the melamine plates. She steadied herself against the counter and then looked down at her son. "My father?"

"He wasn't at breakfast ... Did he go to work?"

She knelt in front of him. "Jimmy ... My father ..." She lowered her eyes for a moment then took a breath before returning her gaze to her son. "Do you remember Grandpa Joe?"

He nodded. "Daddy's father."

"That's right. And do you remember what happened to Grandpa Joe last year?"

He remembered that his grandfather had gotten sick and then went to sleep and didn't wake up. No one ever said *dead*, not when he or his sister were around—though that was a word he would learn soon enough. Instead, they called it *passed away*. He didn't understand what it meant except that his Grandpa Joe wasn't around anymore to tell jokes, give him quarters or sips of beer, or tell him stories about *"the way things used to be."*

"My father passed away too ... A long time ago. Before you were born."

He furrowed his brow. "But I saw him."

"You saw him? Where? When?"

"Last night. He was in the doorway of our room ... He waved at me." Then Jimmy showed his mother what he was holding behind his back. "This man."

"This is your Grandpa Bill," she said as she took the picture from him. She stared at the faded image of the paunch-bellied, middle-aged man wearing a gray suit and matching pork pie hat. Her father. "You saw this man?"

He nodded.

"Did you speak to him?"

Jimmy shook his head.

"How did you—" She pursed her lips into a smile as she stared back at him. "Did you tell anyone else that you saw him?"

"No."

"If you see him again, I want you to tell me ... Only me, is that clear?"

"Yes, Momma."

"There are some things other people don't understand or believe ... You are special, Jimmy. You have a gift, just like Mommy."

She looked down at the photograph and, in a hushed voice, said, "Daddy—Grandpa Bill—called it *the light*. He said some people burn brighter than others and *shades* are attracted to their *light.*" She placed the frame on the counter and looked into her son's eyes. *"Shades* are what he called those that had passed away. Sometimes our *light* reflects onto a *shade*, allowing us to see them—like reflections in a mirror." Then as if talking to herself, "Elizabeth won't have *the light*, I suppose ... Just like my siblings don't." She shook her head while thinking this over.

Jimmy's eyes were big, and he was picking at his bottom lip with his thumb and first finger.

She pulled his hand away from his mouth, held his chin, and smiled. "Don't be afraid, sweetheart. There's so much I have to tell you ... For now, just know that nothing you see can harm you."

But that wasn't entirely true. There are all sorts of things that are attracted to *the light*. And some of those creatures are better left to the darkness.

She wouldn't have a chance to warn her son about that or the price that came with his gift.

And Jimmy never saw Grandpa Bill again.

***

Two months after the Moultrie trip, Jimmy's mother stood at the kitchen counter making lunches for her children while they sat at the breakfast table eating Fruit Loops and drinking orange juice. She wore a floral print A-line wrap dress in shades of red, black, and green and red sandals with two-inch heels. Her toenails were the color of a fire engine, and her henna waves swept freely over her shoulders.

It was three weeks into the new school year, and with her children in school, Madalyn Hobart had transitioned from part-time bank teller to full-time—she just had to be home before her small children. Her boss happily agreed to her condition as long as she worked on Saturday. It was an adjustment the Hobart family had to get used to.

His father walked into the kitchen and filled a thermos with coffee. Then he kissed his wife and told his children to have a good day before walking through the living room and out the front door without eating breakfast.

After finishing the sugary cereal, Jimmy tipped the bowl to his lips and drank the sweet milk. Then he carried his dishes to the sink and slid his lunch box from the counter.

"Wait for your sister," his mother reminded him.

Jimmy was in third grade and still getting used to sharing the bus with Elizabeth—a first-grader now. He rolled his eyes and groaned, but she stopped him to kiss his cheek before he could walk away. He breathed in the bouquet of Noxzema and baby lotion then trudged into the living room where his backpack was waiting by the front door. He slung the pack over his shoulders and waited for Elizabeth as his mother instructed, the same as yesterday and every day this new school year.

A few minutes later, he walked through the door with his sister. At the end of their sidewalk, he turned and waved at his mother, and she waved back. Then she closed the door.

Just a typical day. A Tuesday he would never forget.

What happened next, his family has never spoken about. But he'd heard adults talking and noticed things. As a teenager, his curiosity got the better of him, and an internet search filled in the details he wished he didn't now know.

His mother arrived at the bank as the manager was opening. There was light foot traffic between 9:00-9:30 a.m. Then a man wearing a black knit ski mask entered at approximately 9:35 a.m. He turned the key on the inner glass door then demanded the tellers empty their drawers into his pillowcase while he held a blue steel, .357 snub nose revolver.

Once he had the money, he prepared to leave. But someone in the bank had tripped the alarm and he spotted the police cars parked on the street. The masked man grabbed one of the tellers by her arm and pulled her close as he backed toward the door. Her name was Christine LeCroix, but everyone called her Chrissy—and she was eight months pregnant.

According to the bank manager, Mrs. Roberta Simpkins, Jimmy's mother begged the man to let Chrissy go. *"She was crying—we were all crying—but Maddie just kept pleading with him,"* the manager was quoted as saying. *"'Please, don't take Chrissy,' she said. 'Please let Chrissy go.' She kept saying her name like they trained us to do. And it worked. He shoved Chrissy to the floor. Then Maddie rushed to her side to make sure she was okay."*

In a brave move, Jimmy's mother convinced the bank robber to release the young mother-to-be. And that's when he grabbed her instead.

Jimmy wasn't there to see it go down, of course, but he'd often imagined what happened next—he couldn't help it. He dreamt about it too.

While holding Maddie tight to his chest with one arm and pressing the muzzle of the .357 into her side, the masked man pushed through the doorway, using his hostage as a shield as he stepped onto the sidewalk.

"Let her go and drop your weapon!" an officer shouted from the other side of his police car.

"I'll shoot her!" the masked robber shouted back.

"Drop your gun!" another officer yelled.

"You back off and let me through," the man yelled, now with the barrel of the gun pressed against Madalyn's temple.

"Don't shoot!"

"Drop the gun!"

"Let her go!"

That's how it always happened in the movies anyway. Three, four, eight cops all shouting different commands simultaneously while the perp's eyes bug out and sweat soaked through his knit mask.

"There's nowhere to go!"

"Drop the gun! Do it!"

Head on a swivel, the masked man curled his lip over scraggly yellow teeth while tightening his grip around a trembling Madalyn Hobart. But she was shorter than him and slipping on the pavement as she struggled to stay on her feet.

"Let her go!"

"Do it now! Drop the gun!"

According to the police report and all the newspaper articles, the bank robber's gun went off first. Percival Nolan Dent fired one bullet into Madalyn Hobart's right temple. As her body went limp, the perp turned his weapon toward the police officers. He popped off two rounds before he was hit with a barrage of gunfire. His body twisted and jerked as he fell backward into the glass window of the bank and then fell to the ground.

It was over in seconds.

Madelyn Reanne Hobart was dead before her 29th birthday.

For a while, he thought that *dead* and *passed away* were two different things. It wasn't until he was much older that he realized adults didn't know how to explain death to a child in a way that made sense.

Hell, twenty-two years later and it still didn't make sense to him.

Chapter 2

Jimmy mindlessly picked at the dry skin on his bottom lip while gripping the steering wheel in his other hand and navigating the winding two-lane stretch of Woody Creek Lane. On his left was a rocky hillside, slate gray and wind carved. A steep slope at first but then gave way to the gentle rolls that were here long before this blacktop. On the right, the cornflower blue sky and bright sun made a luxurious sea of gold and red and green ever more vivid and regal.

During the two months after that trip to Moultrie, when he believed he and his mother shared a special bond, she had told him about *feeling* and *seeing* things and that these two words had different meanings for people like them. There were times when he *felt* his mother's presence as if she'd never left. Other times, he even *felt* her hand on his cheek or thought he heard her voice. But he never saw his mother in *the light*.

Still, he believed she was a *shade* now. Just a different sort of *shade* than Grandpa Bill ... And the others he saw. It wasn't like he saw dead people hanging around like that kid in the movie. In fact, after the first time, he didn't see another *shade* for years. For a while, he'd managed to convince himself that he'd imagined the whole thing or dreamed it.

But as the saying goes, that was just wishful thinking.

For him, the best part of his gift was his ability to *see* things. Things that may happen or what people are thinking. Some people might call them visions or ESP. He couldn't perform parlor tricks or win the lottery, and if there was a way to control his gift his mother never had the chance to show him. Mostly he felt like a conduit.

He glanced at the passenger seat where Roni sat smiling, watching the fall leaves pass by in a blur while listening to classic rock play through the pickup's stereo speakers. Her long black hair swept over her shoulder in stark contrast to the cream-colored cable knit sweater she wore on this chilly day.

His most robust *vision* came in college, the night he met Veronica Marie Hobbs. *"Call me Roni,"* she said. *"Everyone does."*

Looking into her hazel eyes was like seeing fireworks for the first time—without the *sizzle* and *boom* of gunpowder. Although his heart was pounding like a bass drum. He actually *saw* green and gold flashes. Guessing that was *the light* trying to tell him something, he didn't leave her side for the rest of the night.

After nearly ten years together, they finally decided they were ready to tie the knot. Their engagement was no elaborate affair. They arrived at a simple decision together, followed by the ring, then wedding plans. Everything was falling into place except one crucial piece: the house. They had been living in the same two-bedroom apartment for years, but now that they were getting married, it was time to become homeowners.

The housing market was red hot. And with their wedding date fast approaching, the chances they would find something and be moved in before saying 'I do' were looking slim to no way in hell.

He let that sink in as he continued mindlessly picking away at his lip. *It's already October—Jesus, where'd the time go?*

Pick, pick, pick.

We need at least sixty days to pull it off ... The holidays are right around the corner ... Next it will be winter and with the risk of snow and ice, well that makes it even more—

Jimmy hissed with pain, taking his eyes off the road long enough to see the trace of red under his thumbnail as he rolled his raw bottom lip into his mouth and tasted the blood.

"That's a nasty habit you have," she said. "What's eating you?"

"What are we doing all the way out here?"

She shrugged her shoulders. "I have a feeling."

"Me too," he huffed under his breath. "A feeling I'm being watched. A feeling I'm being hunted—"

"Oh, stop it, Smudge," she scolded playfully. "Besides, I thought you liked the country."

"Country drives, yes. Country living ..."

He didn't have a *feeling*, not really. Not the kind his mother told him about or when he had a *vision*. And even if he had, he couldn't tell Roni. Not now. Not after all these years of keeping *the light* to himself. *"There are some things other people don't understand or believe,"* his mother warned.

He'd thought about telling her many times but then always chickened out. Like the time he saw her grandmother's *shade*. That would have been the perfect time.

They had only been dating a few months when Roni received the call that her grandmother had passed. But from that first night, he'd been all in. So, when she asked him to go with her to the funeral, he said yes.

They arrived at her parents' home the day before the wake and Jimmy was introduced to Mr. and Mrs. Hobbs for the first time. They were happy to make him comfortable in the guest room on the first floor, a level away from their daughter's room.

After dinner, Jimmy found himself alone in her father's study, where he had walls of books. All the classics from Asimov to Twain and an entire section dedicated to Stephen King—there were even a few titles he hadn't heard of. He was just about to slip *The Duma Key* from the shelf when an image appeared in his peripheral vision.

He turned and saw the widow Hobbs standing by the window, gazing upon the rose garden. He recognized her from the photographs Roni had shown him earlier in the evening.

At first, she didn't seem to notice him. But then she waved, and for a split second, he felt like that eight-year-old boy seeing a *shade* for the first time.

His mouth went dry and when he swallowed, it felt like cut glass in his throat. Then he took a deep breath and smiled back at her. He was about to lift his arm and wave when Roni entered the room.

She must have walked right through *the light*—if it worked that way—because at that exact moment, *the shade* that was her grandmother disappeared as if the signal had been interrupted. Maybe it would have been a more exciting story if she had caught him waving to her dead grandmother.

"There's probably nothing out here anyway," Roni said, her voice trailing off as she stared out the passenger window. "At least it's not a total loss though. Just look at that view."

She wasn't wrong. But they hadn't seen a turnoff, road sign, or house for miles and the nearest patch of civilization was at least a thirty-minute drive back the way they came. It felt like they were the last two people on Earth until he spotted three helium-filled mylar balloons flapping in the autumn breeze through the thinning trees. The way the sun reflected on the foil, they could have been a silver, red, and blue flashing neon sign outside a Vegas casino, beckoning them to come inside and take a turn on the roulette wheel.

"Slow down, slow down," she urged.

He lifted his foot from the gas pedal and the truck engine quieted to a purr as it decelerated. The balloons were tied to a sign staked into the ground at the end of a long driveway amidst a bramble that was sure to sprout white and violet blooms in spring.

"You've got to be kidding," he mumbled, pressing the brake and reading the sign.

OPEN HOUSE

12 – 4 P.M.

"What do you think? Should we check it out?"

He shrugged and leaned over the steering wheel, craning his neck to peer around the corner. It was an impossible place for a home, yet at the end of a long gravel driveway shaded by tall pines lined up like saber bearers was something straight out of a child's fairy tale.

The asymmetrical facade of the Queen Anne design had been a favorite of his and one of the reasons he decided to become an architect. And now, seeing the dynamic bump-outs, turrets, wraparound porch with round support columns, and steeply pitched roof, his interest was piqued.

He turned the wheel to the right and gave the engine some gas. The truck engine roared and began lumbering along the gravel, bobbing and rocking in the divots. Still, Jimmy's eyes remained fixed on the two-story Victorian with decaying art deco accents.

The house had seen better days but as the distance closed, it was easy to imagine the place in its prime. Hiding behind a layer of grime and climbing ivy was what had to be the original clapboard siding painted light olive. This color was once certainly beautifully accentuated by evergreen shutters, some of which were now hanging off-kilter and faded.

The milk chocolate window casings made the traditional stained glass inserts pop as rays of light danced through the swaying pines. Intricately carved window sashes and latticework around the porch were painted a warm pastel red that reminded him of a barn near his childhood home.

Then the curtains over the second-floor windows captured his gaze. They were partially drawn and tied into the shape of menacing jack-o-lantern eyes. It was as if the house was seeing him just as surely as he was seeing it, and he imagined the elaborate entryway curling into the shape of a toothy grin.

He closed his eyes and shivered the image away.

No other vehicles were parked in front, so he let the truck stop about a hundred feet from the porch. "It looks like no one's home."

"The sign said until four and it's only two," she said, looking at her phone. Then she leaned toward the windshield and gazed up at the house. "It won't hurt to knock, right?"

"Is this even a house you would be interested in?"

"I won't know until I see it ... Now come on," she said, squeezing his knee. Fireworks.

He shook his head and sighed then accelerated further until they reached the empty parking pad just feet from the porch steps. He exited the truck and pressed the button on the key fob to engage the door locks.

"Really?" she said. "We're in the woods."

He shrugged. "Habit."

Standing outside the vehicle, he heard the sharp shrieks of hawks and the soft *click-clack* of dried leaves as the wind whispered through the deciduous trees surrounding the property. Then Jimmy looked up at the pine sentries that were higher than the tallest roof turret and for a moment, he swayed along with them. It reminded him of the street in Moultrie ... And his mother.

"Are you coming?" she asked, waiting by the steps.

He slipped the key fob into the pocket of his blue jeans then turned toward the house. And as his boot came down on the first rickety step, the lace covering moved on the left sidelight flanking the entry door.

"I think someone's home after all," he said.

There was a *clack* as the deadbolt turned then the door opened. An out-of-breath woman with oversized plastic-rimmed glasses stood in the doorway. She took a deep breath and smiled, the air inflating her round cheeks like one of the mylar balloons. "I was beginning to think today would be a bust," she said with her hand outstretched. "I'm Millie."

"I'm James—Jimmy," he said, shaking her hand. "This is my fiancé, Roni."

"Nice to meet you, Millie. Your home is lovely."

"Oh, it's not mine. I'm just the realtor. No one here but me." Then she stood quietly with her hands folded over her lumpy Chanel tweed suit while nodding at them. Then abruptly, she raised her hands to her cheeks and said, "Oh, how silly of me. Please come in." She stepped backward and welcomed them into the vestibule. "Will your agent be joining you?"

"No, it's just us," he answered.

"Wonderful."

The walls in the entrance foyer were papered in a velvety floral pattern. A series of wooden coat hooks adorned one wall where a simple beige puffer coat hung in the middle by its hood. It was chilly inside the home, so Jimmy kept his jacket on.

The entrance opened into two bright rooms on either side. He stepped in further and glanced right into what would have been called the parlor when the house was young. A large bay window with a built-in bench seat looked out onto the front porch and yard. On the outside wall, a single lonely window overlooked the south lawn. The third wall was closed off from the rest of the house.

Around the right corner of the parlor, the velvety flower garden continued up a prominent wooden staircase leading to the second floor. Beyond the stairs, the entrance hall continued to the back of the house.

But first, he walked across the foyer and entered what would have been known as the sitting room. Two single windows looked out to the front. In the far-right corner, an elaborate wood-burning fireplace accented with glazed tiles and a thin coating of soot was left bare on this chilly day. The walls were papered in vertical stripes of various shades and widths of green velvet and cream. His eyebrows raised as he suddenly recalled a DIY he'd watched a few months back showing how to remove wallpaper and wondered if he could still find it—just in case.

Looking to his right, the sitting room opened into the lime sherbet dining room toward a hinged door that presumably led to the kitchen. But for now, he roamed left, eyeing the sitting room's cracked and stained plaster ceiling and worn wooden floorboards. Except for the staircase banister, all the wood trim appeared to have been painted white and was chipped and peeling like the porch railing, no doubt releasing toxic lead and asbestos into the room.

Now, he wouldn't consider himself an expert on how to sell a home—although after as many showings as they've been through maybe he should—but it seemed a bit 'green' not to have staged the home, especially on the day of an open house. "How long have you been a realtor, Millie?"

"Oh, just a few months. Truth be told, I'm still trying to get my first sale."

"What firm are you with?"

"I'm an independent agent. The property owner is my only client right now."

He smiled and nodded as she confirmed what he had already surmised.

"I know what you're thinking," Millie said with a sly grin as she directed him to an open guest book and a stack of fliers lying on a small round table he passed on his way into the sitting room. "Why didn't she pay for all the fancy staging? That's what all the affiliated realtors would have done, right? Sure, I could have done that. And that's what you would have noticed: the beautiful furniture perfectly positioned according to *feng shui*," she said with air quotes. "The beautiful drapes and knickity-knacks ... I could have lit candles and baked cookies, taken an ad out in the newspaper—"

Newspaper? he thought with a smirk as he wrote his and Roni's names on the first line of the blank page. *Hasn't she heard of Zillow?*

"I could have done everything the so-called *experts* do," she said, again using air quotes but this time adding a sideways swish of her round hips. "But all that work would have attracted the wrong sort of buyers."

"What do you mean?" Roni asked.

"The sort that's always in a rush ... Circling listings on a page in red marker—"

There's that newspaper reference again, Jimmy thought, trading the ink pen for one of the fliers.

"—trying to see how many showings they can squeeze into one day without taking the time to get to know any one house ..." Her voice trailed off as she meandered with her back turned until she became quiet.

Is she waiting for a response? he wondered. Uncomfortable in the silence, he decided he wanted her to elaborate. "What sort of buyers is the homeowner looking for?"

She spun around, smiling, looking pleased that he asked. "Most people that end up on Woody Creek Lane drive right by this old house without so much as a second glance—like it's not even here. Why, just before the two of you arrived, I was beginning to think my sign had fallen over, leaving the balloons to drift away into the blue sky."

That wasn't an answer.

She took a deep breath, lifting her full breasts before letting them drop. "So, what brought the two of you to this quiet part of town?"

"We were just out driving and—"

"—We ended up here."

She laughed heartily as they spoke in tandem. Then once she had her breath, she teased, "Just stumbled upon a quiet estate as if it had been waiting for you all along. And for reasons you can't understand, you were inexplicably compelled—though reluctant—to wander in for a look." Her eyes were big brown saucers peering at them through thick plastic lenses, bouncing left to right between them. But when they failed to respond to her taunt, she *clip-clopped* toward the entrance, singing out, "The universe works in mysterious ways."

Spoken like someone that had been known to wander herself from time to time, Jimmy thought. But he wasn't house hunting for an ugly duckling waiting to be transformed into a swan—even if he did have the skills and tools to do it. He did, however, believe in *feelings* and *signs*. And while he didn't see fireworks when he turned off Woody Creek Lane, he felt something. He just wasn't sure what.

He spun around toward her. "So, you're suggesting that since we were out for a country drive and just stumbled upon this house by sheer dumb luck that—what? That makes us the right sort of buyers for this house?"

Millie closed the guestbook with a slap, tucked the pen into her suitcoat pocket, then held the book to her bosom and smiled. "Well, that's what we're here to find out."

Chapter 3

"The house sits on twenty acres of private land and is nearly a century old—when things were built to last if you ask me," Millie said, walking the perimeter of the sitting room while Jimmy stood in the center watching her. "You'll notice the house still has all the original floors, baseboards, and crown molding—all maple," she added, turning her head quickly to meet his gaze.

"The ornate crystal doorknobs throughout the interior are all original, as is the fireplace," she said, patting the stone chimney. "You also have radiator heat in each room."

He had recognized the white cast iron coils placed against the walls—until now something he'd only seen in movies or television shows set in New York City. "No central air?"

"I'm afraid not," she answered, "but the trees offer plenty of shade. And with the windows open, you'll find a cool breeze coming off the creek that runs along the eastern border of the property line." Then, having reached the end of her speech, she twisted her hips left and right like a fidgety child while drumming her fingers against the back of the guest book.

It was as if she sensed that he had questions building inside him. And she was right—Jimmy was ready to spar. "The boiler in the basement—it'll need to be replaced, right?"

She shook her head. "It's in perfect condition."

"How's the electricity?"

"Temperamental ... Next question."

"Hmm," he scowled, shuffling his feet. "And the roof?"

"It might get you through another year or two. But then you'll have to replace it."

Honesty—another indication of a green realtor.

He didn't understand why, but he believed her—though it was an interesting sales pitch. Presenting the house in all its naked glory, exposing all of its flaws, could backfire—unless the pitch was directed toward the right sort of buyers.

Is she just that honest? he wondered. *Or were we lucky enough to meet her before the killer instinct took hold?*

"The appliances are all in good working order—I know you didn't ask," Millie said with a flip of her hand as she crossed the room. "I'll let you two look around. If you need me, I'll be on the porch." She stepped through the entryway, closed the door behind her, thumped across the porch, and took a load off in a recently wiped-down rocking chair.

"Creepy," Jimmy muttered as he watched her through the window.

"Come on, let's look upstairs," Roni said.

"You can't be serious. Did you hear what she said about this place? It's a money pit."

"What's the harm? We're already here." She trotted past him to the staircase, where she paused to admire the intricately carved newel post. "Have you seen anything like this?"

"Hmm?" he grunted, finally tearing his gaze from the strange realtor resting on the porch.

"Nevermind," she moaned as she continued up the steps.

He slowly made his way over to examine the antique banister, waiting to be restored to its original glory. The spindles that lined the staircase were in character with the style of the home. As he climbed, he let his hand slide softly up the railing through a layer of dust and noticed it severely needed sanding and refinishing.

Creak.

He paused on the fifth step up from the bottom and shifted his weight forward and back. *Squeak, squeak.* He added the repair to the mental list he began in the driveway and then continued to the second-floor landing.

He turned left into the hallway and spun around 360 degrees to get a lay of the land. The same hardwood flooring continued on the upper level, but it appeared to be in a better state than what he'd already seen, likely due to scatter rugs that had long since been removed.

From this vantage, he could see seven doors. One was undoubtedly a linen closet and another the bathroom—he hoped not the only bathroom. Customary of the period, the bedroom doors had glass transom windows overtop to let in natural light and promote airflow. The seventh door probably led to the attic. *What treasures might have been left behind in a century-old house?* he wondered.

Roni was nowhere in sight, but he could hear her footfalls in the back of the house. He decided to start with the bathroom, straight ahead.

It was fitted with what appeared to be the original claw foot tub and badly damaged floor tiles. This was obviously the source of the water stains on the downstairs ceiling. A shower stall had been added to the corner, and the toilet seemed to have been replaced at one time. A window on the back wall gave him his first glimpse of the rear of the property.

The house sat secluded in the middle of miles and miles of trees proudly displaying their fall colors over rolling hillsides. And somewhere in the middle of it all was a creek. He wondered how much of the vast countryside would be theirs—not that he was considering buying the house.

He scanned over the realtor's flier to remind himself. Twenty acres, it read. But he had no idea what that might look like. They would need a surveyor to stake it out. *How do you even secure twenty acres?* he wondered. *And what about the creek? Is that part of the deal?* The flier didn't specify.

He sighed while turning away from the view and noticed the mirrored medicine cabinet over the pedestal sink. Recalling a segment from a recent documentary, he pulled the knob and opened the cabinet door. "I'll be damned," he mumbled with a grin as he noticed the tiny slit on the back. It resembled a coin slot but was supposedly used to dispose of old razor blades. He closed the door and then made a mental note to show Roni if he ever caught up with her.

He made a right turn in the hallway and was drawn to the bay window in the bedroom on the north side, above the sitting room. It had a built-in seat that opened for more storage. Mahogany-stained crown molding framed the room setting off the textured gold plaster on three walls. The back wall was papered in a worn red and gold pattern that was in keeping with the season. He saw no stains on the ceiling, but he did notice a long crack that reached from the front corner almost to the overhead light fixture.

With his hands in his pocket, he tallied the growing to-do list in his mind as he shuffled toward the exit. Before breaching the threshold, a chill like the air around an ice cube grazed the skin on the back of his neck. He stopped and as he began to turn, he heard whispering.

His first thought was that Roni was on her phone but then he realized it wasn't her voice he heard ... or even two voices involved in a hushed conversation. He stepped into the hall and the sound became louder, like the drone of hundreds of voices whispering at once, hissing like a den of snakes coiling and wrapping around one another.

Jimmy stood still and listened, trying to pinpoint where it was coming from—and *what* it was coming from—but it was too chaotic to track. *Could it be steam escaping from one of the radiators?* He stepped softly across the hall toward the open bedroom door, then through the doorway, this time not in a quiet way but at the same time not eager to give himself away. Still, the voices became louder, drawing him closer and closer.

This empty room was larger than its neighbor. No bay window though. Just two single-hung sash windows overlooking the front lawn. Ahead, a door hung ajar, and the serpentine hiss seemed to grow louder when he crept in that direction.

He inched closer, eyes fixed on the opening, one foot in front of the other, holding his breath, stalking his prey until he was close enough to peek his head around the corner—

"Jesus, you scared the hell out of me," Roni said as she flung the door open.

He jerked backward, feeling the sting of surprise and snapping his body straight so quickly that he slammed his head against the door jamb.

"What are you doing, sneaking around?"

"I thought I heard voices," he said, his back still against the wall as he rubbed his head. "Is Millie in there with you?"

"No. She's still on the porch, isn't she?"

"Who were you talking to?"

"Talking? I wasn't talking to anyone," she scoffed as she walked past him. "Can you believe this house has a walk-in closet?"

"It's a dressing room." The adrenaline buzz now subsided, he decided to step inside the small room for a better look, and it was empty. No Millie, just like she said.

"Whatever you want to call it ... I can picture my wardrobe in there."

Old houses are drafty, he thought as her voice drifted further away. *Was it the wind?* He shrugged his shoulders and visualized the dressing room as a walk-in closet. It would be another use for his tools and skills, in case they were crazy enough to buy the old—

"Let me out."

Gasping, he quickly spun around but there was no one there. This time, the voice—and the message—was quite clear. The silvery sound grated his spine like ice water poured down his back.

"Roni?" There was no answer. He stepped into the bedroom and heard the hiss again, coming from his left, softer now than before. He stepped toward the nearest window and realized it was open just enough to let the air sneak between the sash and the windowsill.

He pushed it down and then waited, listening. But there was only silence. The serpent voices were quiet.

He twisted the window lock and then walked out.

***

After a quick tour of the two bedrooms at the back of the house, Jimmy found himself at the seventh door—what he presumed was the attic. He turned the ornate crystal knob, but the door wouldn't open. He smiled and thought, *This must be where the owner hid the bodies.* After all, there was always something sinister in the attic of an old house—especially behind a locked door.

He shook his head, rolled his eyes, and mumbled, "I've read too many horror novels."

On the staircase, he was careful to avoid the loose step. Then at the bottom, he peeked into the parlor—no Roni. He walked through the sitting room and into the green sherbet dining room to the swinging flap door where, on the other side, Roni's inspection of the kitchen was already well underway.

"Appliances are a little dated but clean," she said.

He nodded, walking around the bar-height butcher block workstation built into the center of the room. An L-shaped maroon countertop started on the right and finished on the back wall of the house where two windows overlooked the backyard. The Formica was peeling at the edges but appeared otherwise in good condition. The dark-stained kitchen cabinets and drawers had flat fronts with non-descript door pulls and knobs. A door on the left outer wall led onto the wrap-around porch. He stopped his lazy tour to gaze upon a row of bare dogwoods and imagined their sweet scent filling the kitchen when they bloomed in the spring.

"Where in the world does this go?"

Jimmy turned away from the view toward Roni's voice. Along the shared wall with the dining room, and obscured by the refrigerator, were four steps that led to another door. She already had the door open when he climbed up behind her and looked over her shoulder.

She activated the flashlight on her cellphone and shined the light into the windowless darkness. The walls were bare masonry with cobweb-coated shelves and toppled glass jars—hopefully empty. A Hoosier cabinet with upper and lower storage and a counter-height workstation stood on the back wall. A two-foot-long string dangled from a lonely bare bulb hanging from the ancient wood rafters.

"Looks like a pantry," he said as he backed down the steps and opened the side door onto the porch.

In the shade of the roof overhang, he inhaled the crisp October air and then exhaled, expelling the particulates he'd likely breathed in while in the musty old house. Naked of their leaves, rose bushes grew on either side of the steps, and he wondered what color their buds would be this summer. For some time, Jimmy's favorite had been coral—because it was somewhere between the deep red, maroon-blue petals adored by his mother and the yellow rose favored by his father.

Beyond the row of dogwoods he spied from the kitchen window, the lawn sloped down at about a 30-degree angle toward a horseshoe-shaped tree line. Otherwise, there was no fence around the yard. And other than the young dogwoods, the backyard had been cleared of trees long ago—most likely to create a spot for beautiful garden parties. He closed his eyes and imagined a large gathering, playing croquet and sipping lemonade, children running around, dogs barking ...

A soft breeze rustled through the distant trees and tussled his hair. Then in the calm that remained, he thought he could hear water moving gently along the creek bed, between and over rocks, to some faraway river.

"Let me out."

He opened his eyes and stumbled backward a step, right into Roni. He jolted forward and spun around, nearly losing his balance.

"Geeze," she gasped, grabbing his arm to steady him. "I didn't mean to scare you."

He hadn't realized it, but while the creek was lulling him, he'd managed to walk past the dogwoods and was standing at the crest of the hill. One more step and—

"Didn't you hear me?" she said.

"That was you?"

"Of course ... Who else—"

"Let me out? Why would you say that?"

"Let me out?" she repeated, wrinkling her nose. "No. I called your name ... Twice."

He turned away to survey the surrounding countryside. There was something eerily familiar about this place. What he'd heard was a *shade*, he was sure of it. He wasn't frightened. Hearing strange sounds and seeing things was something he'd grown used to. But he'd never been visited by the same *shade* twice—until now.

A tremor spread through his bones as he started up the slope, backward to keep watch on the forest. There was something out there.

He could *feel* it.

***

On the porch, Jimmy fished the flier from his pocket and began reading again as he strolled toward the front of the house.

Roni slid her hand inside his. "So ... What do you think?"

"I think it needs a lot of work ... And our daily commute to work would be twice as long as it is now."

"We could fix it up ... Maybe resell it or make it a bed and breakfast and quit our jobs."

"Before making long-range plans, did you see the price?"

"It's within our budget."

"With all the work that it needs—"

"I don't mean to butt in," Millie said as she appeared from around the corner, "but for the right sort of buyers, I'm sure the seller would negotiate a fair price."

"Was she listening to us?" Jimmy whispered in Roni's ear.

She squeezed his hand and smiled at the realtor. "We can see the potential."

"I don't think your man is so sure."

Jimmy turned to his fiancé and watched her green eyes dance above her quivering, upturned lips that held back a stampede of excitement.

Fireworks.

There were a million reasons to walk away from the house on Woody Creek Lane but only one reason to stay and make it a home.

He glanced down at his boots to stave the geyser of doubt building inside him and said, "How can I say no?"

She squealed and hopped into his arms then kissed him repeatedly on his cheeks. Millie adjusted her glasses and looked away as the plump rounds under her eyes bloomed like the roses eventually would. Jimmy braved a stoic grin.

The house had won.

Chapter 4

It turns out there were hundreds of ways to remove wallpaper—though hundreds may be an exaggeration. When Jimmy searched the internet for advice, it certainly felt like hundreds. After hours of research, he settled on a mixture of one part fabric softener to three parts hot water. He could have used vinegar, but he couldn't stand the smell.

A steamer would have been less messy and faster, but steamers can damage the wall if they weren't primed or if the paper were pasted on plaster. Given the age of the home, he didn't want to take any chances.

They started in the entrance foyer. After scoring the paper and covering the wood flooring with a tarp, they sprayed the homemade mixture from top to bottom in small sections. Once the solution was soaked in, Jimmy used a putty knife to peel back a corner of the floral print.

"It works," Roni cheered.

"Did you have doubts?"

"Well, it does seem kind of silly that water and fabric softener removes wallpaper."

It was their first day as homeowners and they had a long list of to-dos to cover during the first week of their two-week vacation before moving in. Wallpaper removal was only the beginning, but they were off to a good start.

By the time the first long piece had been removed and stuffed into a trash bag, they had found their rhythm. An hour later, they had finished with the foyer and had started up the staircase.

"So," Jimmy said, stuffing another strip of wallpaper into the bag. "Are you gonna take my name after we say 'I do'?"

She laughed from a lower step. "Well, I don't see any choice ... Otherwise, we'll sound more like a pair of detectives from Law & Order than a married couple."

He looked down at her, brow furrowed, fabric softener solution dripping from his yellow kitchen gloves.

"Hobart and Hobbs?" she said.

"Damn, you're right," he said, scraping another piece of paper loose. "I never realized how our names sound together ... We could be a law firm."

"Pretty bad, right?"

"No worse than Hobart and Hobart."

She swatted him on the back of his pants and sneered, "Don't tempt me, Smudge."

"Okay, okay." He smiled and stuffed another strip of wet paper into the over-flowing bag when his foot came down on the loose step. The wood protested under his weight with a high-pitched, drawn-out *screech*.

"We'll have to get that repaired. I think a friend at work knows a guy."

"I can do it," Jimmy said.

"Oh, so suddenly you're a woodworker?"

"How hard can it be?"

"This is the original wood ... You don't want to mess this up."

"What makes you think I'll mess it up?"

She didn't respond. Instead, she tied up the bag, tossed it over the railing, and opened a fresh bag. "Besides, we need someone to refinish these floors anyway. Maybe my friend's contact can do both."

Jimmy shrugged as he sprayed more solution onto the wall. That was one less item on his list, so it was okay with him. "Hey, when is the technician coming to turn the power on?"

"Between two and six."

"We didn't bring any lamps, did we?"

"Shoot!"

"I hope some of these old bulbs work, otherwise, we're quitting at sunset."
Jimmy made a mental note: *pack light bulbs and lamps in the truck for tomorrow.*

***

After removing the wallpaper throughout the house, they spent the next day patching and priming the walls. On the third day, the parlor, sitting room, dining room, and kitchen all received two coats of paint in a warm yellow shade, like a field of daffodils.

On the fourth day, while Roni painted upstairs, Jimmy hung drapes over the downstairs windows. For their bedroom—the room with what would become a walk-in closet—she selected glass sapphire, a calm hue meant to promote sleep. The other rooms were still under negotiation as to their purpose, so paint colors were put on hold.

Around noon, they stopped for lunch, which they decided to have outside under the sun on this unseasonably warm November day. They spread a blanket on the back lawn beneath the dormant dogwoods for shade, then unpacked their sandwiches and chips.

While they ate, they tried again to decide which room would be which. He needed an office, and she needed a studio. Their *al fresco* lunch convinced each of them that they wanted to claim one of the back bedrooms because of the view. The remaining space would become the guest room. Then they went over what still needed to be done before moving day. Cleaning, grocery shopping, upstairs drapes. But Roni was too distracted to continue.

"It's too beautiful to be stuck inside the rest of the day," she said. "Let's explore the property."

"Babe, we still have a lot to do … The movers come in two days. We'll have plenty of time to explore after we've moved in."

"True, but do you really want to pass up a day like this?" She stood up and stretched out her arms, closed her eyes, then twirled around in a circle with her head tilted back. "We might not get another chance like this for months."

He couldn't argue with that. They cleaned up what remained of their picnic then, with the property map and two bottles of water, they shirked off the rest of the household chores and set off beyond the dogwoods, down the slope.

***

The map led to a roughly blazed circular trail just beyond the opening in the trees. Nothing more than a deer track, it ran north and south parallel to Woody Creek for a mile in either direction through the wild hilly country. A pedestrian bridge crossed the creek at either end.

They decided on the north track with only their footfalls and the chatter of curious crows to keep them company. The otherwise quiet forest was a welcome reprieve from household chores.

After twenty minutes, they stumbled upon a suspicious clearing on a bluff. A closer inspection revealed the peak of a gable roof sticking up above the brush as if it had been dropped there. A lower path that didn't appear on the map ran ten feet below.

They gave each other a sideways glance, then descended to find a deep notch cut into the hillside, shored up on each side with rocks. A narrow, overgrown opening led to a wooden plank door directly beneath the mysterious roof.

"I think it's a root cellar," Jimmy said.

"Shouldn't it be closer to the house?"

It was strange for the outbuilding to be so far from the main property but that was only a fleeting thought as he jiggled the door handle. "Is this ours?"

37

She studied the map and then answered, "It appears to be on our land, so yes ... I think so."

"Do we have a key?"

She reached into her pocket for the key ring that came with the house. There was a spare key for the front door, another for the back door, one for the attic, and a skeleton key for the other interior doors. "No, nothing. I can call Millie later and ask."

"You're sure this is on our land?"

"Yes. Positive. Why?"

Jimmy handed her his water bottle and then rammed his shoulder against the wooden door. It *cracked* against the frame but didn't budge, so he hit it again, wincing in pain.

"Do you know how sexy you are right now?"

He laughed, standing with his hands on his hips. "Well, now I *have* to get it open." He stepped back, rubbing his shoulder and breathing heavily at the exertion. Then with a deep breath, he lifted one leg and kicked the door hard.

The door gave in to the force of his kick and fell into the room, releasing a gust of stale, dank air that pushed past them and shook the trees. A flurry of squawking crows took flight in a massive black cloud, abandoning their tree-top perches as if rattled by some seismic force.

What remained in their wake was the serpentine hiss of a thousand whispering voices. A sound he'd forgotten. It echoed in the trees, circled around and around until only one voice remained.

"Jimmy!"

And then, as if the sky inhaled a deep breath, all sound was sucked away at once, and it was quiet. The crows had settled on some distant tree limbs. Calm had been restored.

"Did you hear that?" he asked her.

"The birds? Yeah, that was weird."

Of course, he wasn't talking about the birds. She didn't hear it—the voice that sounded like a thousand snakes. *The shade* that shouldn't still be here.

"God, what's that smell?" she said, tugging her shirt collar up to cover her nose and mouth.

He entered the stone building and directed his phone light toward moldy, dusty jars on wooden shelves, sitting among the cobwebs. In the dirt, broken glass and animal bones were strewn amongst empty baskets. "It's been left unattended for quite some time by the looks of it."

"What are we supposed to do with it?"

Good question, he thought. *Board it up? Bulldoze it?*

"I don't know ... But I think we should leave."

On the way out, he propped the battered door against the frame as best he could, wondering if breaking into the root cellar had been a mistake. He hadn't learned much from his mother about his gift but she told him it wasn't up to him to help a *shade*—and he never tried. But the first time he heard the serpentine whisper, it had said, *"Let me out."*

Jimmy was suddenly filled with dread as he climbed up the slope and returned to the trail.

Did I just give the shade *what it wanted?*

Chapter 5

Moving day arrived sooner than expected and with the silvery whisper all but a faded memory, Jimmy was ready to spend the first night in their house. Except the movers were running late and there was nothing left to do but pace and wait.

He parted the plastic window blinds and searched the parking lot again but there was still no sign of them. He looked at his phone and the screen lit up: 8:03 a.m. *They should have been here thirty minutes ago.* He was sliding his phone into his back pocket when finally, he heard the groan of a diesel engine and a twenty-six-foot-long white box truck wobbled around the corner.

"They're here," he shouted toward the back of the apartment. Then he opened the door and stepped onto the concrete porch.

He thought about all the door slams, thumping footfalls, and bumping cabinet doors; every argument overheard through thin walls; every loud party that spilled over into the parking lot; all the neighbors they watched come and go over the last ten years. And now it was finally their turn.

With his hands in his pockets and without a hint of sentimentality, he breathed in the morning and watched the truck come to a stop. *Moretti's Movers* was imprinted in large green letters on the side of the cargo area and on the passenger door, though in a much smaller print.

The driver smoothed his sausage-like fingers over his thick black mustache before scratching the heavy stubble coating his cheeks. And as he barked orders, the other two men nodded like dashboard bobbleheads until the driver waved his meaty paw and tucked a pencil behind his ear.

Then the passenger door opened, and a man much younger than the driver slid off the tattered bench seat, his brown Timberlands landing with a *thump* on the asphalt. After pulling his curly blonde hair into a man bun on top of his head, he leaned his back against the side of the truck and yawned wide while slipping on a well-worn pair of leather gloves.

The other young man took a final sip of something in a white paper cup and then hopped out. Shorter than his 6'2" partner—but by the size of his guns, every bit as capable—the second man let his untamed brown curls flap in the breeze.

They were the muscle of the operation—and both looked like they had just rolled out of bed twenty minutes ago.

As they laughed and playfully shoved each other, preparing for what was sure to be a long day, Jimmy imagined they were bragging about their escapades from the night before, remembering all too well what the morning after 'tying one on' looked like. He didn't miss it one bit.

They settled down as the pudgy driver rounded the front of the cab, silver clipboard in hand, and said a few more words to the rambunctious man-boys. They stood tall, nodded like good little bobbleheads, and straightened their uniforms. By all accounts, it could have been a father reprimanding his sons.

The older man turned and noticed Jimmy watching and promptly dismissed the boys. Then he slicked back his black hair, put on a smile, and hustled across the parking lot as the muscle began unloading heavy blankets and thick canvas straps and laying them on the street.

"Mr. Hobbs, I'm—"

"It's Hobart. My fiancé is Roni Hobbs," he said, smiling as he remembered their previous conversation. *Hobart and Hobbs, attorneys at law.*

"Sorry," he said, scanning the paperwork until he found what he was looking for. Then he tapped his thick finger on the page and looked up. "My mistake, Mr. Hobart."

"No problem."

After a firm—yet sweaty—handshake, he added, "I'm Enzo Moretti. Those two are Leo and Eddie." As he said their names, he held his hand out to the side to indicate Leo was the tall one and Eddie was the shorter one.

The knuckleheads had resumed their shenanigans.

"Got it. And please, call me Jimmy."

Enzo shook his head and snickered as he watched them. "Kids. Their mother spoils them but if it were up to me ... "

Father and sons, Jimmy thought to himself. Then he smiled and nodded.

"Anyways, if you want to show us around, Jimmy, we can get started and get you folks on your way."

***

It took the Moretti boys three hours to pack ten years of memories—most happy but others not—and load them into the moving truck. When they were finished, Jimmy and Roni conducted one last walk-thru of the empty apartment to ensure nothing had been missed.

It's incredible how much dust collects in the nooks and crannies, hidden away from view. A few coins were on the living room rug where their leather sofa once was. A forgotten coffee mug on the drainboard. A magnetized dental appointment reminder in the shape of a tooth clung to the refrigerator door. *It was as if we were never here,* he thought to himself.

It's a strange thing, leaving one home for another. Buried feelings come bubbling to the surface. Like when an eight-year-old boy loses his mother and then finds himself and his sister relocated to a strange new town, living in a new house with their widower father, and making new friends at a new school.

Where did that come from? he wondered as he stuffed the dental reminder into his pocket.

Outside, the Moretti boys were still horsing around while closing the back of the truck. Roni was signing the paper on Enzo's steel clipboard, undoubtedly reminding him of the address of their next destination—classic Roni. Jimmy locked the apartment door and then stepped into the sun. "Adventure awaits," he said under his breath as if he had to remind himself.

Enzo was waiting for him when he finished saying goodbye to Crestview Apartments. "Everything look okay to you, Mr. Hobart?"

"Jimmy," he reminded. "Yep. Looks like your boys got everything."

"We'll give you some time to get to the house before we start unloading—I've gotta feed these two anyway. Meet you there at one?"

"Sounds good." Another handshake and Papa Moretti was on his way to the truck's cab.

Jimmy found Roni behind the wheel of her SUV. While the wonder twins took care of the heavy stuff, she had packed what remained in the refrigerator into coolers and the pantry items into tote bags. Then she loaded all of it into the cargo area of her Ford Edge. The passenger and back seats were crammed with everything she didn't want going into the moving van and wouldn't fit in the bed of Jimmy's truck.

When she rolled her window down, he was reminded of his little sister on that trip to Moultrie, stuffed into the back seat of the silver Taurus. "You look snug," he said with a smirk.

"Ha, ha. What'd he say?"

"They're gonna grab lunch then meet us at the house around one."

"Thank God. I'm starving."

"Me too." He leaned through the window and gave her a kiss. "I'll grab us something on the way and meet you there." Then he took a few backward steps and winked before jogging to his pickup.

***

When he arrived with fast-food cheeseburgers, room-temperature fries, and two fountain drinks, Roni had already unloaded the cold stuff from her vehicle and was halfway through with the totes. She joined him in the cab of his pickup where it was warm. They ate lunch and rehashed the exciting morning.

Then with renewed energy, she took the trash inside and started unpacking the coolers. At the same time, he hauled the remaining pantry bags from the cargo area of her SUV.

She was bent over in front of the fridge when he entered the kitchen. He squeezed by her with his arms full then climbed the four steps to the elevated pantry. Once inside the unfinished cubby, he sat one of the bags onto the floor and reached for the pull cord hanging from the bare bulb—

"Jimmy."

The silvery whisper cut through the darkness. His heart leaped to attention, pounding hard beneath his thin T-shirt. *The shade* was getting personal, but he knew something it didn't. *Nothing you see can harm you.* The mantra his mother taught him brought some comfort, but he remained frozen in place, his fingers pinched around the pull cord. In his other hand, the canvas bag straps were cutting through his sweaty skin.

He swallowed a mouthful of saliva, then finally gave the cord a tug. Jimmy's eyes narrowed as the sudden flash of light sent shadows scurrying along the stone walls and under the shelves. He turned in circles, looking up and down, searching all corners for *the shade* that knew his name. But as his eyes adjusted, he saw nothing. No one.

"What's taking so long," Roni said, feet pounding on the steps as she ran up behind him.

He spun wild-eyed toward her, kicking over the tote bag on the floor by his feet. A plastic container of parsley toppled from the bag, rolled toward the open door, then down the steps with a *tap-tap-tap* until eventually falling onto the kitchen floor and up against the center island.

"Smudge ... Are you okay?"

As his breathing settled, he answered, "I thought I heard something."

"What did you hear?" she asked, looking around the room.

"I thought ... It sounded like ..."

Don't say it, he told himself. *Don't say it, don't say it, don't—*

"... Like someone said my name."

Idiot.

She placed her hands on her hips and stared at him with one eyebrow raised. "Someone? Like who?"

He could almost hear his mother's scolding voice. *"See, Jimmy, what did I tell you? No one will understand."*

"I don't know ... It was like a whisper ... I know, it sounds stupid, right?"

She shrugged and let her gaze fade from his. "Well ... The fridge is right on the other side of the wall. Maybe that's what you heard?"

"Yeah, maybe," he said, bending to the floor to pick up the toppled tote. But he knew that wasn't true.

"What else do you think it could be?"

Demon. Evil spirit. Poltergeist. He could imagine many terrible things, none of which he was willing to say out loud. He had never been afraid of *shades,* but he had a feeling this one would change everything he thought he knew. And that scared the hell out of him.

He closed his eyes, drew a deep breath then placed the totes on the workstation along the back wall. "Why don't I leave this to you while I finish emptying our vehicles."

"Suit yourself." Then in a whisper, she said, "Jimmy."

She was laughing—he wasn't.

***

By the time the fresh air nipped at his cheeks he'd almost convinced himself the voice he'd heard *had* been the refrigerator, as Roni suggested. Almost. More than anything, that's what he wanted it to be. But first in the bedroom, then the root cellar, and now the pantry. Could they all be explained away so easily?

He decided to put it out of his mind and focus on what needed to be done. Six totes remained in the cargo area of Roni's SUV. He slung one over each shoulder and carried two in each hand, up the porch steps, through the entry door, then into the kitchen, where he plopped them at the foot of the pantry steps. *No reason to go back in there just yet,* he thought.

Then he sprinted through the front rooms and out the door for another load. After closing the SUV's hatchback, he jerked one of the suitcases from the back seat and set it on the gravel driveway. When he leaned in for the second one, he heard the deep drone of a diesel engine and the hiss of air brakes as the moving van decelerated and turned off Woody Creek Lane and into the driveway.

When the truck came into view, he waved and then continued sliding the enormous suitcases through the car door. The bags flopped across the gravel like fish out of water as he pulled them toward the porch. He carried them up the steps then rolled them the rest of the way to the door. He propped the storm door with his butt, then dropped the bags into the foyer one at a time.

"Roni ... They're here," he called out as the door slammed shut. Not waiting for her response, he got a grip on two bags and then started up the steps.

When he reached the top, he extended the handles then rolled the bags the rest of the way to the front bedroom on the left side of the hallway and into the dressing room—the future walk-in closet. Out of breath, he paused at the window in time to see Leo and Eddie exiting the passenger side of the cab in a flurry of crumpled fast-food wrappers and paper cups.

He shook his head as he watched them collect their trash and stuff it into an empty bag before their father could see. Then he realized Roni hadn't responded when he alerted her that the movers had arrived. He left the room and, trotting down the steps, called out, "Did you hear me? They're here."

Still no answer.

Enzo was already scolding his sons for the trash or some other infraction by the time Jimmy reached the front door. He leaned through the doorway to see if Roni was out front before returning to the back of the house to look for her.

In the kitchen, he immediately noticed the side exit door was open. But before going out to investigate, he checked the pantry. The light was still on, but she wasn't there. Cans and other items were still packed in the grocery bags on the shelf where he'd left them. It looked like she'd gone out the back door right after he went to the car to retrieve the rest of their luggage.

His mind started to go to an uncomfortable place. *What if the door had been unlocked? What if a drifter made his way from the woods, into the kitchen, and—*

He spun around, stepped into the kitchen, and went through the open door onto the porch. He looked right then left, but there was no sign of her. His heart had sped up by now, blood pumping with worry, panic ... Dread.

He stepped into the side yard and turned toward the back, his head swiveling left to right, searching for a clue, forgetting all about the Moretti comedy team in the driveway. Before he reached the row of dogwoods, the wind had picked up, rustling through the dry leaves of the surrounding forest, blowing against his back and pushing him toward the downward slope, toward the opening in the brush—

"Jimmy."

He froze as the familiar whisper slithered into his ear canal and chilled his bones faster than the November air. *What if something worse than a drifter came for her?* He brought one hand up to his forehead as if he could massage that thought out of his mind. He was sweating, actually sweating.

The wind calmed and it was quiet again. Still.

He took a step forward ... slowly ... then another—

"Gotcha!"

He didn't hear Roni run up behind him until she was on his back with her arms and legs wrapped around him. He stumbled forward and launched a series of 'f-bombs' but managed to stay on his feet. He was so relieved she was safe that it didn't occur to him to be angry. Then his legs gave out and they fell to the ground in a heap, laughing.

"I'm sorry," she said, trying to catch her breath through hearty laughs. "I just couldn't resist."

"Where the hell were you hiding?"

"Over there." She pointed toward the tree line bordering the side yard. "In the trees ... I heard you call out when the movers arrived, and I knew if I didn't answer you'd come looking for me ... So, I ran out the back and waited ... I thought you saw me at first."

He shook his head. "I thought you'd been kidnapped."

It felt good to lay there in the dormant grass, staring up at the blue sky, listening to the gentle *whoosh* of the wind, and inhaling the earthy pine aroma surrounding their yard. Their *home.* He propped himself on his elbow so he could face her. "You know I have to get you back for this?"

"Bring it on, Smudge," she taunted.

Then she reached for his neck and pulled him toward her. And as their lips met, the weight that had been wedding plans, mortgage papers, and moving men suddenly lifted from his body. He wrapped her up in his arms and tasted the hint of salt and melty cheese lingering on her tongue. As she rolled on top of him, the scent of raspberries brushed across his cheek and mingled with the hint of vanilla wafting from the open neckline of her blouse. And for a moment, it was just the two of them.

"Ahem."

He opened his eyes and saw Roni looking behind him. He craned his neck and found a red-faced Enzo Moretti standing about twenty feet away, averting his eyes. Roni smiled and sat up as she slid from Jimmy's body. They both hopped to their feet, brushed the debris from their clothes, then walked toward the house.

"I'll let you handle this," Roni muttered. "I'll get back to sorting the pantry." Then she scooted past the elder Moretti, up the steps and disappeared into the kitchen, closing the door behind her.

Now alone with Mr. Moretti, Jimmy suddenly felt like a horny teenager caught by his girlfriend's father. "We were just—"

"No need to explain," Enzo said with a wink. "I was young once too." Then he turned and started walking toward the front with Jimmy beside him. "Didn't like the city?"

He furrowed his brow. "Why would you say that?"

"Well, you're about as far away as you can get and still have city water."

Jimmy shrugged. "I guess."

Leo and Eddie were on the front porch when they rounded the corner.

"If you want to show us around, we'll get you moved in," Enzo said.

"Sounds good."

***

After the tour, Jimmy opened the storm door wide and adjusted the pump mechanism's washer so it would stay open. Then he stepped into the living room and awaited the first of many trips the Moretti brothers would make today.

At the truck, the elder Moretti appeared engaged in a heated discussion with Eddie—his shorter and presumably younger son—while Leo watched with delight.

"I told you not to stay out late, eh?" Enzo said as he thumped his clipboard. "Maybe next time you'll listen to your papa."

Leo laughed and gave his brother a shove. Eddie shoved him back. And before it could escalate further, their father smacked them both across the back of their heads and told them to get to work.

At thirty years old himself, Jimmy figured the boys couldn't be much younger. In fact, it wasn't that long ago that he'd been doing all the heavy lifting. Fresh out of college and just starting their careers, they didn't have the money to afford movers—back then, they didn't have much of anything really. But they did have friends that would work for beer and pizza. And in your twenties, what's one grueling, physically exhausting day?

But now, Jimmy would rather eat dirt than carry two boxes at a time while his heart pounded in his ears and sweat dripped down his aching back. *This is what growing up is all about,* he told himself. Then he smiled, standing in the doorway of his first home with clean hands tucked into his pockets while someone else broke a sweat.

Eddie emerged from the back of the truck with his thick arms around a two-foot-long by two-foot-high quilt-wrapped bundle, climbed the porch steps then approached Jimmy. "Where do you want this, sir?"

Sir? Did he just call me sir? Jimmy recognized the object as one of a set of living room end tables, but he couldn't come up with the words to respond to the man-child. He wanted to take the thirty-pound piece of furniture and carry it the rest of the way himself—

"Sir, it's getting kind of heavy."

"Eddie, I asked you before to call me Jimmy."

"My dad won't let us. I could call you Mr. Hobart if you prefer?"

Jimmy sighed and shook his head, then pointed into the sitting room, suddenly feeling ... old.

***

For as long as he'd known Roni, she'd always been squeamish when it came to watching furniture—or anything large and heavy—as it was carried through narrow doorways or up flights of stairs. Which is why she wasn't present to witness the brothers stumble while carrying the mahogany and poplar wood king-size headboard over the threshold into the foyer, nearly jamming a corner through one freshly painted daffodil yellow wall.

Jimmy didn't mind her charming quirk. It was just another reason why he fell in love with her.

It was one of the last things off the truck, and now, two hours after arriving, the Moretti boys were busy assembling the king-size bedframe in the master bedroom.

Jimmy decided to make himself useful by finding the box labeled 'bath towels,' so he and Roni could get showers tonight.

All boxes labeled '2nd floor' had been crammed into the smaller of the two front bedrooms and were stacked in no particular order. He removed them one after the other, shuffling them around while trying hard to ignore the banging coming from the front bedroom, until he found the box he was looking for. Then he carried it to the linen closet. Roni had scrubbed the shelves and lined them with red and white floral paper. The lavender-scented pouch at the back of the second shelf was emblazoned with the word CALM. So, he breathed in a deep helping, hoping it would push away the image of two hammer-wielding apes jumping up and down on the mahogany headboard.

He unboxed one towel at a time, refolding each before placing it on a shelf until the box was empty. Then he decided to hunt for the box labeled 'sheets.'

But first, he decided to take a detour to the larger back bedroom. This is where he'd instructed the muscle to bring his desk, ergonomic chair, printer, and file cabinet. It was the only upstairs room with a view of the backyard—perfect for his home office.

While mentally repositioning the desk, he became aware of how quiet it had become. *Could they be finished already?* Taking care to avoid the creaky spots, he stepped into the hallway and toward the master bedroom to check on the movers.

He could hear their lowered voices as he stepped closer, but their words were garbled. He needed to move closer ... Slowly ... Carefully. He hated to eavesdrop, but he was curious what they were being so secretive about. *Women? Their father? Me?* When he reached the doorway, he craned his neck just enough to get a peek. The boys were holding their tools while sitting close together on the floor inside the bed rails. He only heard four words before ducking back around the corner.

"... shanty in the woods."

Eddie was speaking the tail end of a sentence that, without context, had no meaning. So why was he so sure they were talking about the root cellar? *His* root cellar. There was only one way to know for sure. With his back against the wall, he slid closer to the doorway.

"Bullshit," Leo said.

"It's true," Eddie hissed.

"You'll believe anything."

Jimmy smiled as he pictured Leo's eyes rolling at his younger brother. Then he heard the familiar *click-click-click* of the socket wrench signaling a return to work. But Eddie's voice persisted, his words coming rapid fire as he tried to convince his brother.

"Me and my friends drove out here one night, planning to sleep over, but it was just too creepy. Later, I googled the old house and—

Creak.

Eddie and the socket wrench both fell silent.

Jimmy closed his eyes and cursed the squeaky floorboard under his breath for giving him away before he could get the whole story. Seeing no other choice, he stepped into view. "How's it coming, guys?"

"Oh, hey, Mr. Hobart," Leo said, practically jumping to his feet.

Mister, is it? He suddenly felt ancient.

"We're almost finished."

While Leo secured the last of the bolts, Eddie wiped the sweat from his forehead and picked up the wooden slats that would lay across the bedframe to support the mattress.

"I couldn't help but overhear your conversation. Were you talking about our house?"

Eddie stumbled over the rubber mallet lying on the floor and dropped the wooden slats in a *clatter*.

"*Goffo*," Leo said.

Eddie stood there, gut-punched, his big brown eyes locked on Jimmy's gaze, while his brother began gathering the slats.

"Sorry, Mr. Hobart," Leo added. "My brother is a klutz."

Neither brother answered his question. "If there's something I should know—"

Leo patted his brother on the arm, knocking him out of his stupor. Then to Jimmy, he said, "Don't pay him any mind ... We never do."

Jimmy nodded then watched the brothers position the eight wooden slats inside the frame. Every few seconds, Eddie would make eye contact with him but then quickly look away.

Before putting the mattress in place, Leo said, "How's it look, Mr. Hobart?"

"Jimmy. Call me Jimmy."

"Oh, I can't do that—"

"Right. Your father," he sighed.

Jimmy directed the Moretti boys to center the frame along the north wall then they carefully laid the mattress onto the frame and placed the end tables beside the bed.

"That looks great. Thank you."

"We're all finished," Leo said, "but you'll want to double-check the truck in case something fell out of a box or something ... Once you sign off, we'll be on our way."

"Okay. I'll meet you downstairs."

Jimmy hoped Eddie would lag behind and maybe fill him in on the secret about 'the shanty in the woods,' but he was already out of sight.

***

With The Moretti Movers long gone, the fictional detective team of Hobart and Hobbs was alone in the woods and settling into their new home. But Jimmy couldn't stop thinking about Eddie. He sat on the naked king-size mattress, staring at nothing, picturing the boy's deep well-like eyes. At the same time, Roni busied herself, unpacking her suitcase.

"Something had that kid worked up," he finally said. "You didn't see his face."

"The house has been empty for a while—Millie told us that," she reminded him. "I'm sure there are plenty of rumors swirling around about the creepy house in the woods."

He nodded, his brow furrowed, as he watched her go happily back and forth between the suitcase and the dresser, seemingly undisturbed that their house may have a checkered past. But she didn't know the things that he knew. She hadn't heard the voice—*or was it voices?* He felt the mattress bounce and turned to see her sitting beside him.

"I think you're overreacting," she said.

"Yeah, but what he said—"

"You're going to take the word of Eddie Moretti?"

He chortled at her point.

"Besides, you don't believe in evil spirits."

He believed there was a presence in this house. But was it evil? Suddenly he was that little boy that had just seen his dead grandfather. But this time, his mother wasn't here to brush the hair from his forehead and tell him, *"Nothing you see can harm you."* He believed her then but what if she was wrong? These recent encounters were different than anything he'd experienced in the past. And he hadn't *seen* this *shade* ... Not yet.

Roni put her arm around his shoulder and squeezed. "You don't believe in evil spirits, do you, Smudge?"

Finally, he smiled and shook his head. "You're right."

"Can I get that in writing?" she said, howling with laughter.

"Plausible deniability."

"Coward," she said as she rose from the mattress. Then she zipped up the empty suitcase and carried it to the dressing room—which for now had become a catchall until it could be converted into a walk-in closet.

He sat on the mattress, twisting his bottom lip between his first finger and thumb as he fought the urge to pick at the raw skin with his nails.

She returned from the closet and folded her arms across her chest. "If you're not going to unpack, why don't we get some dinner? I'm starved."

"Sounds good." He released his lip and stood up. "If it's all the same to you, I think I'll board up the root cellar."

"You can demo it for all I care ... That place creeps me out."

***

Just a twenty-minute drive north, they found a small shopping plaza and a locally owned pizza parlor called *Franks*. They sat at the bar and ordered two draft beers and one large hand-tossed garbage pizza to go—that's what Roni called a pizza with everything.

Ten minutes later, they were on their way home, basking in the aroma of melted cheese, greasy meats, and bubbly red sauce spiced with garlic and oregano wafting from the pizza cooling on Roni's lap. Lightning flashes lit up the night like paparazzi flashbulbs as a regiment of violet clouds marched closer.

As he turned into the gravel driveway, the first drops of rain dotted the windshield. The house was a gothic silhouette against the backdrop of the coming storm. They hadn't considered the hour when they left, and now, with no lights to warm the windows, it looked as cold and empty as the day they first found it. He also hadn't started the boiler in the basement, so there would be no radiator heat. Not a good start to their first night.

After parking the truck and cutting the engine, Jimmy grabbed the pizza box and followed Roni to the porch. They had barely stepped across the threshold when the downpour began, hurling fat water droplets against the house. He flipped up the light switch in the foyer and nothing happened. He flipped the switch down and up several more times to no avail.

"Power's out," Roni said as she jiggled another switch.

"There's that temperamental electricity," he laughed, recalling Millie's unique flaw description.

"There're some logs on the back porch. Why don't you get a fire started?" she said as she disappeared into the kitchen through the swinging door.

He made his way to the dining room, avoiding shadows that may or may not be furniture. By the time he'd set the box on the table, she was back with two long-stemmed lighters. After handing one to Jimmy, she began touching the flame of the other to scented candles she had strategically positioned around the room for just this sort of emergency. Never had he been more grateful for her love of candles.

He retrieved an armload of logs from outside and then stacked them in the hearth in the sitting room. Using the lighter, he lit the kindling. The room began to glow with dancing flames reflecting on the dark window glass while the storm blew fiercely through the surrounding forest.

Meanwhile, Roni had rounded up two paper plates, two bottles of cold beer, a roll of paper towels, and a blanket from the upstairs linen closet. He spread the blanket in front of the warm fire and while thunder rumbled in the distance, they talked and laughed, drank beer, and ate room-temperature garbage pizza.

The house was different at night ... In the dark.

Shadows lurked in every dark corner, shifting and squirming, trying to stay hidden from the dancing flames and flashes of light outside the windows. Phantoms that watched as the new lord and lady of the manor made love in front of the hearth where eventually, with their heads on sofa pillows and their nude bodies covered under a blanket, they fell asleep.

Chapter 6

"*D*OO WAH, DOO WAH, DOO WAH, DOO WAH!*"

Jimmy sat straight up on the floor, awakened by the gravelly voice and screeching orchestra playing at a volume he hadn't heard since his college bar-hopping days. He squinted his eyes to block out the light that seemed to be coming from every bulb in the room as the chaotic mixture of brass and percussion played on.

"What is that?" Roni shouted, with her hands over her ears.

"The radio. I guess it came on when the power was restored."

"Turn it off!"

The logs had burned down to ash with only a few glowing embers remaining in a pile and, without the boiler pumping steam heat through the radiator, the room had grown cold. But the music had to be stopped. Jimmy slipped from under the covers and sprinted into the dining room. As the next chorus started, he fumbled, still half asleep, through the clutter piled on the buffet table until finally, he found it. Resisting the urge to throw it against the wall, he pressed the on/off button instead.

"*DOO WAH, DOO WAH, DOO—*"

No more music.

Peace.

"Oh, thank God," Roni groaned from the other room, her head emerging from beneath the blanket where she'd been taking shelter.

It was only then that it occurred to him he was standing naked under the lights and in front of the open curtains—something he could never do while living at the apartment (too many neighbors). The corner of his mouth turned up into a smirk. *No neighbors here, though.*

Then he jerked the electrical cord from the wall and began winding it around the radio. *Why was it even plugged in?* he wondered. *And why was it tuned to that station? We're not fans of big band music—and certainly not at that volume.* Bewildered, he set the radio onto the chaotic heap—*Moretti's! Of course it was them ... Stupid kids playing a prank. I wonder what other surprises they left for us.*

"What time is it anyway?" Roni asked.

"I dunno. Late by the looks of it ... Storm seems to be over, though." He turned off the lights in the dining room and then checked through the butler door into the kitchen. Sure enough, that light was also on. He flipped that switch down then found his phone lying on one of the end tables in the sitting room. "It's 2:20."

"Hurry up and come back to bed ... I'm freezing."

He flipped the switch in the foyer, killing the light from the floor lamp, then turned off the overhead chandelier sending the sitting room into darkness. A memory of the room remained burned onto his retinas like on a negative from a film camera.

All was quiet around their home in the woods.

Before returning to Roni, he stopped at the front window. In the distance, velvety amethyst clouds followed remnants of the storm like a coronation robe trailing behind royalty. Through the clearing, he could see stars—more than he ever saw from the parking lot of their old apartment in the city. *Old apartment,* he repeated to himself. As if they hadn't just woken up there yesterday morning. That felt like so long ago.

As he started to turn away, his eyes settled on where the trees opened onto Woody Creek Lane. A streetlight shined over what appeared to be a man standing at the end of the gravel driveway. Jimmy's stomach fluttered as he leaned toward the glass and rubbed his eyes, staring unblinkingly at the shadowy form.

A gust stirred in the night, swaying the pines. The streetlamp flickered and the phantom's skinny torso bent forward in an unnatural way. The wind swirled around, bending the figure backward until its long limbs touched the pavement. Then it grew still. The gangly thing popped upright, swayed, and then stood straight once again.

Jimmy released his breath. *Just a tree.*

"Now that the power's back, can we turn the heat on?" Roni asked.

"Tomorrow," he said, not at all interested in going into the basement just now. He placed two logs into the hearth then stoked the embers with the cast iron poker. Fresh flames quickly took hold and began *crackling* and spitting with delight. He repositioned the fireplace screen then crawled under the blanket next to her and she promptly snuggled close to him.

As his eyes began to close, he caught a glimpse of movement in the periphery. He spun his head toward the shadows in the room's northwest corner but there was nothing there. Just his eyes playing tricks while the house settled down.

He wanted to believe that.

But he couldn't shake the feeling that he was being watched.

Chapter 7

After the big band wake-up call, Jimmy never fell back to sleep. His eyes remained trained on the northwest corner of the sitting room until dawn finally arrived, and he could see precisely what had been 'watching' him during the night and he remembered what had happened.

Last night in his haste to get naked, he had tossed his T-shirt over a decorative owl lantern light perched on a box in the corner (they had actually laughed about the peeping eyes of Mr. Owl). When he returned to bed at 2:20 in the morning, the T-shirt had slid from the owl's head, exposing its large saucer-shaped eyes. It freaked him out to the point he couldn't go back to sleep.

It was kind of funny now that he knew what had happened. But thanks to the storm, the temperamental wiring, the damn owl, and the Moretti's—don't forget them—his back ached from sleeping on the floor, and he was too tired to laugh. Still, he'd resolved to tackle the ancient boiler in the basement. And with the satellite dish installer coming later and his heart set on a full day of football on the big screen, he needed to take care of it sooner rather than later.

He'd been in the basement once, the day of the open house. That day, with Millie and Roni, it hadn't seemed so bad, but that was two months ago and this time, he'd be alone.

After a breakfast of cold cereal and orange juice—neither of them was up for cooking a big meal considering the night they'd had—he stood at the top of the stairs, staring into the darkness and inhaling the blend of damp concrete and stale earth before finally flipping the light switch. He also had a flashlight just in case.

He started down the steps, thumping his feet loudly on the wood as a warning to anything—or anyone—that may be prowling in the shadows. This seemed like perfectly reasonable behavior to someone who's seen his fair share of *shades* and read more than his share of horror novels.

The basement was lit up by six bare bulbs hanging from the rafters. He paused at the bottom of the steps to scan the room and found no shadows or lurkers scurrying into the concrete corners. It looked the same as it did a little over a month ago. He was starting to feel like that scared kid that used to read Stephen King novels late at night and then wondered why he couldn't fall asleep. A feeling he thought he'd left behind when he entered high school but apparently there were some things you never outgrow.

He slipped the flashlight into his back pocket, having no need for it just now, and approached the boiler standing in the far-left corner of the room. It looked suspiciously like the robot maid from that futuristic cartoon that aired in the 1960s. *What was the name of the show?* "Come on, Jimmy boy," he muttered in his best, high-pitched Brooklyn accent. "What are you waitin' for?" Then he rolled his eyes and laughed to himself. "How can a robot be from Brooklyn?"

Two months ago, he knew absolutely nothing about electric boilers so he'd devoured as much information as he could find on Google and by chatting up the know-it-alls at the local hardware store. Essentially, what he'd learned was that it worked a lot like a hot water tank: fill it full of cold water, which was then heated and transferred through piping that leads to cast iron radiators positioned around the house that may be turned on or off to provide on-demand, zoned heating.

Standing in front of Rosie—as good a nickname for the boiler as any—he unlocked his cell phone and pulled up his notes. First, inspect all ventilation and combustion air openings to ensure they are clean and debris-free. "*Ya' hafta' do the startup checks,*" he recalled one leathery-skinned man say. There was no water in the boiler—which was to be expected since it had been off for some time. He pulled the handle of the water feed valve and watched with amazement as water flowed into the tank. When the water reached the appropriate level, he pushed up on the handle, closing the feed valve.

"So far, so good."

He ran through the rest of the series of checks and, as time dragged on, he couldn't help picturing Roni wearing a knit hat and mittens with a blanket draped around her shoulders yet still shivering. But he wanted to do everything by the book and make the old know-it-alls proud.

Finally, it was time to start old Rosie up.

"Operating controls closed," he said. Then, after performing the task, he responded, "Check." And so it went, down the list as he sounded like the flight commander at NASA mission control calling out the requirements of a safe startup and the astronaut completing each assignment as they prepared for launch.

"Interlocks closed ... Check ... Start fans and purge boiler ... Check."

When he reached the last item on the list, he paused. It was the moment of truth.

"Energize igniter." After a deep breath, he pushed the button and said, "Check."

The boiler began to rumble and shimmy. Jimmy took a step backward, bracing himself for what was sure to be an explosion. But there wasn't one. Instead, the rumble settled into a soft, continuous purr. He stepped closer and placed his hand on Rosie's tummy—it was warm.

"Yes!" he exclaimed, vigorously pumping his fist to celebrate his accomplishment.

"What's going on down there?" Roni's muffled voice called out from above.

"Almost done," he yelled at the ceiling. Then, picturing the know-it-alls that were skeptical he'd be able to get the old girl working, he pointed and mumbled, "Take that."

Rosie seemed to smile back at him as he gloated, so again, imitating the cartoon robot's voice, he said, "Well done, Jimmy boy." Then he laughed at himself as he turned around and surveyed the basement. Then he thought to himself, *This isn't so bad. What was I so afraid of?* He slipped his cell phone into his back pocket and started toward the steps when he saw movement in his peripheral vision.

He quickly turned in time to see a shadow duck behind the water heater. He wasn't half asleep this time, and that was no decorative owl light with saucer-shaped eyes. "What the—"

He was interrupted by a low, guttural growl, like the *thump-thump-thump* of a Harley just getting warmed up—or was that the sound of his heart? Either way, he couldn't move. Upstairs he heard Roni's footfalls. He tracked her movement as she crossed the room and approached the basement door.

"You've been down here forever," she said, stomping down the steps. "When are you—"

"Shhh ... Over there," he whispered, pointing toward the water heater.

"What is it?" She stopped halfway down and ducked her head under the ceiling, trying to find what he was pointing at. "I don't see anything."

"Behind the water heater."

Grrrrr.

She gasped and pressed her back against the wall. "What the hell was that?"

"I don't know."

He looked around and spotted a broom leaning against the wall to his right. He stepped sideways toward it, slowly, keeping his eyes fixed on where the monstrous beast was hiding in case it attacked. When he reached the broom, he gripped it with both hands and held it across his body as he moved toward the water heater.

"Jimmy," she whispered, "Be careful."

The shadow growled again, followed by what sounded like an unattended pot of water boiling over onto a hot burner—a warning that, whatever it was,

was about to strike. He swept the bristled end of the broom toward the water heater and the thing scurried out of its hiding place.

"Racoon!" Jimmy yelled as he swatted.

But he wasn't fast enough. The creature disappeared under the steps.

"It's a cat," Roni said, sliding her smartphone from her back pocket as she hurried to the floor. Then she opened the flashlight app and shined it into the darkness until she spotted two green eyes glowing like marbles.

Jimmy crouched beside her, still holding the broom, to have a look for himself. The mass of black fur was huddled against the wall, with its long fluffy tail coiled around itself.

"Here," she said, handing him her phone. "I'll be right back."

"Where are you going?"

She was halfway up the steps when she answered, "He looks hungry."

Jimmy stood watch, one hand holding her phone, the other still clutching the broom just in case the cat decided to try something. Two minutes later, Roni was back with an open can of tuna she found in the pantry.

"I can't believe this little guy had you so scared," she scolded as she set the can on the concrete and then slid it under the steps toward the trespasser.

Feeling slightly silly, Jimmy was wondering the same thing. But for all he knew, the creature hiding behind the water heater *had* been a rabid raccoon and he wasn't about to take any chances.

The cat's nose began to twitch, and then carefully, he leaned toward the fishy treat and began to eat as Roni watched on with delight, quietly patting her hands together.

Jimmy could see she was already trying to decide on a name for the intruder, but he had other ideas. "So how are we going to get rid of it?"

She whipped her head around and, with her chin hanging low and eyebrows drawn together, blew out a huff of disgust.

He raised his palms apologetically and didn't say another word.

A few minutes later, the cat emerged from the safety of the cubby beneath the steps, his plush coat rippling in waves over his shoulders and rear haunches with each slinking step. Without a physical exam to confirm the cat's gender, Jimmy was already convinced it was male, just based on his size alone.

He was three feet long from tip to tail and at least twenty pounds. The wide-set almond-shaped eyes and lynx-like tufts of fur poking from the tips of his ears gave him away as a Maine Coon—whose name was derived from the Racoon because of their long tapered tails, hence Jimmy's initial confusion.

Hunkered down under the steps, his fur appeared black as coal but as he gratefully rubbed his head and back on Roni's legs, he looked more silver. She bent over and stroked his arched back then picked him up. "Looks like we have our first pet," she cooed, flashing doe-eyes in Jimmy's direction as the cat purred loudly with approval.

Great. Just what I wanted. He reached toward the cat, but before he could sink his fingers into the silky fur, the creature growled and hissed, baring bright white snake-like fangs. He recoiled his hand to avoid being scratched or bitten. "Maybe we should put him outside."

"Nooo, it's cold out. He can stay inside where it's warm." Then she turned toward the staircase, her face buried in the cat's thick mane as he vibrated in her arms.

It appeared Jimmy was already outnumbered, and it was only their second day in the house. How could he say no? *Can I say no?*

Then, halfway up the stairs, she asked, "What should we call him?"

At least he didn't whisper, "Jimmy."

Chapter 8

An hour later, Roni walked out the door in search of pet supplies for their new addition. There was no pet store in the small town, of that Jimmy was sure. Besides Frank's Pizza, the shopping plaza had a laundromat, liquor store, hardware store, a CPA (closed until tax season), and a nail salon. It also had a mom-and-pop grocery that would likely carry all the basics. If she went there, she could be back in an hour, but knowing Roni, she would want more than just the basics. That meant she was going into the city and could be gone for hours.

Left behind to wait for the satellite installer, Jimmy stood in the parlor watching through the bay window as her SUV disappeared down the gravel driveway.

But he wasn't alone. Not really.

The silence was suddenly interrupted by the hypnotic rumble beside him. He looked down to find Coal perched on the built-in window seat. That was the cat's name now, as in charcoal. Roni liked it because of his beautiful smokey coat.

Coal was watching Roni drive away too. Until her taillights disappeared onto Woody Creek Lane, and he felt Jimmy's eyes on him. Then he cocked his head sideways and looked up. His pupils were thin vertical slits cutting through the center of two large emeralds as he stared contemptuously at his new roommate.

By all accounts, Coal didn't like Jimmy. The feeling was mutual. But apparently, he came with the house as part of a package deal—something that wasn't mentioned in the fine print of the closing documents. He remembered hearing that cats gravitate toward people who *aren't* staring at them—something about being aloof giving off a friendlier vibe than direct eye contact, which cats consider quite threatening.

Jimmy saw this as his chance to assert his dominance. So, he made a point not to look away from the feline freeloader's gaze. Their eyes were locked in a tense stare down for at least ten seconds as the air stung his eyes.

Unimpressed, Coal finally looked away and began grooming one of his front paws.

Jimmy took it as a small victory—a line in the sand. "Now that we know who's boss," he muttered as he turned, "I'm going upstairs."

***

Before moving day, they had decided the room across the hall from their bedroom would be the guest room. But last night, over pizza and beers, Roni suggested that perhaps that had been a mistake. *"Imagine my parents coming to visit and staying in the room across the hall from us,"* she said. *"Wouldn't you rather have them in the back of the house—far, far away?"*

She had a point. But they had already claimed the back bedrooms for themselves. He had made a case for why he should have the southeast room, citing his files, books, desk, and drafting table, and that she, being an artist, would benefit more from the light in the smaller room than he would. Really he just wanted a view of the backyard, something the other back bedroom didn't have. She grudgingly accepted his argument, but now that he thought about it, she had conceded a little too easily. And now he was the one moving.

And what better time to do it than while she was gone shopping.

Thump, thump, creak—

I've gotta fix that step, he thought.

At the top of the stairs, he first decided to peek in Roni's studio on the northeast side of the house beside the bathroom. A cozy bump-out addition with four eight-foot windows overlooking the side yard is where she decided to set up her easel. It was the perfect spot for viewing both the sunrise and sunset. And now he understood.

"She should have been a lawyer." He smirked and shook his head then crossed the hall to the room formerly known as his office. After a quick goodbye to the backyard view, he picked up the first box and carried it to the front bedroom, where several unpacked boxes were stacked along one wall. They would have to be transferred to the new guest room to make room for his office. He let out a heavy sigh, sat down his box, picked up one of the miscellaneous ones, and took it with him on his return to the back room.

After twelve trips back and forth, he stopped counting. The sweat on his brow and ache in his back and knees told him he'd been at this task far too long when finally, he was hauling the last box. He returned to the office empty-handed this time having transferred the miscellaneous boxes three trips ago. He spied the ergonomic chair parked under his desk. His body begged for a break, but if he sat down now, he wouldn't finish.

He slid the chair aside and sized up the desk. It was the first piece of furniture he designed and made himself. Cut from walnut and stained a warm cherry color, the three-drawer writing desk was 60 inches long and weighed over 100 pounds. *Where are those Moretti boys when you need them?*

Usually, he would just slide it along the floor, but he didn't dare do that on these historic natural hardwood planks. He knew he could lift the desk but carrying it the length of the hallway ... twenty-five feet? That was another story. Plus, navigating the narrow doorway on his own would be tricky. He thought about waiting for Roni, but then he devised a plan.

He tore away a piece of cardboard from one of the box tops, divided it into four equal strips, then slid one under each of the four legs of the desk. Once they were in position, he pushed the desk, and it slid easily along the floor.

Next, he covered the desk with a blanket to protect the edges while maneuvering it through the doorway. Then he carefully lifted, tilted, and angled the desk through the opening, allowing the blanket to absorb the bumps.

It was heavier than he remembered, or maybe he was just older and needed to hit the gym more often. *When was the last time I worked out?* he wondered. *Perhaps the basement could become a home gym?* Once he'd wiggled the desk into the hallway, he paused to stretch his back and catch his breath before continuing. He quickly learned it made more sense to pull the desk rather than push—after a few inches, the bulky furniture had slid right off the cardboard sliders.

By the time he'd reached the front room, sweat was creeping down his back. Once again, he stopped for a breather, bending at the waist with his hands on his knees. Sweat dripped from his nose and landed in a puddle on the wood floor. Then another. *Just a few more feet and this part is over.* He forced himself to straighten, then repeated the same lift and tilt technique to get through the doorway—a little less gracefully this time—and became stuck halfway through. If he didn't know better, he would have sworn the desk had doubled its weight since leaving the back room.

"Come on, you son of a—"

One final heave and it was through. He slid the blanket onto the floor then dragged the desk into place in the center of the room, between the two front windows and facing the door, just like James "Wild Bill" Hickok.

Just a few weeks after arriving in the gold rush town of Deadwood, South Dakota, Wild Bill, who served as a spy, a scout, and a sharpshooter during the civil war, decided to join a game of poker. Wild Bill never turned his back to the door at a poker table but, on this fateful day, there was only one seat available—a little factoid Jimmy learned in 2002 while on a family vacation out West.

It was the summer after his mother had been killed and a month before his father moved them to a new town to 'start over'. They were on another road trip, this time with his father behind the wheel of his 1990 Navy Blue Dodge Shadow—the silver Taurus had been sold months ago.

Again, Jimmy was the navigator while his sister shared the back seat with a stack of pillows, a cooler full of canned beverages and cold cuts, and a bag of snacks. But there were no stops at Stuckey's or any other interesting sites for that matter. Only highway rest stops for quick pee breaks before getting back on the road. *"And no shenanigans with truck drivers."* His father was more regimented than his mother had been, and once they were on the road, he wanted to get as far as possible before stopping again.

Somewhere around mile marker 235 in Colorado, his father's white-knuckled death grip on the steering wheel began to relax. Until that moment, Jimmy had felt like they were trying to outrun something. He'd felt that way for the last eight months as Thanksgiving and Christmas passed in a blur like the last thousand miles of roadside scenery. But suddenly, he noticed the white-capped Rocky Mountains in the distance and mountain goats grazing by the side of the highway. His father saw them too.

After eighteen hours on the road, they finally stopped for the night at a motel in Rifle, Colorado. Elizabeth had to be carried into the room and was put straight to bed while Jimmy helped his father unload the car. He was only nine, but he felt all grown up with the added responsibility.

In the morning, Jimmy woke to find his father's bed empty. He could see him standing just outside the room through the open curtains, sipping coffee from a motel mug, far away in his own thoughts. Jimmy got dressed and joined him on the second-floor balcony. And while Elizabeth dreamt of whatever little girls dream of, Jimmy and his father stared at the ring of mountains around them and had the first of what would be many man-to-man talks.

That's when he found out that his mother had planned this trip, not his father. She had used a computer at the local library—they didn't have one at home yet—and mapped their route, including where to stop for the night based on points of interest. They were supposed to go last summer—before she died—but at the last minute, his father couldn't take the time off work. That's why she had taken Jimmy and his sister to Moultrie, Georgia instead.

So, they took the vacation she had planned, and they saw everything she had wanted them to see. Starting with Dinosaur National Monument Fossil Bone Quarry. Then after that, it was the world's largest natural mineral hot spring before more ancient fossils at the Wyoming Dinosaur Center. Then on to The Little Bighorn Battlefield National Monument to see where George Armstrong Custer fell. It was by then that Jimmy realized his mother was a genius.

Later that afternoon, they circled back into Wyoming and visited Devil's Tower and, if he was being honest, he was a bit disappointed when he found out it was more likely to be a 1.5-billion-year-old volcano core than an alien landing site as depicted in that sci-fi movie. But still, it was really cool. Then it was on to see Mt. Rushmore, the Crazy Horse Monument, and more dinosaur fossils at The Mammoth Site.

But before returning home, there was one final stop to make. A self-proclaimed wild West historian, Jimmy's father couldn't resist adding Deadwood, South Dakota to their itinerary. Born out of the gold rush, Deadwood had once been a playground for outlaws, gamblers, and gunslingers—it was also where Wild Bill Hickok lost his life.

On his final night in Nuttal & Mann's Saloon, Wild Bill was forced to sit with his back to the door—so he never saw John "Crooked Nose Jack" McCall coming. While holding a pair of aces and a pair of eights—the dead man's hand—Wild Bill was taken down with a single gunshot to the head.

Jimmy knew how silly it was to imagine an assassin or someone with a grudge trying to get the drop on him. Facing the entryway just made sense—*feng shui* and all that. But telling anyone who wondered that it was because he didn't want to suffer the same fate as Wild Bill Hickok ... Well, that was a hell of a lot more interesting than *feng shui*. And it kept the memory of that summer with his father alive in his mind and in his heart.

That trip was the first time he remembered seeing his father happy after his mother's death. Really happy. And maybe it was the higher altitude, but by the end of their wild West adventure, Jimmy felt lighter somehow. They all did. And on the drive home, his father pumped his arm at truckers along with his children, turned up the volume on the radio, sang at the top of his lungs, and stopped at every roadside attraction as if they had all the time in the world.

Later, during one of their talks, Jimmy's father called that trip a love letter from his mother. He didn't understand that as a boy, but he did now.

Once he was sure the desk was straight, he brought in the ergonomic chair, sat down, then used his feet to scoot it into place. Leaning back, he took a moment to look around the room—trying it on so to speak. He envisioned his bookshelves lining the wall straight ahead. To his left, he saw the tips of trees through the north-facing side window. Behind him, the bay window offered abundant natural light. He spun the chair around and admired the view overlooking the driveway and front yard. In the summer, the sparse trees lining Woody Creek Lane would be full and—

Creee-ak.

His body instantly tensed as the sound of the squeaky step went through him like an electric shock. He spun around, half expecting to see 'Crooked Nose Jack' McCall standing in the doorway, holding his six-shooter at his hip. But there was no one there.

Slowly, he allowed the chair to lean forward until he was sitting straight behind the walnut writing desk. From this vantage, he could only see a sliver of the hallway. The wall would obstruct their assent if anyone was coming up the steps. He shifted his eyes to the right and found his vintage Jackie Robinson H&B Power Drive baseball bat leaning in the corner. Anyone stupid enough to break in would regret it instantly after the first swing of the pine bat made contact with their head—if he could get to it in time.

But he didn't hear anyone break in. And he was sure the doors were locked.

He stood up and glanced down at the driveway through the bay window. Only his pickup was there. He stepped around the desk and toward the corner, grasping the bat in his right hand. Then with his back against the wall, he slid toward the doorway, eyes trained on the hall in search of the slightest movement.

At the threshold, he quickly poked his head around the corner, then with his heart pounding, mouth dry, and ears ringing, he raised the bat over his shoulder. Then he pounced into the hallway, landing with his eyes wide, knees bent, head swiveling, and ready to swing.

But no one was there.

He lowered the bat slightly and straightened his knees while his heart slowed to a trot. Not convinced yet that he was out of danger, he took two steps toward the staircase and turned right into the alcove. At the top of the stairs lay a mound of black fur.

Carefully, Jimmy stepped closer ... closer ... until the lump rose and turned abruptly—

"Maou?"

Startled and apparently miffed at having his daily cleaning ritual so rudely interrupted, a stern-faced Coal aimed two glowing green orbs directly at him and hissed.

Cats were known for their stealth, walking on their toes and the balls of their feet to enable quick, quiet movement. So, Jimmy thought it was uncharacteristic for a cat to cause a step to squeak. Although, for a cat, Coal was on the large side—about the size of a small dog.

Still, something had him unsettled.

He surveyed the hall from the safety of his position while a curious Coal looked on, one paw raised toward his mouth, preparing to be licked. He tried to convince himself that even if someone had managed to enter the house without him hearing and then climbed the steps, there wasn't enough time for that person to have made it into one of the back rooms without him seeing or hearing their footfalls.

Or was there?

He stepped back into the hall, staring toward the open doors in the back of the house and listening for any sounds of movement while Coal moved on to grooming other body parts.

Once he felt it was safe, Jimmy retreated into his new office. He leaned the bat against the wall between the doorway and the closet then proceeded to mentally unpack the rest of his things. He'd already decided where the bookshelves would be set up, so he had to decide where to place his file cabinet and—

Scritch, scratch, screech, scratch.

"Damn cat," he grumbled, stomping through the open door and into the hallway. "So help me, if you're sharpening your claws on the wood, you'll be out on the street—"

"Maou?"

There he was, exactly where he'd left him, now lying quietly at the top of the stairs, having completed his daily bath. *But if it wasn't him making the noise—*

A shadow moved at the end of the hall, cutting through the beam of light coming from Jimmy's former office. *Scritch ... tap-tap ... screech.* He stepped backward slowly, eyes fixed on the back room, until he reached the opening on his left. Then Jimmy reached around the corner and grabbed the bat still leaning against the wall. Holding it with both hands, he tiptoed quietly toward the back bedroom—

"hrn-rhn-hrn-rhn"

—past the murky alcove where Coal had resumed his after-bath nap—*screech, scratch*—darkness fluttered through the soft glow of sunlight illuminating the hallway just outside the room. He raised the bat to shoulder height, ready to swing at whatever awaited him—*Tap-tap-tap ... screech ... Tap-tap ...* He furrowed his brow. *What the hell is that?* Finally, he was just outside the doorway.

On the other side of the wall, silence.

He flung himself around the corner, holding the bat above his head as if it were an ax, and scanned the room for any sign of danger. But there was none. Only stacks of boxes and an empty space where his walnut desk used to be. To ease his mind, he opened the closet door—making sure to step out of the line of fire in case an assassin was hiding inside. When no one popped out, he looked in—empty. He let the bat rest on his shoulder as he turned around—

Tap-tap ... scratch, screech ... tap-tap-tap ...

There, at the side window. He hadn't noticed until now, but the wind had picked up while he was moving furniture and boxes, causing a jumble of scraggly twigs from a deciduous tree to scrape and knock on the glass. He rolled his eyes and sighed.

Between the strange voices, the Moretti brothers whispering about the root cellar and spending the night in the creepy abandoned house in the woods—*his* creepy house—plus finding a feral cat in the basement, he was pretty jumpy. He turned around—

"*Mhr-aou.*"

"Jesus."

Coal was there, sitting in the doorway, tail swishing back and forth along the wood floor as he quietly watched the strange behavior of the new man of the house.

"You can certainly be quiet when you want to be," he said, heart slowing down to a normal rhythm. "Can't you?"

"*Mhrn.*"

Jimmy stepped toward him. "Move aside."

"*Mhrng-a,*" Coal answered as he sprang to his feet and curved his body around the doorframe while sashaying into the hall and out of the path of his indifferent host.

"Don't bitch at me," Jimmy mumbled. "I didn't invite you in here."

When he reached the alcove, he heard the metallic *clank* of the deadbolt. The squeal of ancient hinges, followed by the familiar jingle of a collection of keys that would make any building superintendent jealous.

"I'm home!" Roni called out, entering the foyer with what sounded like the whole store in her arms.

Fondly nicknamed 'the key hoarder,' Roni had a key ring to memorialize every point of interest she'd ever visited—and some she hadn't. Jimmy used to give them to her as gifts until, after one of their dates, she clumsily dropped her purse in his kitchen. It landed with a heavy *ker-chunk* on the cheap laminate flooring. When she bent to pick it up, the contents spilled out, including what must have been ten of the sentimental trinkets. They were all hooked together, each with at least one nickel or brass key threaded on its ring. That was a decade ago, so who knew how many she had now? He was willing to bet she still had the keys to her college apartment somewhere in that jumble.

"I'm up here," he called out as a silvery black blur skittered past his feet, nearly tripping him as he made the turn toward the stairwell.

Coal hurried down the steps in front of Jimmy, eager to greet his new mistress as if he already knew where his bread was buttered.

"Well, someone's happy to see me," she cooed.

"Mhrn-aou, mhrn-aou."

Jimmy rounded the turn at the landing ... *thump, thump, creak—*
I gotta fix that step, he reminded himself again.

Then at the bottom of the stairs, he turned into the foyer where Coal was curling around Roni's legs, murmuring and mewling frantically—no doubt telling her everything that had happened while she was away. Thankfully for Jimmy, she was unable to understand his chatter.

Leaving the pound of keys and keyrings hanging from the lock and *tapping* against the wood door, Roni dropped her bags and began stroking Coal's back while repeating, "I missed you too," over and over. And with each new verse, Coal bumped his head against her knee and fluttered his tail.

Jimmy leaned against the wall, arms folded across his chest, watching as the cat demanded her attention. In all their years together, they'd never had a pet. They had both decided they enjoyed the freedom to be able to pick up and go at a moment's notice—for now anyway. Someday, children would change all that. But seeing her now with Coal ... They were quite the pair already. He could get used to that.

She looked up and caught him staring. "And how did you boys get along while I was gone?"

"Fine," he said, moving toward her. "We mostly stayed out of each other's way." Ignoring the feline suitor's disapproving growl, he wrapped her in his arms and kissed her. It crossed his mind to tell her about Coal lurking about in the hall and sneaking up on him when suddenly his body tensed as he realized—

The step didn't creak.

During the excitement, he hadn't noticed but now ... He thought back to that moment. *I was at the top of the stairs; Coal raced past me and down the steps; then I started behind him; he turned the corner and ran over the loose step—and no creak. Until I stepped on it. If it creaked under his weight on the way up, why not on the way down?*

He let that sink in for a moment.

What if it wasn't Coal that made the step creak? That's crazy though ... Right? He just missed the squeaky spot on the way down ... Or maybe he ran over it too fast ... I mean, what else could it have been? Shades are just reflections so even if there is one here—

"Earth to Jimmy," she said, pumping her arms against his sides.

"Hm?"

"I asked if the satellite guy showed up."

"Not yet."

"It's after twelve," she moaned. "We're gonna miss the football game."

"You know how it is," he shrugged, trying to hide his disappointment. "Our appointment window is ten to two, so we still have almost two hours before he shows up." He felt like *the light* was working his brain overtime and he needed to get out of his head. "Anything else you need me to bring in from the car?"

"No, this is everything," she answered, slipping out of his arms to admire her haul.

There were six bags on the floor—four gray and two white—plus the hooded plastic litter box. He started rooting through the gray bags first and found different varieties of wet and dry cat food, kitty litter, and jingly, feathery toys—these were from the pet store. "Where else did you go?"

"I found another grocery store," she said, smiling, as she snatched the white bags from the floor. "One that carries all your favorite game day snacks."

"No," he said, wide-eyed, forgetting all about the mysterious *creaking* step.

"It's just too bad we can't watch the game," she teased, holding the bags behind her as she eased backward toward the opening into the sitting room.

"We can stream it on my tablet using cell phone data," he said, slinking toward her.

Still stepping backward, she shrugged and said, "If you say so."

"I do say so," he said, inching closer.

"You'll have to catch me first." Then she spun around and sprinted into the sitting room.

Jimmy kicked the litter box with the heel of his sneaker as he rushed to catch her.

"Mhrng-a," Coal grumbled as he leaped out of the way and over the bags to avoid the chaos.

Roni squealed, rounding the turn into the dining room before making another sharp right to get around to the other side of the table, keeping it between her and Jimmy. She looked like a caricature of a bank robber in the way she was holding the white plastic bags at shoulder height, one in each hand like sacks of money.

Then, shaking the bags, she said, "If you want this, you have to do something for me first."

"Name your price."

***

Twenty minutes later, Jimmy had stowed the cat food supplies in the creepy pantry, found a spot in the sitting room for the igloo-shaped sherpa-lined cat bed, and scattered the toys. He found an out-of-the-way place in the kitchen for Coal's food and water bowls and as soon as the kibble *tinked* against the ceramic dish, the cat came running for a taste. Last but not least, as part of the price he promised to pay in exchange for his favorite game day grub, he had to set up the litter box.

Just off to the right of the kitchen was a powder room—the perfect place to keep Coal's toilet out of sight. He put the liner in the base and then poured in a layer of unscented, dust-free, highly absorbent and clumping, odor-controlling litter. *It better be*, Jimmy thought, grimacing as he eyed the plastic scoop and wondered why he had also agreed to litter box duties for one week. Then he snapped on the lid and returned to the kitchen and the buttery aroma of browning ground beef.

Roni had already diced red and green onions, tomatoes, and red and green peppers on the cutting board. She had drained black beans and jalapeños and spread a layer of restaurant-style tortilla chips on a baking sheet. Having finished his meal, Coal watched intently from the floor as she removed the sizzling pan from the burner and poured the meat into the colander.

"All finished?" Roni asked.

"Yep."

"Including the litter box?"

He rolled his eyes, wondering if a promise made under duress would hold up in their household court. "What if he doesn't know what to do with it?"

"All cats know," she assured him as she returned the browned meat to the pan then added water and taco seasoning.

Not even a minute later, as the oven signaled it was preheated, Coal ducked out of the kitchen and into the bathroom, where he immediately began scratching at the litter inside the plastic enclosure. Jimmy was still skeptical. When it became quiet, he snuck to the doorway and peered around the corner, right into the faraway stare of a feline in mid-poop.

"How about that," he said as he looked away, content to give the cat his privacy.

"Told ya'," she said. Then she spread the seasoned ground beef and black beans over the tortilla chips, followed by the onions, peppers, and a pound of shredded yellow and white cheese. Jimmy left to find his tablet as she stuck the nachos in the oven.

***

After watching the pregame show, Jimmy returned to the kitchen and was met by a bouquet of surf and turf that held his senses captive. He paused to enjoy it, almost tasting it without taking a bite. "It smells awesome."

"It's almost ready," she said, preparing a tray with bowls of green onion, diced tomatoes, jalapeños, sour cream, and guacamole, leaving a space in the middle for the plate of nachos.

He reached into the refrigerator and grabbed two bottles of beer. After tossing the metal caps into the trash, he pulled two plates from a cabinet and a handful of spoons from a drawer. He set them on a different tray just as Roni opened the oven. The cheese was perfectly browned and melted into the layer of meat and beans and chips. But that wasn't even the best part.

The *pièce de resistance* was on the second baking sheet. Jimmy's favorite, and nearly impossible to find unless you go to the restaurant, Phillips Maryland

Style Crab Cake Minis, cooked to a mouthwatering golden brown. Coal's nose twitched and his pupils dilated to the size of dimes as she set the crab cakes on the tray with the beer, plates, and a bowl of tartar sauce.

They settled in the sitting room in front of Jimmy's tablet, ready for kickoff.

The Ravens had already put up one touchdown when a scruffy-faced kid named Bob arrived wearing a zipped-up too tight around the middle company jacket. Three hours later, Jimmy and Roni watched Tampa Bay trounce the Chiefs on the 65-inch flatscreen while finishing up leftover bits of nachos and flakey crab cakes. Then it was on to the main event: Steelers at Patriots.

It had been a while since he allowed himself to watch the entire Sunday night game, but thanks to the move, he was still on vacation for another week, so he decided to treat himself. Roni had her fill around halftime and had already gone upstairs. And by the time the game ended at eleven fifteen, Jimmy was ready for bed too.

It was their second night in the house and, now that the heat was on, it would be the first they spent in the upstairs bedroom. After turning off the television, he made a sweep around the downstairs, checking all the windows and doors to ensure they were all locked. Then before turning out the light, he glanced at Coal, snuggled into his igloo bed.

He yawned then said, "Goodnight."

Coal stared back longingly then slowly blinked his green eyes but made no attempt to follow Jimmy up the steps.

On the second floor, Jimmy confirmed everything was locked up tight, then joined Roni in the master bedroom. She was tucked beneath a white and blue floral-patterned quilt, reclined against the matching pillow sham while reading *Fairy Tale* by Stephen King in the glow of the bedside light.

"Who won?" she asked.

"Who do you think?" he grumbled. Earlier in the day, his beloved Ravens had defeated the dreaded Browns. Still, even that couldn't take the sting out of a Steelers win—Pittsburg was now within a game of taking the lead in their division.

"Sorry," she said, her bottom lip turned out in her best sympathetic pout as she slid the bookmark between the pages and placed the book on the nightstand.

He slipped out of his T-shirt and blue jeans, climbed into bed next to her then kissed her bare shoulder before kissing her lips.

"Goodnight," she giggled.

Then with a click of the bedside lamp switch, the room was black. The streetlight filtering through the drapes cast a strange web of shadows on the far wall. And as his head lay on the pillow, eyes closed and waiting for sleep to come, he recalled the blast of big band music from the night before—almost certainly a Moretti prank.

Then the image of the mysterious silhouette at the end of the driveway entered his mind. Only a misshapen tree but still ... disturbing. He furrowed his brow and pushed it away. But then he thought about the owl eyes, watching as they made love in front of the fire.

He sighed and tried to think of something else.

Something to lull him to sleep.

He thought of that trip out West. His father behind the wheel, singing as "Don't Stop Believing" blared through the car speakers. Jimmy in the passenger seat, smiling and dancing to the beat. Elizabeth in the back, clapping and laughing. But instead of a pile of pillows and snacks beside her, it was their mother, singing along with their dad.

A perfectly unbroken family.

Chapter 9

"*Jimmy.*"

The breathy voice stirred him from sleep. He opened his eyes and whispered, "What?"

Silence answered.

In the quiet, he could hear Roni breathing beside him in effortless slumber. He lifted his head from the pillow and blinked his eyes, bringing the red LED numbers on the bedside clock into focus. It was 2:20 a.m. and he was inexplicably awake.

He dropped his head and laid there, wondering if he'd been dreaming. But then he realized they weren't alone. There was something else in the bedroom with them ... A presence.

He didn't see it at first. It took a moment for his eyes to adjust to the low light filtered through the curtains. And then, bit by bit, a shadowy figure came into view. A hunched-over shape with unnatural protuberances on its arched back was kneeling beside the bed with its head lowered as if praying.

He stared at it for what seemed like minutes as his brain tried to make sense of the featureless profile, like one of those black-card silhouette portraits that were popular before the invention of photography.

Am I dreaming?

2:21 a.m.

Forced by stinging dryness, Jimmy blinked his eyes. Two quick blinks, to be exact. But the shadow remained. It was a *shade*, he was sure of that now, but he'd never seen one like this. It could stay hidden, just out of reach of *the light* so that he couldn't quite see it.

"Nothing you see can harm you."

His mother's words did little to calm his racing heart as he struggled to bring *the shade* into *the light*. If only he knew how. She died before she could teach him what his gift really was or how to use it—if she even knew herself.

As it lifted its head, Jimmy could make out the sharp points at the end of its nose and chin. Then it rolled its shoulder forward as it turned and crouched on all fours, ready to pounce. It leaned toward him, its two amber eyes glowing in the murky darkness.

"I sssee you," it hissed, breathing out a stench of rot and decay.

Jimmy refused to turn away. His mouth was dry, his tongue like dehydrated meat. His breaths were shallow and quick. He swallowed the fear trapped in his throat and kept his eyes fixed on the figure as it leaned closer. Then *the light* shimmered over its blackened hide as its lips peeled back over its jagged teeth.

"I sssee you, James Massson."

Jimmy sat straight up and reached for the bedside lamp, squinting as the shards of light stabbed at his eyes. He struggled to remain focused on *the shade,* but it was gone, back into the shadows.

"What's wrong?" Roni asked, rolling onto her back with her arm shielding her eyes.

He flipped the covers back, swung his legs over the edge of the bed and propped himself up with one hand on his knee. He shivered as the cool air touched his sweaty skin and wiped his hand across his forehead and hair. *That was no ordinary* shade ... *It wasn't human ... Wasn't ever human; it couldn't have been ... It's—*

"Jimmy?"

"Huh?" was all he managed to say as he stood from the bed.

"Are you okay?"

"I just had a nightmare. Everything's fine."

"What was it about?"

He was standing where it had been, on the very spot where it hissed his name. That had never happened before either. *Maybe it was a dream?* But that was just wishful thinking. He looked at the clock. 2:23 a.m. He scanned the room, but again, there was no trace of it. Anywhere. Everything was as it should be.

"Jimmy ... Do you want to talk about it?"

"No, I'm uh—I'm just gonna run some water on my face."

"Turn out the light first," she yawned, rolling over onto her left side.

"Okay."

He leaned over and pinched his fingers around the switch on the lamp. But before cutting off the light, he noticed the bedroom door was ajar. *Didn't I close the door last night?* It had been a habit of his since he was a kid. On bring your parent to work day, one of his classmates brought his father, a volunteer fireman. Jimmy was fascinated by the man's uniform and the equipment he used. The man took the opportunity to teach them about fire safety and tell them that they too could be firemen—or women—someday.

He couldn't remember that man's name—or the name of his classmate—but he never forgot what that fireman said: closing the bedroom door at night could substantially improve the chance of surviving a house fire. Jimmy had always been terrified of a house fire. And ever since then, he always closed his bedroom door before going to sleep.

It was possible that the stress of moving, lack of sleep, and a full day of football caused him to forget to close the door, but he wasn't sure. Then something moved in the dark hallway, just outside their room, and he stood up a little straighter, fingers still gripped around the light switch—

"Jimmy, please ... I'm trying to go back to sleep."

"Sorry, babe."

Click.

Darkness.

He shuffled through the room, hands outstretched until he found the doorway. He closed the door behind himself and searched the shadows for movement. All clear. Ambient light from the street showed him the way to the bathroom.

Once inside, he closed the door and turned on the light. His reflection in the medicine cabinet mirror was pale. His hairline was damp with sweat. His hands shook as he reached for the faucet.

He leaned over the sink and splashed cold water on the back of his neck, then on his face ... once ... then again. Eyes closed, he turned off the stream and felt for the hand towel. He held the soft terry cloth to his face, drying the water away, before daring to have another look.

James Mason Hobart was officially terrified.

He rehung the damp towel and then relieved himself in the commode—meeting new *shades* in the middle of the night tended to overact one's bladder. Or so it would seem. It had never actually happened to him before. He flushed the water down, closed the lid, and washed his hands.

He reached for the door handle and then took one more glimpse of himself in the mirror. It occurred to him to stay in the bathroom until sunrise, but how would that look? He sucked in a deep breath and slowly exhaled through puckered lips, letting his cheeks puff out as the air escaped. Then he switched off the light and opened the door—

"*Mhrng-a!*"

"Dammit," he gasped, nearly tripping over Coal lurking outside the door. Then he felt the cat's soft tail wrap around his calf, followed by a head bump.

"*Hrn-rhn-hrn-rhn ...* "

The gentle purr followed him as he walked away, reverberating in the dark, empty hallway like a motor through still water. Perhaps, under different circumstances, Jimmy would have found it soothing. Maybe he even would have picked Coal up, held him to his chest, and relished the vibration.

Perhaps, he thought as he closed the bedroom door and returned to bed.

But not right now.

Not on this night.

Chapter 10

J immy couldn't fall back asleep after the wee hour's visit from the mysterious *shade*. So rather than lie in bed, staring at shadows of tree limbs dancing across the ceiling and listening to the deep, rhythmic vibrations of peaceful slumber beside him, he palmed his cell phone and then crept from their room and down the hall to his office.

Earlier, between the end of Tampa Bay vs Chiefs and the beginning of Steelers vs Patriots, he had convinced Roni to help him relocate his bookcases to his new office. And now, he was glad he did. He had something to occupy his mind: plenty of empty shelves waiting to be filled with memories and books.

It was in between shelving *The House at the End of the World* and *Carrie* when his olfactory senses detected the first hint of bacon frying in a skillet over the hot burner.

It was 7:19 a.m.

He'd been so focused on his books he hadn't realized how hungry he was. But now, all he could think about were the caramelized fatty tips of browned strips of bacon and how they would practically melt in his mouth. So, he decided to save the rest of the boxes for later. He turned the door handle and pulled—

"*Mhrng-a!*"

"Jesus!" Jimmy blurted out as Coal sprang to his feet. As he stood there trying to catch his breath, the cat sashayed into his path and swept his long, flowing tail across his legs. "Are you trying to give me a heart attack?"

"*Mhrn,*" he answered, while bunting his head against Jimmy's knee. Then he looked up sideways and slowly blinked his emerald eyes before continuing to rub his head, exchanging scents with the new man of the house.

Jimmy bent over and stroked Coal's fur. "Are we friends now?"

Coal stood on tip-toes and arched his back. "*Hrn-rhn-hrn-rhn ...* "

Like it or not, it seemed that they were.

***

Once dressed, Jimmy meandered down the steps, yawning so wide his eyes were forced to close. Surprisingly, he was able to navigate their new stairwell without any issues and even sidestepped the loose board. Maybe it would start to feel like home after all.

Maybe, he thought as he shuffled into the dining room.

It was their first Monday in their new home and it felt every bit like a Monday. Roni had already set two places at the table and two glasses of orange juice. He picked up one of the glasses and took a sip as he pushed open the swinging door. A blur of charcoal fur brushed past his legs while he stood in the entryway and breathed in the mixture of cinnamon and salty bacon.

"You look like shit," she giggled, taking a moment to acknowledge him before returning her attention to the hot pans on the stovetop.

"Thanks ... I feel like shit."

"Where were you? I don't like waking up to an empty bed."

"In my office, unpacking ... I couldn't sleep."

"Must have been some nightmare."

The eerie visitor's susurrous voice slithered into his mind like a serpent as he remembered they weren't alone in their Victorian abode. A *shade* was living amongst them. But maybe it was wrong to call it a *shade*.

"Reflections in a mirror." That's what Grandpa Bill thought they were. But this one was no reflection. It was different. I smelled its foul, sour breath as it said my name. And when it leaned closer, I sensed its desire ... it's longing ... but what does it want?

"Hello?" she said, looking over her shoulder.

"Hm?"

"Can you feed Coal? I'm kind of busy."

Jimmy sat his glass on the counter and then retrieved the kibble from the pantry. Coal responded with excited chatter while rubbing against the center island cabinets and flittering his tail. And as the tiny brown pieces landed in his dish, he was ready to scoop them up.

"Anything else I can do to help?" he asked, secretly hoping she would say no so he could return to the dining room.

"Nope. It's almost ready ... Go sit down."

***

Minutes later, she pushed open the butler door with her backside while carrying a large serving tray. At the same time, Coal somehow managed to escape the kitchen through the open door without tripping her, then scurried through the dining room on his way to the sitting room.

"Let me help," Jimmy said, rising from his chair.

"I got it," she assured him.

He sat down and watched as she delivered the tray, loaded with plates of French Toast, scrambled eggs, and thick slices of bacon, along with a bowl of powdered sugar, salt and pepper shakers, and a jug of warm syrup—*she even managed the time to warm the syrup.* It sure beat the hell out of the cold cereal he ate for breakfast yesterday morning.

"You've been busy," he remarked as he politely waited for her to be seated before getting started. "How long have you been up?"

"Since 6:45," she answered while scooping scrambled eggs onto her plate.

Jimmy's first stop was the bacon, moving half of the slices from the serving tray onto his plate. Then before taking anything else, he savored a bite. Tasting the hickory-smoked goodness brought back Sunday morning memories of his mother in the kitchen while he watched cartoons with his sister and his father drank coffee and read the paper. His father must have felt the same way because he only cooked bacon once after his wife died. He found the memories too painful and shied away from most reminders of her.

But not Jimmy. He relished anything that reminded him of his mother: her favorite song, red roses, Elvis Presley. But like silver flatware, some memories become tarnished if you touch them too often. This was precisely why he didn't allow himself to enjoy bacon every day or even once a month. He didn't want those Sunday morning memories of his family to fade away. So today, he would think of them for as long as the aroma lingered.

"Don't get used to this," Roni warned.

"What's that?" he asked as he filled his plate with generous portions of French toast and eggs to accompany what was left of the bacon.

"This," she said, pointing at the feast before them. "Once we're back to work it's everyone for himself again."

He nodded and laughed. For Roni, the desire to cook was like the cycle of the moon, waxing and waning during the month. Apparently, they were in the full moon phase while on vacation and settling into their home. Jimmy intended to take full advantage of that. But mostly, he was jealous of her energy as it seemed she'd gotten a full night's rest, unlike him. He hoped a belly full of protein would perk him up.

While they ate, they talked about where the sofa and armchairs would work best now that the TV was set up, which turned into a discussion about when they should have their housewarming party. They both agreed that first, they had to get the house in order. Next thing he knew, they were discussing Roni's walk-in closet.

And suddenly, he'd forgotten all about *the shade*—or whatever it was.

***

After cleaning up the breakfast dishes, they went upstairs to the master bedroom so Roni could explain her vision for the dressing room/walk-in closet. Jimmy measured the walls and took notes, all while nodding dutifully.

Then they locked up the house and drove thirty-five minutes to the nearest big box hardware store where an aisle the length of a jumbo jet was dedicated to closet organization and systems. They selected several pieces in Coastal Teak—a beachy shade of grayish green—that included adjustable hanging rods, shelves, and drawers.

The various pieces would need to be cut to fit their space. If he was going to do that himself—which he insisted on doing to save money, plus he knew his father would roll over in his grave if he allowed anyone else to do it—he was going to need a workshop for his tools that were still in storage. So, while they were at the airplane hangar-sized store, they decided to look at sheds.

They came in various sizes and materials, from 2' x 4' x 6' resin gardening tool sheds, to 32' x 16' wooden barns. Jimmy decided on a 120 square-foot wooden shed with a 10' ceiling, barn door opening, and operable windows for plenty of natural light and airflow. It even came in a shade of green that matched their house.

What really sold Jimmy was that they had the shed in stock at the store and could deliver it on Wednesday and even assemble it for him on site if he wanted. He protested at first to make sure the salesman knew he was perfectly capable of doing it himself before finally agreeing—but only because his tools were in storage.

After paying, they scheduled the shed delivery and onsite setup for the same date as the closet system delivery. After all, there was no point in bringing it home until he had his tools out of storage—something he was looking forward to.

Three hours after arriving, they left the big box store tired and with several bags of odds and ends, including an outdoor fireplace with a cast iron cooking grate. He felt very accomplished—and hungry as he spotted smoke billowing from the roof of a nearby fast-food restaurant, carrying the aroma of grilled beef with it. They pulled up to the drive-through window and ordered two cheeseburgers with fries and soft drinks that they consumed on the drive home.

***

After 32 liquid ounces of carbonated caffeine, Jimmy felt ready to tackle the rest of the day, despite his lack of sleep. After parking the truck, he climbed the porch steps and stuck the key into the front door lock. When he pushed the door open, the lingering aroma of Sunday mornings at the Hobart house greeted him like an old friend. He welcomed the image of his mother that it stirred in his mind, pausing momentarily on the threshold to enjoy it.

The rest of the afternoon passed in a blur as he unpacked and polished knickknacks. But not even wiping away the dust that should have been left behind in their old apartment could ruin his euphoric state. He didn't even mind scooping clumps from Coal's litter box.

Around three o'clock, Jimmy stepped into the crisp November air and walked to the mailbox at the end of the driveway to retrieve their first delivery at the new address. It was mostly junk mail since they took advantage of online bill pay from their joint bank account. Still, he took his time rummaging through the advertisements on his way back to the house, enjoying the break from inside chores.

On the porch, he gripped the front door handle and anticipated the bacony scent that awaited him on the other side of the door. And he wasn't disappointed. It had faded somewhat but was still detectible over the bouquet of lemon-fragranced dust spray and cardboard. Just enough to make him want to go back outside so he could come in and enjoy it again.

Instead, he found Roni in the parlor and suggested they enjoy a fire in their brand-new fire pit and watch the sunset on what was forecast to be a cold but clear evening. She agreed.

While she continued working in the house, Jimmy gathered some wood from the nearby tree line and then set up two lounge chairs in the driveway. Next, he unloaded the fireplace from the flatbed of his pickup and placed it in front of the chairs. After tossing balled-up strips of newspaper into the belly of the iron hearth along with some of the smaller sticks, he ignited the long-stemmed butane lighter, and flames appeared.

As if drawn out by the radiating warmth, Roni appeared behind him, offering a cold beer and a blanket. They settled into chairs and watched as the sun descended behind the trees until the only light remaining was the glow of the flames before them and the waxing gibbous moon above.

In the embrace of the flames, they chatted about nothing in particular as, one by one, tiny pinpricks of light appeared in the blackness. And even though he hadn't stargazed since boyhood camping trips, he still remembered a thing or two. Using the bright asterisms, he pointed out the constellations Pegasus and Andromeda, Cassiopeia, Aquarius, and Pisces, dazzling his betrothed until their stomachs began to protest.

Then Jimmy dropped two thick sirloins onto the slide-out cooking surface of their brand-new fireplace. In the house, Roni cut and steamed broccoli crowns as an accompaniment. Once the steaks had cooked for seven minutes on each side, maintaining a juicy pink center, he removed them from the heat and then closed the fireplace flues to smother the flames. They feasted in the dining room, musing over their eventful day while the wood turned to ash outside in the fire pit.

By the time they finished eating and cleaning up the kitchen, it was nearly midnight. Roni proceeded upstairs while Jimmy completed a security sweep of the lower level to ensure everything was locked up tight. His last stop was the sitting room where Coal was snuggled in his cozy bed, eyes closed with his nose tucked firmly under one leg.

As Jimmy reached for the light switch, he whispered, "Goodnight."

The cat opened his emerald eyes to mere slits and let out a faint squeak as he raised his head. Then he yawned wide, bearing his pink tongue and white teeth while stretching one leg out in front and spreading his clawed toes before finally returning to his former posture.

Then he extinguished the light and began the climb in darkness, stepping over the loose step.

Chapter 11

For the third night in a row, Jimmy was mysteriously stirred awake. After checking the time, he closed his eyes and inhaled a deep, exhausted breath. The sweet hickory aroma from breakfast had long faded, taking with it the memories of his mother. What remained in the air was a pungent odor, not unlike the stench of rotting roadkill.

A smell befitting a creature of the night.

His heart rate intensified. He opened his eyes, and while lying very still, he searched the murkiness for the sinewy, disfigured shape from the night before. But nothing was lurking in the shadows. Nothing kneeling beside the bed. No amber eyes staring back at him. Only his mind playing tricks.

As his heart slowed, he flipped the covers back and sat up on the edge of the bed. He looked over his shoulder where Roni's delicate silhouette rose and fell with each soft breath beneath the blanket. He smiled, then turned away and rubbed his eyes—

Something like soft down feathers brushed against his right ankle, and his body stiffened. His heart pumped faster, sending blood to his limbs in preparation for an attack. Then the fluffy plumage moved beneath the bed and grazed his left ankle. The hair follicles on his skin rose to attention in a wave starting from his legs and up to the nape of his neck—

Coal, he thought. *I must have left the door open again.*

He furrowed his brow, frustrated that he could have done that two nights in a row. He shook his head and dared to breathe again. Then he hunched forward and rested his elbows on his thighs. Sitting there, he wondered if he could fall back to sleep or if he was doomed again to remain awake until dawn. Then he felt the pressure of his bladder and regretted the fourth bottle of beer he drank over dinner. He straightened his back and prepared to stand—

"Jimmy."

As the voice crept into his ears, he felt cold, spindly fingers clench around his ankles. Nails, filed into sharp points, scratched at his skin. His protesting bladder shrunk away, replaced instead by a pounding, consuming fear. His ears cried out a high-pitched tone in search of any sound in the silence as the grip on his legs slid higher. First around his right calf, then around his left, pulling with it the sound of a dried husk swishing along the floorboards.

"Jimmy," it whispered again.

A shiver spread over his sweat-dampened skin as he slowly lowered his gaze. *Swish, swish* it went as the coarse grasp climbed to his knees, bringing the foulest stench of death so sickening that it caused the stomach acid to rise into the back of his throat. He wanted to turn away, but he couldn't ... He had to look ... He had to know—

From between his knees, two amber eyes, unblinking and full of hate and pain, stared back with horizontally elongated pupils. For a moment, neither of them moved. They were locked in on one another—predator, and prey.

Then the creature reached for the target of its misery as it hissed, "*I sssee you Jamesss Massson.*"

"No!"

Jimmy stood on unsteady legs and shoved the thing away, sending it tumbling across the bedroom floor, toward the future walk-in closet.

"What—what's wrong?" Roni cried as she awoke.

Coal growled and wailed from the hallway as his paws thumped desperately against the bedroom door.

Gasping for breath, Jimmy stumbled toward the lamp on the bedside table and turned the switch. Momentarily blinded by the flash of light, he was determined to maintain a visual lock on the creature. But he quickly saw there was nothing there.

The yowls continued in rapid succession on the other side of the bedroom door. "*Mhr-aou, mhr-aou, mhr-aou ...*"

"Jimmy?" Roni was sitting up, poised for battle, while looking toward the walk-in closet for some sign of danger. Anything. "Jimmy, what is it?"

He didn't know how to answer her, not yet. He wiped his brow and walked toward the darkened opening leading into the closet. There were no shadows in the bedroom to hide in, so it must be in there. When he was close enough, he reached for the light switch—

Coal let out a frightening, primeval shriek and then became quiet.

Except for a few boxes, the closet appeared to be empty. He walked in for a closer look, nudging the cardboard with his foot to shake loose anything that might be hiding inside or behind it. But there was nothing. He brought his hands to his face, rubbed the stubble coating his cheeks, then let his hands move up, spreading his fingers through his hair.

When he turned around, Roni was on the edge of his side of the bed, perched up on her knees, mouth agape as she watched him. Then his eyes trailed to the bedroom door—it was closed. He walked out of the closet and turned off the light. The sweat had dried on his skin, and he suddenly felt the chill in the air. The pressure from his bladder had returned as well. Then his eyes returned to Roni.

"Another nightmare?" she asked.

Was it? he wondered. He wasn't sure anymore.

"Jimmy?"

"I don't know," he finally said as he rounded the foot of the bed on his way toward the bedroom door.

"You don't know?" she huffed.

"I need some air."

"Jimmy," she said, turning as he walked by.

But he didn't answer. He was exhausted and wired all at once and he knew he wouldn't be able to sleep after what happened. He opened the door—

"*Maou?*"

"You could've at least turned out the light," she complained in a last-ditch effort to get him to respond.

Instead, he closed the door without looking back.

***

In the morning, breakfast was served cold—like the mood in the house had become.

They sat at the rectangular table in the dining room—him on the long end, her on the short end—scooping spoons of vanilla almond bran flakes into their mouths to keep from speaking to one another. He understood her anger. He was keeping something from her, and she knew it. And it wasn't like him to keep secrets. It left his stomach knotted up.

The spoon came to rest in the bowl as another cramp gurgled within his gut. His brow furrowed and he squirmed in his seat as he waited for the tightness to subside before taking another bite. He half expected her to ask if he was okay, but she didn't. He wanted to glance in her direction to see if she even noticed he was in pain, but he didn't.

She had done nothing wrong, yet he was waiting for her—expecting her—to make the first move toward a peaceful resolution. She always did. She was the peacemaker in their relationship. A role she neither campaigned for nor was elected to ... It just happened. Probably something from her childhood, watching the parts her parents played.

Jimmy stayed quiet, brooding, like his father.

Coal finally broke the ice, twirling his fluffy tail around Jimmy's leg and then sitting on the floor beside him, mewing mournfully as if he sensed the tension too and wondered if there was anything he could do to help. A silly thought. Jimmy knew that. Nevertheless, he stroked the cat's head to soothe him. Coal reacted by extending his neck and pressing his forehead against Jimmy's palm while emitting a gentle whirring noise from within his throat.

Then Coal arched his back and stepped toward Roni. He bumped his head against her leg, purring loudly and coiling around the chair legs beneath her until he was on the other side of the table, out of Jimmy's reach.

"*Mhrn?*"

She reached down and scratched Coal's head which he gratefully accepted. Then, while still gazing upon the feline, she said, "You didn't come back to bed last night."

Jimmy shook his head. "I didn't want to keep you up."

"I noticed the blanket on the couch."

It was true. He ended up on the couch in the sitting room, where he sat in the darkness ... thinking. There was so much he didn't know about *the light* and *shades* ... Things he didn't get to learn from his mother ... Things he hadn't worried about until now.

"Did you get any sleep?" she asked, now looking across the table at him.

"No. That couch sucks."

She smiled. He smiled back.

And just like that, a new peacemaker had been elected. Before wandering off to his igloo bed, Coal mewed one last time—a catlike victory lap—leaving his humans to return to their cereal.

"You know you can talk to me?"

"I know," he said, reaching for her hand. "I'm fine. I just need time to settle in." Another lie.

He wanted to tell her everything. Everything he'd been keeping from her since the day they first met. The reason he was able to guess her birthdate, how he knew her deceased grandmother had blue eyes, what really kept him up at night. He knew he could trust her from the moment they first met, but his mother's warning prevented him from telling her about his gift. And once he started keeping a secret, it was difficult to stop.

Now for the first time, that secret had come between them.

How much longer before it destroys us?

Chapter 12

What is it this time? Jimmy wondered, lifting his head from the pillow and staring at the red glowing digits through the darkness.

It was the fourth night he'd been awoken at 2:20 a.m.

First, the big band music—which he no longer believed was a Moretti prank—then the mysterious creature praying beside the bed, the frightening encounter last night, and now what—

For one blissful moment, he'd forgotten what an ass he'd been yesterday. But now, before he could search for amber eyes and foul breath, he was beginning to remember ...

After breakfast, the peace treaty negotiated by Coal fell apart. Fueled by sleepless frustration and long days of working to the point of physical exhaustion had led him to snap at Roni for no reason. They were hanging framed art in the parlor—a chore he could handle with the household tool set he brought along with the move—when she pointed out that one frame was crooked. And no matter how often he adjusted it, he couldn't get it straight (according to her).

So, he exploded.

He regretted it immediately and apologized profusely—it wasn't her fault he wasn't sleeping. She accepted his apology but decided to give up on the picture and give him some space. The rest of the day was a return to their frigid silence.

Now that he was awake in the middle of the night and still feeling bad about the whole stupid incident, he got the bright idea of how to put an end to their cold war. He rolled over beneath the covers, preparing to wrap his arm around her and pull her close against his body, but before he could make his move, the sour stench of the creature's breath belted him across the face.

He recoiled and lifted his head from the pillow, his gaze landing squarely on the murky form seated on the bed beside his beloved Roni. Its long boney black fingers were spread around her shoulder, holding her like a lover would as it leaned over her body.

At first, Jimmy couldn't move. He could only stare at the creature's twisted shape as it whispered its disgusting secrets into Roni's ear. Then, it opened its amber eyes and stared back at him, turning its lips into a wide toothy grin while still holding her in its grasp.

Jimmy pushed himself up, and in one clumsy motion, he lunged all of his 198 pounds at the thing. But instead of making contact with *the shade*, his stomach landed squarely on his fiancé's hip with enough force to nearly knock the wind out of him.

Pinned beneath him, Roni let out a piercing scream and began thrashing, smacking him with her free hand as she tried to dislodge the weight across her body.

From the hallway, Coal wailed and slapped his paws against the bedroom door like a boxer with a speed bag.

As Jimmy struggled to catch his breath, his hands kept slipping on the blanket while his head and shoulders were assaulted with a barrage of slaps. Until finally, he was able to get enough traction to push himself off her and sit back on his knees. "It's all right!" he shouted. "It's me ... It's me."

"*Mhr-aou ...*"

She slid from the bed and switched on the light. "What the hell, Jimmy?"

"I'm sorry," he said, holding his hands up. "I—I thought I saw something."

Thump, thump, thump, thump ...

"*Mhr-aou, mhr-aou, mhr-aou ...*"

"What?" she demanded as she scanned the room. "What did you see?"

But just like the other times, there was nothing there ... No mysterious creature with glowing eyes and razor-sharp teeth. No one ... Nothing.

Thump, thump, thump, thump ...

"*Mhr-aou, mhr-aou, mhr-aou ...*"

"And what the hell is wrong with that cat?" she screamed toward the ceiling. The hallway fell silent.

She brought her hands to her cheeks and shook her head. "Jimmy ... Please tell me what's going on."

He was still in the middle of the bed, confused, trying to catch his breath, squinting and rubbing his eyes as he looked around the room. He envisioned the misshapen thing hovering over her like an animal, feeding. He wasn't sure what to make of it. He'd never seen anything like it before—

"Jimmy."

"Nothing, I ... I must have been dreaming."

"You're lying."

"Roni, I'm not—"

"Yes, you are. Or at least you're not telling me everything."

"You're right," he said reluctantly. "I don't want to tell you about the dreams." *Not dreams, liar.* "I just don't want to talk about it."

"I'm worried about you, Smudge," she said, settling onto the bed beside him and wrapping her arms around him.

He let his head rest on her shoulder and encircled his arms around her waist. "I don't want you to worry."

"Tomorrow, I'm getting melatonin from the drugstore. That should help you sleep."

"It's already tomorrow," he mumbled.

She playfully jabbed her fingers into his sides before he could block her hand. He flinched and jerked sideways.

"You're lucky you're cute," she teased.

He kissed her on the forehead and said, "I know." Then he scooted to his side of the bed where the covers were still flipped back. He slipped back into place and closed his eyes.

She switched off the light and shimmied beside him.

"Goodnight," she whispered.

But he didn't sleep.

Chapter 13

After another sleepless night, all Jimmy wanted was to lounge on the couch while binge-watching the latest series on one of the streaming services. But there was work to be done.

It was Wednesday—the day the shed was scheduled to be delivered and built. It was also the day he promised he would build Roni's closet. Although right now, he was wondering what the hell he'd been thinking when he made that promise. In fairness to himself, he didn't know his nights would be haunted by a *shade*. If he'd known that ...

Well, let's just say he would have done a lot of things differently.

He got dressed and ate a quick, cold breakfast of cereal with milk. Then, with a thermos full of high-octane, he slipped behind the wheel of his pickup truck. With Roni in the passenger seat, they were ready to embark on the forty-minute drive to the self-storage facility, where Jimmy's tools were locked in a 10' x 15' steel container. To be more accurate, the tools had originally belonged to his father until a year ago when the senior Hobart told his only son he wanted him to have them. Not because he knew he was dying—he didn't.

Before retiring five years ago, Benjamin—Benji to his friends—worked as a foreman at a large construction firm, reading plans someone else drew and building what other people dreamed up. It was a well-earned promotion—that's what his boss had told him—and he accepted it for the money. But if he was being honest, he preferred the feel of calluses on his hands to paper cuts.

Benji had started laboring with the firm right out of high school, shadowing the more experienced tradesmen to learn everything he could while collecting tools along the way. And after a decade, he became their youngest foreman. So, when Benji Hobart asked Madalyn McSally to be his wife, he was able to buy a fixer-upper in a nice neighborhood where they could start their family. She was nervous about the repairs the house needed, but he said it was more economical than buying a new home—really, he just missed getting his hands dirty. Plus, the house had a two-car garage he could use as a workshop. So, he assured his betrothed he would handle the repairs. And that's what he did, adding more tools to his collection whenever a new household project called for something he didn't have.

Maddie hardly recognized the old house by the time their son was born. And Benji decided he didn't want his son to follow in his footsteps. He wanted his son to be the dreamer who drew up plans for someone like him. He wanted his son to be an architect.

Even before his boy was putting together complete sentences, the senior Hobart taught him how to read construction blueprints. They spent hours together in that two-car garage, tinkering with this, repairing that. After his wife died, Benji moved his children to another town and into a 2,200 square foot four bedroom/four bath split level with a detached shed larger than their old two-car garage. And ever beside him was Jimmy.

By the time the senior Hobart retired, he had just about every tool there was, from socket wrenches and screwdrivers—in metric and imperial measurements—to a double-bevel sliding compound miter saw with interchangeable blades.

Then last year, Benji announced he was selling the home where he raised his children as a single father and moving to a more modest 1,100 square foot two bedroom/one bath apartment. There simply wasn't any room for his tools, so he wanted his son to have them.

At the time, Jimmy also lived in an apartment. So he rented the storage container and packed everything away until the day he had his own workshop.

But Benji didn't survive long enough to move into his downsized apartment. He was on his way to sign the lease when a drunk driver veered across the highway divider and into the front end of his four-door sedan. The coroner's report listed the cause of death as blunt force trauma to the brain and heart. Benji was dead on impact.

It was barely light as Jimmy pulled out of the gravel driveway and turned left onto Woody Creek Lane. He sipped his coffee and realized history was repeating itself in a way.

Like his father, he too bought a fixer-upper as his first home and he already had a long list of repairs. He thought about those hours spent in the garage and everything his father taught him. As he imagined setting up his own workshop, he only wished he'd done it sooner so they could have shared time together tinkering in it.

***

It had been months since they last visited the self-storage, but Jimmy still remembered all the turns leading to locker number 410. He backed the pickup into the parking space just outside the orange roll-up door and cut the engine. Then he finished the last of the coffee in the thermos before stepping out onto the blacktop.

Roni had already released the tailgate and was waiting by the steel door. "You remembered the key, right?"

"You mean you don't have it?" he said, wide-eyed.

Her shoulders sunk, and she groaned, "Jimmy."

"I'm kidding," he said as he fished the padlock key from his front pocket. "But you deserved it for waiting until now to ask me that."

She playfully smacked him on his rear end, then folded her arms across her chest.

He laughed as he released the lock and then pulled up on the metal handle. The door rattled in the ceiling track as it rolled up and let the light shine on his father's expansive collection.

For a moment, he stood by the truck tailgate, skimming his eyes over the boxes and plastic containers as he slowly returned the padlock key to his pants pocket. He realized it was a good thing he'd opted for one of the larger sheds. *Maybe I should have gone even bigger.*

"Do you know what we're looking for?" she asked, stepping into the cardboard maze.

He wanted to free all of them but there was no time for that—no room in the pickup either. If the builders were running on time—which would be a miracle in and of itself—they only had an hour to grab what he needed and get back home by 8:30.

Luckily, there was order in what appeared to be chaos. The boxes were labeled; small power tools were along the right-side wall; bulkier tools were in the back. There were tools he needed today—like the handheld drill and drill bits, the meter-long level, and circular saw—and tools he needed for other household projects—like the belt sander and nail gun. He also knew that this small lot wouldn't even take up half of the trucks' flatbed, so he planned on adding whatever else he had room for.

"I'll grab the power tools," he said. Then he pointed to bankers' boxes stacked along the left-side wall. "Why don't you start loading those."

"All of them?"

"As many as will fit."

***

Twenty minutes later, the truck bed was full, and they were behind schedule. He pulled down the orange steel door, letting it land against the concrete floor with a *clunk*. The door rattled, echoing in the empty parking lot. Then he replaced the padlock and closed the truck's tailgate. Roni was in the passenger seat, buckling her seatbelt when he opened the driver's side door.

"The one time you want 'em to show up late, they'll probably be early."

"We still have time," she said.

"We're cutting it close though." He buckled up, started the engine, put the truck in drive, and pulled out of the parking spot.

"I guess there's no time to stop?"

He'd forgotten all about the Melatonin. That's why she got in the truck. He was supposed to stop at the drugstore on the return trip so she could run inside and pick up a bottle of the sleep aid because she knew he wouldn't do it for himself. She was worried about him. Worried he might not stay awake to drive because he hadn't been sleeping. Worried he might not sleep tonight, and the next night, and the next.

He turned to meet her gaze. "I'm sorry. But I don't think we have time to stop."

"It's okay. I'll do it later."

He didn't like the idea of taking a sleeping aid, even if it was all natural. And if she knew the real reason he wasn't sleeping then she'd know that Melatonin probably wouldn't solve his problem. But for her, he was willing to try.

***

As luck would have it, there was no heavy traffic on the way home, so they made good time, arriving fifteen minutes before the scheduled delivery. Jimmy drove slowly along the gravel driveway, careful not to jostle the tools, then parked in front of the house.

By now, the sun was above the tree line but still behind the house, so the parking pad was in full shade. He felt the chill in the air when he stepped out of the warmth of the truck's cabin. The sky was clear, so he didn't mind leaving the boxes of tools in the bed of the truck until the shed was built—it didn't make sense to move them twice. He only needed the drill, drill bits, level, and circular saw, all of which he made sure were stowed near the tailgate so he didn't have to unpack the whole truck to get to them.

While Roni climbed the steps to unlock the front door, he looped his arm through the shoulder strap of the red tote bag stuffed with the tools he needed for the closet project. Then he grabbed the meter-long level and the 25' long orange sixteen-gauge-wire extension cord before closing the tailgate.

He tried more times than he could remember to convince his father to upgrade to a cordless drill, but every time, he refused. Jimmy finally bought one for his father as a gift three years ago. Lightweight with 280 in/lbs of max torque and two batteries for a full day of drilling, driving, and fastening. It was perfectly built for any project. By now, the batteries were certainly dead, and given that they hadn't been charged in over a year, they might be useless. He didn't know why he hadn't thought to keep the drill set at the apartment—he didn't have one of his own so it may have come in handy. Now he was just thankful that his father had been a stubborn man that wouldn't let go of his electric drill. Otherwise, Roni's closet would have to wait.

His foot landed on the first porch step when the diesel engine revved at the driveway's entrance. He turned around and watched the driver navigate the flatbed truck onto the gravel and begin the lumbering journey toward the house. Then he set the bag, level, and extension cord inside the foyer and closed the front door.

There was no need to hurry down the steps to meet the builders, but Jimmy was naturally a fast walker. Always had been. He stood beside his truck in the shade of the house and motioned for the driver to pull to the left, knowing that would make it easier for them when they were ready to leave. Also, he didn't want them blocking Roni's car on the right side of the parking pad.

Once they were parked, Jimmy approached the driver's side. It was at least another minute before the door opened and a fifty-something man hopped out wearing permanently stained bleached denim pants, a green flannel shirt, and black-rimmed sunglasses with blue mirrored lenses.

"Mr. Hobart?" he said.

Jimmy nodded, nearly wincing as his hand was swallowed up in the man's firm grip. "Call me Jimmy."

"All right. I'm Roger; he's Glen," he said, his head tilting back toward his partner. "We're building you a shed today, that right?"

"Yes, sir."

"You want to show me where?"

As Jimmy led the way, he couldn't help but notice that Roger smelled like a 1950's diner—what he imagined it would smell like anyway. Perhaps his perception was formed by what he saw watching *film noir* alongside his father but, having grown up in the nineties, the depictions almost felt like science fiction to him. And now, being in the presence of it, he wouldn't say the odor was pleasant—or unpleasant for that matter. It was the memory it carried with it that he appreciated. And for that, he liked Roger instantly.

They stopped on the south side of the house where the parking pad opened into a wide enough space to park two rows of three cars each. Jimmy mused this was likely where guests of the previous owners would have parked while attending a party thrown by their hosts. The rest of the time it was just wasted space.

Glen joined them to survey the spot. He was the opposite of his partner. Quiet, his indigo jeans unwrinkled, red flannel tucked neatly into his waistband, and no stirred-up memories hiding in his musky aftershave. He concluded the space was suitable for the shed, although they may need to use shims to level it out.

On the way back, Roger said, "We've also got a closet system on the truck, but I don't see an order for us to install it. Does that sound right to you?"

"That's right," he confirmed. "I'm installing the closet."

"You're the boss. You want us to bring the pieces in for you?"

"I wouldn't want to trouble you," he said, while secretly hoping Roger would insist because honestly, the thought of making God only knows how many trips up and down the staircase while carrying long boxes that weigh—

"It's no problem, Jimmy."

"If you're sure."

Roger lifted his mirrored sunglasses and winked. "Just point us in the right direction."

"Great ... Um, they're going up to the second floor," Jimmy said, backing toward the house.

"Come on, Glen ... Let's get these closet boxes off the truck."

On the porch, Jimmy opened the storm door, set the brake on the pump so it wouldn't close, and waited as they unloaded the truck. Roger and Glen trudged across the gravel, each with a box propped on his shoulder, between the pickup and Roni's SUV and up the steps. They followed Jimmy to the upstairs bedroom, deposited the boxes on the floor, and returned for the rest.

Jimmy slipped each man forty bucks for the extra effort, then left them to the business of the shed while he went back inside to tackle the closet. It wasn't until he was halfway up the staircase that he realized he hadn't seen Roni since before the truck pulled up. He paused on the landing and called out, "Roni?"

When she didn't answer after a few seconds, he assumed she was in the basement doing laundry and then finished the climb to the second floor.

***

For the next three hours, Jimmy was the lead musician to Roger and Glen's accompaniment in a heavy metal concert comprised of power tools and testosterone. But when they failed to pick up the last three refrains, he set the drill down, wiped the sweat from his brow with the back of his forearm, and listened.

In the silence, two voices, gruff from years of hard days and long nights, carried up from below. The conversation appeared lighthearted, intermingled with laughter—different than the sparse words he'd heard previously. He walked into the bedroom, pausing in the doorway to turn and admire his work before continuing to the front window, where the voices were louder and a faint, familiar melody played in the background. He concentrated on the music, trying to bring it into focus until he could finally sing along.

They must be on their lunch break.

He removed the phone from his back pocket. 12:35 p.m. He'd been so preoccupied with the closet he hadn't even realized he was hungry. Now that his stomach had his attention, he decided taking a break was a good idea.

At the foot of the steps, he clapped along with Queen's "We Will Rock You" and danced/walked across the foyer and through the dining room on the way to the kitchen—

"*Maou?*"

As Jimmy's hand pushed the butler door open, Coal was on his feet, back arched and caressing the corner of the center island cabinet.

"Have you been trapped in here all morning?"

The cat twitched his tail and stared at Jimmy, slowly blinking his emerald eyes. On the floor, the ceramic dish was empty—*Did we feed him before going out?* He wasn't sure. He'd been so tired that he barely remembered having breakfast himself. The bowl should still be half full if they had. Coal was a grazer, after all, not a gobbler.

"All right," he finally said. The sound from the porch now out of reach, Jimmy continued bobbing his head to the beat and sang the refrain while he stepped up into the pantry. With the bag of kibble in hand and Coal chattering as he led the way, he started across the kitchen. "Just don't make a habit of this—I don't want you getting fat."

Coal's head tilted side to side as the tiny brown and orange pieces landed in the dish—a few even bounced off his head but he didn't seem to mind. Then, unable to wait any longer, the cat began devouring the meal, a clear indication that they had indeed forgotten to feed him earlier.

"Sorry, Bud," Jimmy said while scratching Coal's back. "It won't happen again."

After replacing the bag of kibble, Jimmy's next stop was the refrigerator where he found thin-sliced Virginia baked ham, Cooper sharp cheddar cheese, mayo, and Romaine lettuce. He took a plate from the cabinet and set it on the counter with the rest of his haul. Then he slathered mayo on two slices of seedless rye bread, followed by two slices of the rectangular cheese that he had to trim to fit—the excess went promptly into his mouth. The masterpiece was topped off with a layer of ham and three leaves of lettuce, ribs and all.

He couldn't resist taking a bite before putting everything away. Then he returned to get a second bite, savoring the creamy, sweet and tangy flavor combo between the bread slices as he strolled to the south window, taking the plate with him to catch crumbs.

There, he admired Roger and Glen's progress on the shed. The floor was set, as well as the two short walls. *They work fast*, he thought while chewing and nodding his head. Then movement in the tree line to the left of his peripheral vision caught his attention.

He walked to the closest east-facing window for a better look while crunching into the sandwich for another bite. He squinted and leaned toward the glass ... It was Roni, stomping up the incline that was their backyard. *What the hell was she doing in the woods?* he wondered, swallowing before taking another bite.

He tracked her as she crossed the yard, moving out of view from one window before reappearing in the next. Then he popped the last of the sandwich into his mouth and placed the empty plate on the center island. When he did, he saw the empty bowl on the floor. A grazer no more, Coal had finished every morsel. Now he really felt bad.

Footfalls from behind told him Roni had arrived at the porch. He turned around in time to see her open the side door. "Where've you been?" he asked before she was barely inside.

"I went for a walk."

"You've been gone hours."

"Have I?" She took the knit hat from her head, laid it on the island, and then went to the sink to wash her hands. Brown grass and prickly burs were stuck to the hat and woven into her hair.

"Did you fall?"

"No," she huffed, wiping her hands on the towel. "Why would you ask that?"

"Your hair," he said, plucking some debris from the clutches of her shoulder-length raven locks.

Her eyes grew wide. "Oh, I laid down for a bit to watch the clouds."

"What clouds? It's a clear sky."

"Well, there *were* clouds," she insisted as she opened the refrigerator door.

He shook his head. "I don't think so—"

"Just drop it," she said, shooting him a glance as she removed the same deli items from the fridge he had replaced moments ago.

He held up his hands and stepped aside to give her some room. She didn't bother getting a plate from the cabinet, opting to prepare her sandwich right on the countertop instead—a little out of character for her, but then again, she appeared to be ticked off about something. As she spread a thin layer of mayonnaise on the slices of bread, he wondered if he should bother trying to find out what it was. She took only one slice of cheese, topped by four slices of ham. Then she stopped to fetch a tomato from the windowsill.

Trying to be helpful, he retrieved a serrated knife from the butcher block and set it next to her half-made sandwich.

"Thanks," she said.

"You're welcome." He leaned against the counter and decided against digging deeper, opting instead for a less triggering topic. "Did you feed Coal this morning?"

She stood straight, knife halfway through the second slice, closed her eyes, and said, "I knew I was forgetting something." Then she completed the cut, and the sliver of tomato flopped over onto the first slice. "Did you feed him?"

"Yeah, he wouldn't stop crying."

Buzz-buzz-buzz.

The vibrations from the cell phone in his back pocket were amplified against the wooden cabinet to sound more like a power tool. He leaned forward and reached around to retrieve it.

"Who is it?" she asked as she finished constructing her masterpiece.

"It's Bette."

"Tell her I said hi."

He pressed the answer button on the touch screen and then brought the phone to his ear. "Hey, troublemaker ... Oh, you know, living the dream of home ownership. Roni says hi ... She says hi," he relayed in a hushed tone, then returned his attention to the caller. "So, what's up?"

Roni bit into her sandwich and dribbled pink drops of tomato pulp onto the counter. She fished a napkin from the holder and wiped her chin.

"Hold on," he said, lowering the phone to his shoulder. "She says she's in the area and wants to drop by."

"Gw-ate," Roni answered, covering her bulging mouth. "When?"

"When do you think you'll get here?" He looked down while listening to the voice on the line, then to Roni, he said, "30 to 40 minutes."

As he finished the call, he balanced the phone on his shoulder and began putting the food back into the fridge. He hoped that would be enough to get him back on Roni's good side, but something told him it would take more than that.

Chapter 14

Forty-five minutes later, Jimmy heard the purr of a 396 cubic inch engine block pumping out 425 horsepower as it rumbled off Woody Creek Lane and onto the gravel driveway—an unmistakable sound that, even though a football field length away, overpowered the construction noise and reached his ears in the confines of the walk-in closet. Once again, he set his tools down and went to the bedroom window.

At first, he didn't see the car—he didn't hear it anymore either. Perhaps he'd been fooled by some other sports car passing by. He was just about to return to the closet when there was a flash of light in the pines, like sunlight reflecting on a mirror. And then she appeared, preceded by loud music playing like the fanfare heralding the arrival of a monarch.

The Nassau Blue 1965 Corvette Stingray convertible was moving at the speed of a parade float. Uncharacteristically slow, but a gravel driveway will do that to most drivers, especially one as protective of her classic car as Bette.

Finally, the engine revved as the car glided to a stop between the flatbed semi and his pickup truck. The parking pad was in full sun by now, and with the convertible top down, the light glinted on the wild auburn curls that framed her movie star sunglasses. She let the motor grumble and growl a bit longer while she peeled brown leather gloves from her hands.

Bette saved almost every penny she earned since she was twelve, working odd jobs for the neighbors: babysitting, mowing lawns, and walking dogs. Until she was old enough to get a real job. First at a local fast-food restaurant, after school and on weekends, and then in retail. Always with her eyes—and heart—set on one thing.

She enrolled in college because that was what she was expected to do but she couldn't decide on a major. She had a passion for psychology and the supernatural, astronomy, and the occult—sciences that don't easily overlap in the world of academia. After two semesters, she dropped out and returned to retail full-time while following her passions in her free time. Eventually, she secured an administrative position at the local military base, where she's thrived ever since. And when she turned twenty-five, she purchased her dream car—her baby as she liked to call it.

Jimmy was proud of his younger sister—and she was proud of her car.

Their parents always called their daughter Elizabeth. Her friends called her Beth. No one ever called her Bette—at least not twice. No one except Jimmy. And if you asked him why, he would either say he doesn't remember or it's a long story. But neither would be true.

The truth was that his younger sister was far too sassy and feisty to be called Elizabeth. Too combative and confrontational for Beth. To him, she would always be Bette—like the movie star from Hollywood's golden age.

Eventually, she cut the engine and stepped out of the sports car, wearing knee-high brown leather boots over blue jeans. A braided white and maroon plaid sweater coat was cinched around her waist. After tucking the keyring into her pocket, she swung the door closed. Then, for good measure, she gave the door a final nudge with her hip before sashaying around the car's front end to survey her brother's new purchase.

＊＊＊

On his way down the steps, Jimmy noticed how quiet it was inside the house.

After finishing her sandwich, Roni had left in her SUV to retrieve the Melatonin that they failed to get earlier that day. Otherwise, he would have called out to her—though, as previously mentioned, she probably would have heard the car pull up herself.

But that wasn't the only reason it was quiet. The *whir* and *ca-chunk* of power tools had stopped—not just his, but Roger's and Glen's as well. That meant they noticed Bette pull up too. But then, everyone noticed Bette. And once they got to know her, they never forgot her.

In the foyer, Jimmy heard the pathetic sounds of middle-aged men flirting with a woman half their age. Bette didn't need rescuing—he'd felt the force of her punch against his arm enough times to know that. But since he was her older brother, and he would like to have his shed finished today, he needed to break things up.

He opened the door and stepped out onto the porch. At first glance, it would appear to the untrained eye that the predators had her cornered by the cab of their truck. But things weren't always as they seemed.

He let the storm door slap against the frame to announce his presence. Roger and Glen snapped to attention like good soldiers.

Bette whipped her head around, her curls bouncing across her shoulder. Then propped her hands on her hips and said, "Back to work, boys ... The boss is here."

Jimmy smirked and shook his head.

Roger and Glen protested as she walked away.

"You sure know how to make an entrance," Jimmy murmured.

"Haven't I always?" She wrapped her arms around his neck.

"Always causing trouble," he whispered in her ear while giving her a squeeze.

"I'm just having a little fun."

Roger turned around for one last glimpse of his would-be prey, taking two backward steps before finally giving up altogether and joining Glen inside the unfinished shed. With the back wall in place, all that was missing was the front wall, barn doors, and the roof.

"Why don't you show me around this dump of yours," she said, slipping her arms away from her brother. Then she took hold of his elbow and led him toward the porch, out of reach of the middle-aged suitors.

***

"Wow, Jimmy," Bette said, spinning in the entry hall and taking in the natural beauty and charm of the Victorian treasure.

"I know the outside doesn't look like much ... We're focusing on the inside for now and then when it warms up—"

"You know I was just kidding with the 'dump' comment, right?"

"I know." He never took offense at a little good-natured ribbing. That's what siblings were for. But he did feel a little self-conscious about the outside of the house.

"Where's Roni?"

"She had an errand to run but she should be back soon. She wants you to stay for dinner—that is, unless you got a better offer."

She gave him a curious look.

He responded with a head-tilt toward the *whirs* and *ca-chunks* that had resumed outside.

She punched his arm. "Ha-ha."

After peering into the parlor, she continued her self-guided tour by strolling into the sitting room. She ran her fingers along the daffodil walls and nutmeg wood trim like she was communing with the house. Then she spotted the igloo-shaped bed tucked into the far corner and twirled around with one eyebrow raised.

"We have a cat now," he said.

"You have a cat!" she exclaimed, scanning the room for the tiny creature. "Since when?"

"Since we found the little stowaway in the basement ... And he likes me, too."

"Why James Hobart, I never thought I'd see the day."

"So? Will you stay for dinner?"

"Of course," she answered as she wandered into the dining room. Then, as she pushed the butler door open, she looked over her shoulder. "But only because Roni invited me."

***

On the second floor, Jimmy resumed the tour first with a visit to Roni's studio, where colorful canvases leaned against one wall amid the half-unpacked boxes of supplies. The paint-splattered easel and the empty chair were still in the bump out.

"She has a beautiful view," Bette said, looking out the window at the forest. "Should be very inspiring."

Jimmy nodded.

"So, where's your office?"

"Right this way."

He led his sister to the front of the house for a quick look at his office in progress, then they were in the master bedroom.

"What's going on in here?" she asked, walking past the bedroom furniture, draped in dust-coated plastic, then onto the painter's tarp, stepping over wood scraps and around empty boxes scattered about the room.

"I'm converting the dressing room into a walk-in closet."

In the entrance to the closet, she eyed the frenzy of horizontal metal support braces screwed into the walls. Power tools lay on the floor amongst a heap of modular pieces that had yet to be hung. "Has she seen it yet?"

He shook his head. "I don't think so."

Bette looked at him seriously now. "Are you guys okay?"

He furrowed his brow. "Why would you ask me that?"

She didn't respond. She simply held his gaze, mentally decrypting the password that unlocked his emotions and thoughts like a common thief.

Bette had an irritating intuition when it came to her brother, always able to sense when he was lying or hiding something. Jimmy had often suspected that perhaps the family 'gift' hadn't entirely skipped over her like his mother intimated it would.

Powerless against her methods, he quickly glanced over his shoulder to ensure they were still alone, then in a hushed voice, he said, "We had a little argument yesterday ... I snapped at her."

Bette folded her arms across her chest and shook her head as she rolled her eyes, scolding him with her steely blue stare.

"I know. It was my fault." Then he lowered his eyes and shuffled his foot. "I haven't been sleeping since we moved in."

"What's going on?"

He had to be careful here. Bette didn't know about his 'gift' any more than Roni did. He couldn't reveal the truth to his sister and not his fiancé ... *Can I? Maybe I should tell her—she always knows when I'm lying anyway.* But after so many years of keeping the secret, the thought of coming clean was agonizing.

He took a deep breath and again met his sister's gaze. "I'm having nightmares."

She leaned closer, her eyes wide with excitement. "Nightmares?"

Since she was a teenager, studying and analyzing dreams had been a hobby of hers as it dealt with the mind and behavior. She'd been documenting her own dreams in volumes of journals—probably dozens by now. She read her copy of Freud's *The Interpretation of Dreams* until the paper cover fell off and had to be held in place with clear packing tape. She'd researched the theories of Jung and

Hall, Faraday and Clift, and anyone else with letters behind their name who might have an opinion.

"What are the nightmares about?"

"I'm being chased by ... a shadow." When lying, it was always best to keep it simple, stay as close to the truth as possible, and believe what you were saying. He only hoped he could fool his lie detector/sister.

"I'm sure I don't have to tell you this," she said, leaning her back against the door jam, "but buying a house is very stressful. And being chased in your dream could signal that you're anxious. It's the second most common recurring dream."

"What's the first?

"Falling."

As she turned and began walking into the bedroom and toward the hallway, Jimmy realized he'd successfully thrown her off the trail and felt simultaneously vindicated and guilty. Perhaps if she'd called him out for lying, he would have decided to tell her the truth. And perhaps that wouldn't have been so bad.

"What's Roni say about your nightmares?"

"She only knows I'm not sleeping. I haven't told her about the ... shadow. And I don't want you to tell her either."

She stopped in the bedroom doorway and turned around. "Jimmy—"

"She wants me to try Melatonin ... Maybe it will help."

"It might also help if you tell her."

He gave her a gentle nudge into the hallway. "Come on ... Let me show you the backyard."

***

"You can't beat this view," she said, standing at the crest of the slope that led to the tree line.

He nodded. "I can't help thinking about how much Dad would've loved it here."

Then for a moment, the construction noise faded away, and in the manufactured silence, Jimmy imagined it was twilight in the yard. Flames danced in the firepit. His arms were around Roni as they swayed to Elvis' soothing baritone crooning his rendition of "Can't Help Falling in Love". And in the background, his parents cradled their grandchildren that hadn't yet been born. It was a dream worth holding on to ...

"Beth!"

Roni's voice carried from the back porch and into his fantasy world, ripping him back to reality with the pinch of a bandage peeled from an unhealed wound. When he turned around, Bette was already sprinting toward her future sister-in-law.

"You're here," Roni squealed, leaping off the porch and quickly closing the distance between them.

It wasn't lost on Jimmy how rare it was for a man to fall in love with a woman who would become his sister's best friend. Others might say he was lucky. He knew it was something else and was glad he didn't ignore *the light* when he was led to Roni. Because he couldn't imagine his life without either of them.

The women collided with a kinetic force he saw and felt, even from twenty feet away. His 'gift' was keener around Bette—as if she helped him focus it somehow. He knew there was so much more to learn if only he had a teacher.

"I'm so glad you're here," Roni said.

"I got tired of waiting for an invitation."

"Blame that on your brother. You know what a perfectionist he is."

"Yes," Bette said, turning to give Jimmy a disapproving look while still holding one arm around Roni. Then, to her sister-in-law, "Your house is fantastic, by the way."

"Not yet," Roni said. "But it will be. Are you staying for dinner?"

"Well, that depends." She turned up the corner of her lip and raised one eyebrow while pumping her thumb toward the shed. "Are they staying?"

"You will never change," Roni scolded. Then she laughed and hooked her arm around Bette's as they began walking toward the house with Jimmy following steps behind.

"Speaking of hairy beasts," Bette said. "I hear you have a cat."

***

While his two favorite women visited, Jimmy drove into town for takeout pizza from Frank's. He returned home at seven with two large pies just in time to witness Roger and Glen fix the last of the asphalt shingles to the shed roof.

It was dark by then, but the south lawn was lit up in the white glow of utility lights. Jimmy offered the builders one of the pizzas before thanking them and going inside.

Roni and Bette were on the couch in the sitting room, their voices just below the volume of the syndicated detective show playing on the flatscreen. The women followed Jimmy and the spicy aroma of pepperoni, sausage, and oregano to the dining room table, where plates, silverware, and napkins were waiting.

After setting down the box, Jimmy went into the kitchen where Coal was waiting, hugging the center island with his fluffy body. "Why are you hiding in here?"

"Maou?"

He looked at the floor. "Empty again, huh?" *Or had his bowl remained empty since lunch?* He peeked through the butler door. "Babe, did you feed Coal?"

"Shit," she sighed. "I've been so preoccupied with your sister that I forgot."

He ducked back into the kitchen. "Sorry, Bud," he said on his way to the pantry. Then softer, "You know how ladies are."

While Coal ate, Jimmy took three bottles of beer from the fridge and then returned to the dining room where the trio devoured six slices of gooey deliciousness while talking and laughing. At 7:30, he heard the diesel engine roar as the flatbed truck rumbled toward Woody Creek Lane. Then he took one of the last two slices from the box. The women split the other.

Before Bette left, she let him know that, while he was getting the pizza, Roni confided that she was no longer angry over yesterday's argument. She'd been suffering from a headache and needed to get away from all the banging. Considering she'd disappeared before the banging even started, that only partly made sense to Jimmy, but he kept that to himself and thanked his sister for letting him know.

By 9:30, the house was quiet and empty without his sister's vibrance.

Jimmy was exhausted.

Before heading up for bed herself, Roni reminded him to take the Melatonin, which he did, right before checking that all the downstairs windows and doors were locked. Then before switching off the light, he glanced toward the igloo in the far corner of the sitting room.

It was empty.

***

After brushing his teeth and emptying his bladder, he went to the master bedroom, where he found Roni in the doorway to the unfinished walk-in closet. He wrapped his arms around her waist and rested his chin on her shoulder. "Are you disappointed?"

"No," she said as she folded her arms over his. "Because I know you'll finish tomorrow." Then she turned her head around. "Right?"

"Promise." Then he kissed her cheek and swapped his dirty clothes for a fresh T-shirt and sleep shorts before hopping into bed beside her. As he reached for the bedside lamp, he glanced at the bedroom door to ensure it was closed.

It was.

Then he brought on the darkness and waited for the Melatonin to kick in.

Chapter 15

Jimmy gasped as he opened his eyes, jolted awake as if he'd been shaken.

He was on his back, arms by his sides, bedcovers pulled up under his chin. Unable to breathe. Unable to see anything in the darkness—not even the glowing red numerals on the bedside table.

Creases formed along his forehead as he grimaced from the discomfort of what felt like a knee pressing against his sternum. He shouldn't be on his back. He was a side sleeper. Had been ever since one terrifying morning before his mother died.

He needed to roll over. He pressed down with his right shoulder and left foot, but the pressure on his breastbone intensified, pushing him deeper into the mattress. With each shallow breath, pain radiated through his chest. He tried raising his left leg to get more leverage, but his leg wouldn't obey. Then he felt the gentle tension of the bedcovers pulling taut across his skin. He told his arms to fight back but they were pinned—yes, pinned—and unable to move.

Paralyzed.

It was amazing what fear can do, imprinting in your brain like a tattoo. A particular sound, smell, or circumstance can awaken that fear and transport you to an exact moment in time ...

He was seven or eight, asleep in his tiny bed when suddenly he couldn't breathe. He sat up straight, clawing at his throat, mouth wide, chest sinking with each shallow gasp. But the air couldn't get in no matter how hard he tried to inhale. It was as if invisible hands were clamped around his airway. He scrambled from his bed, tumbled through his bedroom door, then ran down the hallway toward his parents' room, bare feet slapping against the Pergo flooring. He tried calling out for help but only managed gurgles and grunts. He opened the door and flopped onto his mother, gasping and wheezing. Startled but alert, she did the only thing she could think of doing. She pounded on his back several times until his airway finally opened, satiating his starved lungs ...

Since then, he trained himself to be a side sleeper, every night repeating the same mantra, "Don't roll over. Don't roll over." And it worked—until now.

He struggled, but the weight on his chest only grew heavier. His fingers curled around the fitted sheet. He tried to cry out, but there was no breath in his lungs to produce sound. He gulped greedily at the air but was unable to pass oxygen through his compressed airway.

He wished for his mother to appear. To roll him over, and pound on his back like he was that scared little boy again. He wished for Roni to wake up, see him struggling and blow air into his lungs. He even wished he'd left the bedroom door open so Coal could jump on his chest.

But no one came to his aide.

As he felt himself slipping away, *the shade* revealed itself. It was sitting on top of him, its full weight leaning into the knee on Jimmy's chest, its boney arms pulling the bedcovers tighter, cotton threads cutting into his skin.

It slowly opened its amber eyes, first into mere slits, like twin crescent moons, until they were fully open, and the oblong pupils dilated to twice their normal size.

The creature opened its mouth, lips splitting like a broken scab as they turned up into a haunting grin. Its ashen tongue, dripping with a vile acrid slime, slipped between its yellow teeth.

It leaned closer and hissed, "*I sssee you, Jamesss Massson.*"

All at once, Jimmy's muscles contracted and he was upright on the bed, gasping deep, raspy breaths. His arms now free, he repeatedly slapped the palm of his hand against his chest as if to wake up his lungs.

"*Mhr-aow.*"

Coal's guttural growl followed desperate thumps against the bedroom door, rattling the wood in its frame as he tried to enter the room.

Roni was up and around the bed to Jimmy's side. She tossed the bedcovers off and took hold of his legs, spinning his body and setting his feet on the floor. Then she sat beside him and gently leaned him forward until his head was between his knees.

"Breathe, Jimmy," she said as she rubbed his back. "You're okay. Just breathe."

He took slow, deep breaths through his nose, then blew out from his mouth as she stroked his back. The compression of his torso helped to normalize his blood pressure as oxygen reached his brain, and he could think clearly again. He was safe.

He turned toward the clock.

The glowing red digits showed 2:20—no, 2:21 a.m.

***

A few hours later, Jimmy sat quietly, staring at his breakfast with his chin propped on one hand as steam wafted to his cheeks.

"It probably takes a few nights for Melatonin to enter your system," Roni said from across the table. Then she lifted a spoonful of peaches and cream oatmeal and held it in front of her mouth, cooling the temperature with her soft breath as she scrolled on her tablet.

Too exhausted to spoon the food into his mouth, too disturbed to want to eat, he twirled a half-empty mug of coffee on the wood veneer and thought about *the shade*—which he doubted it was, at least not by his grandfather's definition, but he didn't know what else to call it.

Grandpa Bill surmised that sometimes *the light* reflected onto a *shade* like reflections in a mirror. His mother told him this happened when *the shade* wanted to be seen and that he couldn't control it. But this creature was not a 'reflection' of a deceased person. And while he could only see it when it wanted to be seen, it also wanted Jimmy to know that it saw him.

But what else does it want? he wondered. *To kill me?*

"Could've been the beer."

"Hm?" he said, looking up to meet her gaze.

"The beer ... Alcohol, when taken with Melatonin, can cause anxiety," she said, reading from her tablet. "Google says you should take it 30 minutes before bed and practice a regular bedtime routine ... And no alcohol."

"Great," he said, straightening in his chair and raising the mug to his lips. "I'll remember that tonight."

"Just give it time, Smudge ... And eat your breakfast."

Chapter 16

After quickly checking the time, Jimmy sighed heavily and closed his eyes. *2:20 a.m. again. So much for Melatonin.*

Then he nestled his head deeper into the down pillow and scootched the bedcovers over his shoulder to ward off the chill. In the silence, he heard the *whoosh, whoosh* of blood rushing through his veins. The endearing *snort-chuff* of Roni's breath moving in and out (although she professes not to be a snorer). The *creek* and *crick* of the clapboard siding as a gust stirred outside.

Determined to fall back asleep, he sighed again and then imagined Freddie Mercury singing the opening lines of the masterful rock opera "Bohemian Rhapsody" ... Enter John Deacon on base ... Like a lullaby, ranging in intensity and timbre, Freddie Mercury conveys emotion with every dramatic note ... Queue Brian May's guitar solo and then ... The piano picks up the pace, and the ballad transformed into an opera ... The percussion section joins in as Roger Taylor builds toward the dramatic falsetto B♭ in the fifth octave—

A tickle on the back of Jimmy's neck broke the spell. The music faded, and he was back to reality, back in his bed. He opened his eyes and glimpsed the numerals on the clock again: 2:25 a.m.

He sighed, closed his eyes, and called the band back for an encore performance, attempting to recreate the atmosphere of the private concert. But before

Queen could retake the stage, again he felt a tickle. This time, he reached around to scratch the itch but instead felt the cold, leathery epidermis of the night *shade* crack and flake under his fingers.

He opened his eyes, his breath coming short and shallow. He felt its presence, lying beside him—between him and Roni. He swallowed and slowly brought his hand back under the safety of the bedcovers. He lay still ... Silent. Waiting for *the shade* to make its move.

Then the sheet shifted as the creature forced its charred body against his, spooning him. He heard three short rushes of air enter its nostrils as it inhaled his scent. His hair tussled with each exhalation of its hot, sour breath. Its scaly tongue slid along the nape of his neck, licked up, and then snaked around to his ear, leaving behind a trail of warm, sticky slime.

Jimmy's breath quickened, anticipating the bite of its sharp fangs that was almost certain to come as its cracked lips grazed his earlobe.

"*I sssee you,*" it whispered.

Jimmy sprang from the bed and spun around to look upon the beast.

The bunched up white sheets took on a washed-out periwinkle tint in the moonlit glow. Beside his empty spot laid Roni's silhouette, peacefully unaware that he'd been roused again in the middle of the night.

But nothing more.

He brought his shaking hands to his head.

What's happening to me?

Chapter 17

Roni had no idea about Jimmy's most recent 'nightmare,' and he saw no reason to tell her. He figured the less she knew, the better. But when she noticed he looked every bit as haggard this morning at breakfast as the day prior, she suggested they take a walk in their woods. *"The fresh air will do you good," she'd said.* He didn't argue with her. Besides, she might be right. Also because debating with Roni was about as pointless as the diamond thieves on *Lost.* You may start out with a good argument, but in the end, you'll end up buried alive like Nikki and Paulo.

So, here he was, in the woods in the middle of the afternoon ... Alone. Because, after stopping to relieve himself, he'd lost sight of his fiancé. *Where the hell could she be anyway?*

"Roni!"

He was also lost, not unlike the aforementioned castaways—though still unwilling to admit it. He stood in one spot and spun slowly around, examining the landscape for something that looked familiar: a broken limb, a large rock, anything. Something. But one tree looked like all the others and there was no discernible path to follow because they had decided to 'off-road' their little hike.

"Roni!"

His voice echoed between the bare trees and traveled up the limbs until it disappeared into the heavy cloud cover where the sun remained hidden. He removed his cell phone from his back pocket and opened the compass app. The trickle of the creek was to his right—east according to the compass—meaning he needed to cut through the woods to the west to find the house. He started walking again, crunching over dead leaves and small twigs as he pushed branches aside.

"Roni," he yelled again, then mockingly to himself, he mumbled, "Let's take a walk in the woods ... It'll be fun ... Yeah, right."

He stood sideways between two young trees when a short burst of childlike laughter stopped his progress. He turned, thinking the sound came from behind, but with all the noise he was making—on top of talking to himself—he wasn't sure.

He carefully squeezed between the trees, eyes fixed on where he'd come from, when another giggle erupted. Certain it came from the north, he spun around 180 degrees—

More laughter, this time from the south—no, east. Or was it west? It was all around, confusing like the echo inside a bell tower, spinning him round and round until he tripped over a fallen branch and fell to the ground in a pile of leaves—

The laughter stopped.

He stayed there, crouched on his knees, listening ... two seconds ... four seconds ... six—

Hurried footfalls, running west—toward the house.

"Gotcha," he snarled.

He jumped to his feet and started running, ducking his head under taller branches while pushing low-hanging limbs aside until finally, he saw something familiar: a large rock resembling one of the monolithic stone figures carved by the Rapa Nui people on Easter Island. He turned left and was on the trail heading south, closing fast on the opening to their backyard.

"You'll be sorry when I catch you," he said.

There was no response except his own rhythmic breaths as his heart galloped in his chest and his feet hammered the earth. He hadn't been running since they bought the house, and he hadn't realized until now how much he missed it. She was right: the fresh air was doing him good.

He broke right through the opening in the tree line, and the house was in sight, just a hundred yards up the hill. He slowed to a stop and placed his hands on his hips as he surveyed the yard. But Roni was nowhere in sight.

"Damn," he said, panting and doubling over to rest his hands on his knees as he tried to catch his breath. "She's fast ... And I'm ... out of shape."

After a short break for recovery, he stood straight and again sized up the incline. There was no need to run; she'd already beaten him. So, he began the climb by taking long, slow strides up the grassy slope, and at the halfway point, something plopped onto the top of his head.

He felt around but found nothing. Then another plop, this time on his cheek. And another on the back of his hand. Rain. He looked up at the darkening clouds just as more droplets began to fall, landing on his shoulders with a steady *pat-pit-pat* before becoming a full-on shower.

"Perfect ... Just perfect."

He resumed his assent, but in the downpour and under the darkening storm clouds, he lost sight of the house. Determined to get home, he powered upward, slipping on the slick grass until he had to claw his way uphill, digging his fingers into the earth and pulling away muddy clumps with each grasp as water flowed into his eyes.

He sputtered his lips to keep the rain from going into his mouth. He grunted and groaned against the force of the wind, the sound of his voice lost in the fury of the storm, just as he'd been lost in the woods.

Exhausted by the time he reached the summit, his clothes soaked through, he wiped his eyes and saw the row of dogwood trees. *Almost there*. He leaned into the torrent and continued forward. But each step seemed to take all his strength.

"Jimmy!"

Her voice was salvation though it seemed miles away. A gust thrust him a step backward, but he fought, flinching as thunder clapped overhead. He was in the open now, vulnerable to the strike of lightning that was sure to follow, so he fought harder until finally, he saw Roni waiting for him on the back porch, waving her arms and calling his name. As he reached the steps, a light flashed behind him, cracking over the rumbling clouds as it struck its target.

Roni wrapped a towel around his shoulders as she directed him into the kitchen, where another towel was spread out on the floor. He shivered and grabbed the corner of the center island while she removed his muddy shoes. Then she peeled his sopping jeans from his cold, pink legs as the overhead lights flickered but stayed on. She dried his hair and then dropped the damp towel to the floor before helping him out of his wet jacket and T-shirt.

He wrapped his arms around his shivering body and asked, "W-where did you go?"

"Home, silly," she said as she pulled a clean, dry sweatshirt over his head.

"I l-lost you."

"Well, I'm right here."

After stepping into a pair of warm flannel pants, he followed her into the dining room, where a mug of hot chocolate awaited him. He sat at the table, gripping the warm mug and inhaling the sweet cinnamon scent as she returned to the kitchen. Then the lights went out, and the room glowed with the soft flicker of fall-scented candles. In the sitting room, burning wood *snapped* and *popped* in the hearth.

And he wondered, *How did she do all of this? How long was I gone?*

The butler door opened, and Roni emerged carrying a sheet cake with chocolate icing, decorative piping around the edges, and two candles in the shape of a three and a one. She sat the cake on the table before him, sliding his mug of hot chocolate aside.

Suddenly it was standing room only in their dining room as his friends crept from their hiding places and shouted a collective "SURPRISE!" followed by a verse of Happy Birthday as he sat in the seat of honor, smiling.

When the song finished, he made a wish, then blew out the candles—took him two breaths, but he did it. Bette stepped forward and kissed him on the cheek before removing the candles and putting them on a plate.

Roni handed him an 8-inch chef's knife. It was a bit more powerful than what this task required, but he accepted the polished stainless-steel blade. Holding it horizontally, he caught a glimpse of his reflection in the mirrored finish. His hair looked like ruffled bird feathers from being towel dried. The skin under his eyes shaded gray like overdone stage makeup.

"Go on ... Cut it," Roni said as she leaned over his shoulder.

He slid the knife into the gooey buttercream frosting and through the spongy yellow cake as his friends applauded. For his encore, he cut a second slit and removed a corner piece for himself onto a plate. Bette plopped a scoop of vanilla ice cream on the side, then handed him a fork while Roni began dishing out the rest to their friends. He had barely tasted the celebratory confection when Greg presented him with a glossy black gift bag.

Jimmy laid his fork on the plate and removed the bottle of caramel liquid. Large white letters on the black label read, *Dead Rabbit ... a golden blend of aged Irish single malt and grain whiskies.*

Chase stepped up with a box wrapped in red and blue patterned paper. Jimmy peeled away the wrapping to reveal a box of twelve Callaway Chrome Soft Truvis USA Golf Balls.

"But I don't play golf," he said.

"You will," Chase said with a wink.

Next was Bette's gift. The new Dean Koontz novel he'd been wanting to read. A box of assorted Primrose candies and popcorn from Jack and Cara. Then finally, the traditional gag gift from Libby: a DVD box set of all 117 episodes of *Charlie's Angels.*

"I've actually been wanting this," Jimmy said, laughing while holding up his present.

"Don't you regift that," Libby warned.

"Nope, I'm binge-watching it."

"Okay, okay," Roni said, holding a shiny navy-blue paper-wrapped box bound around the sides with a white ribbon and topped with a fluffy white bow. "Now open my gift."

It was almost too beautiful to tear apart—but he did. First, removing the bow and sliding the ribbon away. Then he tore through the heavy metallic paper until he was holding a brown shoebox. The lid was emblazoned with the logo of a women's footwear line and one of the short sides of the box depicted a running shoe, size 10.

A reused box. There could be anything inside: plane tickets, a Rolex, a can of soup. The possibilities were endless. Excitement swelled in Jimmy's stomach as he flipped up the hinged lid and revealed a layer of bright white tissue paper, one end folded over the other.

His eyebrows pulled together as he noticed one corner of the paper was stained with a red smudge. This sometimes happened when you recycled—papercuts were a bitch. Still, he found it strange that Roni would overlook something like this. But he couldn't contain his curiosity. He reached inside the box and unfolded the paper—

His heart thumped heavily in his chest as a chill spread up his spine, consuming his neck in the cold grip of fear. It wasn't a watch or a can of soup or a surprise vacation. It was something he never would have guessed ... Not if he'd been given a hundred tries or a thousand.

Is this some kind of a sick joke? A mistake?

"Do you like it?" Roni asked.

He looked up at her, and she was smiling, waiting for his response. Sweat dotted his forehead. He lowered his eyes to the box, blinking two ... five ... eight times. But it was still there ...

The box of bones.

A mixture of small ribs, femurs, tibias, ulnas, and radius bones. Animal bones from various donors had been skinned, cleaned, and boxed ... for him. And on top of the pile lay the freshly severed hock of an Eastern cottontail, the speckled brown fur matted with dried blood. The same blood that was smeared on the bright white tissue paper.

His friends were smiling and clapping and laughing. Celebrating Roni's gift.

He wanted to scream out, *Can't you see!* But he couldn't scream. He couldn't speak. He was shaking. His mouth dry, his throat closing up. Their voices drifting, overtaken by the rising tone in his ears—

He smelled *the shade's* sour breath as its gnarled tongue swept across the back of his neck. Its gangly fingers wrapped around his shoulders. He struggled to escape, but the tips of its claws pierced his fleece sweatshirt as it squeezed and held him in place. Then it leaned over and pressed its cracked lips against his ear—

"*I sssee you, James Massson.*"

Adrenaline rushed through his veins, and he pushed up and backward in his chair, slamming his left hand and knee on the floor with a *thud*.

"Oh shit," Roni gasped. "Jimmy, are you okay?"

He was half on the couch, half on the floor. Shaking. Tangled up in a blanket.

"What—What happened?"

"You fell off the couch."

He heard voices ... Felt her arms around him, pulling him backward, and he pushed off the floor until he was sitting on the edge of the sofa in the sitting room. There was no one there but the voices on the TV. He wiped the sweat from his forehead, pushing his bangs aside. There was no party. The room was dark except for the glow of the flat screen and one floor lamp. The curtains were drawn to keep out the night.

"Were we watching a movie?"

"Yes. But then you fell asleep."

"How long?"

"I don't know … Hours. I didn't want to wake you."

"I was having a nightmare … I was lost in the woods … in the rain." He squeezed his eyes and shook away the image of the end of the disturbing nightmare.

Roni stroked his back. "Must have been some storm." Then she clicked off the television and began folding the blanket. When she finished, she patted his leg and said, "Let's go up to bed."

"What time is it?"

"Um … 2:20."

Chapter 18

In the morning, Jimmy sat on the edge of the bed, eyes pinballing, nerve endings tingling in that caffeine-high sort of way. Except, he hadn't had any coffee yet. He'd just woken up.

It was Saturday, 7:14—

No, Sunday.

Without work to ground him, the days were blurring together. He rubbed his eyes, then rose from the bed and wobbled forward, much like that of a marionette under the control of a puppeteer, each step sending a shockwave through his hypersensitive body.

Is this what a Melatonin hangover feels like?

He stood in the doorway of the now-finished walk-in closet. Their clothes hung neatly on hangers from the metal rods that he installed; shoes were tucked neatly in cubbies that he assembled; drawers that he built were now stuffed with socks and underwear; sweaters and jeans were stacked on shelves that he cut. He'd been quite busy.

When did I finish? Friday? Or was it Saturday?

He slipped into a pair of pants and a T-shirt then grabbed a pair of socks and sneakers and shuffled back into the bedroom, stopping to stare at the half-made bed. On Roni's side, the covers were pulled up under her pillow, the wrinkles neatly pressed out. On his side, the covers were folded over into a rumbled heap the way he'd left them when he first sat up.

Only one project was left on his to-do list before returning to work on Monday.

He didn't like the idea of the root cellar door being left unsecured after he forced his way in—frankly, he didn't like the idea of the root cellar at all and planned to have it demoed in the spring. But until then, he needed to fix the door to keep out animals and teenage ghosthunters. And with the closet finished, he should have enough scrap wood to do it.

The puppeteer pulled on his strings, and Jimmy moved forward again until he reached the bed. He turned and sat down, put on his socks and shoes, slumped over with his arms resting on his thighs and waited for the puppet master to wiggle his strings and whisk him away.

***

After breakfast and two cups of coffee, Jimmy felt slightly more human. He made his way from the house to his new workshop, where all of the senior Hobart's tools were now either hanging from hooks, stowed in drawers, or bolted to a table. At some point, he'd found the time to free all of the tools from storage—the canceled contract from the self-storage warehouse lay on the worktable to prove it. He could only imagine how many trips it took to haul everything away because he couldn't remember.

Deciding against dwelling on that fact, he strapped his father's old leather tool belt around his hips and then slid a claw hammer into one of the loops. It was only 8:30 a.m., but already his mind strayed to football. He had over four hours to finish this project before the kickoff of the Ravens vs Steelers grudge match. It shouldn't take him that long, but ...

He scooped a dozen three-inch nails into one pocket of the toolbelt and a dozen three-inch screws into another. Then he removed the cordless drill from a wall hook and snapped a battery into place—apparently, in his brain fog, he'd planned ahead and charged it up. Lastly, he slipped on a pair of leather work gloves.

After selecting several pieces of scrap wood, he balanced them on one shoulder, and while carrying the drill on his other side, he exited through the double doors—

"*Mbr-aou?*"

"Who let you out?"

Coal didn't answer of course. He simply curled his long, fluffy body around Jimmy's legs, staring up with wild curiosity.

Jimmy started walking again before the wood became too heavy.

After a few twitches of his tail, Coal toddled out in front as if he were aware of the plan, leading the way down the backyard hill and through the row of dogwood trees. At the path, he turned south, his hind quarters sashaying as he trotted, his tail twitching.

It was strange for a root cellar to be so far—about a 20-minute walk from the house. It was as if the builder didn't want it to be found at all. In fact, that day exploring the forest, he and Roni had walked directly over the root cellar at least once before noticing the pitch of the gable roof.

Why would you go to the trouble of building a root cellar, filling it up with vegetables, fruit, and whatnot, if you didn't want it to be accessible? It didn't matter since he would never use it and was about to board it up—until the spring when he would likely have it bulldozed—but still, the puzzle confounded him.

The scrap wood on Jimmy's shoulder grew heavier with each step along the winter ground. Then he spotted the clearing up ahead on the east side of the trail and knew they were close. He grimaced as he tilted the timber slightly backward, shifting the weight and easing the pain in his neck—

Coal stopped abruptly, his back arched, hair standing erect, as he cried a long, mournful yowl.

Startled by the cat's peculiar behavior, Jimmy also stopped, heart racing and nearly losing the off-balance bundle on his shoulder in the process. He had been huffing loudly but now he closed his mouth and controlled his breathing. His eyes bugged out as he stood still, studying the brush. Whatever spooked the cat, spooked him too.

No longer advancing toward the root cellar, Coal sidled to the left, intermittently hissing and growling as his eyes remained fixed on something unseen. Then without warning, he turned and skittered back in the direction of the house.

He turned around in time to see the cat disappear into a tangle of bare vines, and then he was gone, leaving Jimmy all alone on the path. After nothing baring teeth and fangs gave chase, he decided it was safe to move forward again.

Once in the clearing, he quickly found the small ventilation chimney sticking up through the grass and twigs. He was careful to stay to the left where the land eased down the ten-foot slope to the lower path until he stood in the embrace of the niche cut into a rock wall. A few steps away, the ramshackle door was as he'd left it, propped against the frame.

The temperature was noticeably cooler. After letting go of the drill, he eased the scrap wood to the ground to the relief of his aching shoulder. A shiver crept along his spine as he stood straight. He pulled the collar of his puffy jacket tighter and wished he'd followed Coal back to the house.

Before securing the door, he wanted to ensure there was no sign of life inside. He slid the door aside, removed the flashlight from his tool belt, and swept the wide beam of light along the dirt floor, into the crevices and corners, up the walls, and along the rafters.

Nothing flapped or scurried or screeched—or whispered, "*Jimmy.*"

Then for reasons he didn't understand, he stepped inside. He only needed to ensure this morbid tomb was empty before sealing it up, yet he couldn't stop himself ... The puppet master was in control again, moving him forward, drawing him into the center of the room where the animal bones were scattered. But now that he looked closer, they seemed to be placed in the shape of a triangle.

147

Just my imagination talking, he assured himself.

He turned to the right and as the flashlight illuminated the wall, he was urged again to begin walking. The beam of light narrowed, focusing on what appeared to be calcification streaks in the stone wall like thin vertical brush strokes. He removed the glove from his right hand and touched his fingers to the cold stone. There was no residue on his fingertips as he rubbed them together and nothing appeared when he held his hand under the light either. He leaned toward the wall, squinting in the glow.

Not calcification streaks ... scratches.

And not just scratches but words. The same three words, scrawled over and over like an incantation or punishment. Over and over like madness. Over and over like a caged prisoner.

He jerked upright and stepped back, the beam of light growing larger as it lit up the rest of the wall. The phrase was etched from side to side, floor to ceiling, on the back and south walls. The same taunt that haunted his nights now surrounded him. He covered his ears as he heard the susurrant voice of the night *shade.*

He turned around and around, kicking up dirt with the thick soles of his boots. His chest heaved to no avail—he couldn't breathe. He dropped the flashlight and clawed at his throat as the walls closed in on him. Again, he was that little boy, awoken from deep slumber, gasping for air that wouldn't come.

He ran, collapsing to his knees outside the root cellar, wheezing and pounding on his chest until his lungs woke up and let in the fresh air. Then he leaned forward, coughing and spitting as if he were breathing oxygen for the first time until muscle memory finally kicked in.

But the slithery voice continued chanting in his mind and he felt the puppeteer tug at his strings. Crawling on hands and knees, he breathed deeply as he inched further and further away from the doorway until the voice was quiet. Then he crumpled onto his side and scooted around in the dirt to face the root cellar.

Inside the cold darkness, his flashlight lay on the ground casting its beam on the stone walls. And suddenly he heard the sound of his own voice, chanting over and over, "Nothing you see can harm you. Nothing you see can harm you. Nothing you see can harm you ..."

***

Once he'd composed himself, Jimmy placed the busted door against the rotten frame. Then he sealed in the voice, the animal bones, and his favorite flashlight, using more than enough wood and every screw and nail in the pockets of his tool belt.

When he emerged from the forest and began the climb up the slope toward the row of dogwood trees, he should have felt lighter, having left all of the scrap pieces of wood and the chill in his bones behind. And yet he carried a weight with him. It felt as if *the shade* were riding on his back like a parasite—

"*Mhr-aou?*"

Coal leaped from the sanctuary of the back porch and trotted to Jimmy's side, seemingly relieved that he made it back alive.

The workshop's double doors were still open as he'd left them. He hung the cordless drill on the wall, then put the hammer and tool belt away as Coal purred and encircled his legs. And he thought about the creature that wouldn't let him sleep, the beast ... It wanted something from him. And it wanted him to go inside the root cellar, although by now he was convinced it was much more than a root cellar.

He looked down and met Coal's gaze. "You know what it is ... Don't you."

The cat blinked his emerald eyes and then bumped his head against his human's leg.

Jimmy closed the doors and went inside, hoping the recent horrors would soon be forgotten.

Chapter 19

J immy woke with a gasp, his head lifting off the pillow.

Too weak to hold himself up, his head dropped, landing in a puddle of spit that had leaked from his mouth during the night. He slid his face to a dry spot and then wiped the mucous from his lips with the back of his hand.

If it's 2:20, so help me—

He tried to open his eyes to check the time, but his lids resisted, still suffering from a Melatonin hangover. But he had to know. He fought through the grogginess, enlisting the help of his eyebrows. The room was black as pitch except for the red blur on the bedside table. He rubbed his eyes to clear the murk.

5:25 a.m.

Yes, he mouthed to himself, pumping his fist under the blanket.

He'd managed to sleep through the night, right through the phantom visitor, and there were no dreams. It seemed his nightmare might finally be over. He closed his eyes and smiled in that self-satisfied way only the Cheshire cat himself could outdo. Then he rolled over and reached for Roni—

But her side of the bed was empty, the covers thrown aside, and the warmth of her body evaporated long ago, leaving only cold Egyptian cotton in its wake.

He propped up on one elbow. Through the darkness, he found a thin slice of horizontal light reflecting on the wooden floorboards in the hallway outside the bedroom. In the residual grogginess, he concluded Roni was in the bathroom.

He was about to lay back onto the mattress when something passed through the light, cutting it off for an instant.

"Roni?" he said.

Thump.

Swish ... Swish ... Swish ...

Backlit by the bathroom light, an elongated figure appeared in the hallway. He swallowed hard, instantly recognizing the unnaturally thin torso, spindly arms and legs, and spidery fingers of the night *shade* prowling toward the master bedroom—

Swish ... Swish ...

—dragging its feet along the wooden boards as it moved closer.

Jimmy's heart thumped in his ears while keeping his eyes fixed on the eerie silhouette. He rose up higher on the mattress and leaned forward, ignoring his eyes as they begged him to blink for fear of what the creature would do next. And then, it was in the doorway.

"Roni?" he whispered hopefully. "Is that you?"

The figure melted into the muddiness of the dark room and Jimmy lost sight of it. But he could hear its raspy breath rattling through its shriveled lungs.

Jimmy pushed the bedcovers away, freeing his legs to make an escape as it was indeed coming for him. Then he steadied his weight on his arms and scooted backward toward the edge as his skin prickled and the hair on his arms and the back of his neck snapped to attention.

The temperature seemed to drop at the same time the other side of the mattress sank under *the shade's* weight.

Intimidated, but not without hope, he told himself, *This isn't real, it's just a dream ... This isn't real, it's just a dream ...* Three seconds passed as sweat stippled his forehead and his heart pounded ... At five seconds, the silence was all but unbearable when a high-pitched tone filled the void.

Then a stench not unlike seeping sewage gas vapors ventured into his air space, followed by the hollow sound of diseased lungs inhaling a deep breath.

Stomach acid backed up into his throat and his mouth filled with water. He turned away to gag, exposing his neck to the warmth of *the shade's* breath.

"Roni?"

"*No,*" it hissed.

Jimmy swung his arms and legs while propelling himself backward. But his punches and kicks failed to make contact with anything but air. He rolled off the bed, landing on the hard floor. He scrambled to his knees, fumbling for the knob on the bedside lamp. But before he could reach it, the room lit up—

He squinted and hopped to his feet, chest heaving, fists in front of his body. Then, as his pupils adjusted and the room normalized, he saw Roni standing in the doorway. Her fingers were still pressed to the switch plate.

She gasped, her jaw hanging agape, "Jesus ... Did you fall out of bed?"

Still out of breath, Jimmy remained in a defensive posture, his eyes shifting left and right, up and down, searching the shadows for the intruder. But, just like the other times, there was nothing there.

"Jimmy?"

He wiped his shaky hand across his brow, then dried it on his T-shirt as he tried to settle down and make sense of what happened. Then, meeting her gaze, he finally asked, "Was that you?"

"Was what me?"

"On the bed just now ... Was that you?"

"No. I was in the bathroom when I heard a thump." Suddenly she was beside him with her arm around him, easing him onto the mattress. "Babe ... What happened?"

"I—"

He wanted to tell her—almost did. But then she tucked her hair behind her ear, and the lamplight glinted on her eyes ... And for a moment, her pupils appeared ... square—

He quickly turned away, pressing his fingers to his eyes. "I don't know." Then he arched forward and began rocking on the edge of the bed, wishing he was back in their old apartment, before this house, when everything was safe and familiar. Where he had a routine and slept through the night without a sleep aid. Where nothing went bump in the night except the neighbor's occasional late-night party.

But most importantly, where there were no *shades*.

Then he felt her hand stroking his back, up and down and across his shoulders in a circular lulling pattern. He took a deep breath. He removed the pressure against his eyeballs, letting his arms rest on his knees. After another deep breath, he was able to raise his head. The tension in his chest eased, and he sat straight.

She touched his chin and turned his gaze toward her. "Jimmy ... You can tell me anything."

Her eyes were like a field of shamrocks, pupils round and contracted. She was right. He could trust her. He could tell her anything.

"I think I'm losing my mind."

They held each other while his words loomed overhead like a tornado threatening to tear their world apart.

Chapter 20

Jimmy turned into the half-full parking lot at 312 Wendo Office Park Drive at 7:20 and parked among the black and silver sedans. He cut the engine, quieting the talking heads on the radio, then reached for his thermos—

"I think I'm losing my mind."

He grimaced and tried to shake away the memory from earlier when those words had just slipped out. He immediately regretted saying it, but now that it was out there, he couldn't take it back ...

Am I losing my mind? Would I know?

He wasn't sure. Maybe it was sleep deprivation. Maybe it was *the shade* somehow messing with his head—if it really was a *shade*. He wasn't sure about that either.

Whatever was going on, Roni wanted him to see his doctor and it was pointless to argue with her. You couldn't just say, *"I think I'm losing my mind,"* to someone you love, that loves you, and then refuse to see your doctor. But he could refuse to take more Melatonin.

And that's what he did. His cover story was that he believed the sleep aid worsened his nightmares. The real reason was much more complicated than that. Jimmy believed *the shade* wanted something from him and he needed to figure out what. He couldn't do that with his senses dulled by Melatonin—or anything for that matter.

Somehow, he needed to regain control. Seeing his doctor was a step in that direction. He grabbed his thermos, slung his leather backpack/laptop bag over his shoulder, exited the truck, and made his way toward the four-story glass building.

***

It was early, so the third-floor wing occupied by PJM Designs was quiet. He entered his office with the view of a pond frequented by wild ducks and migratory geese and closed the door. Then he unpacked the laptop from his leather bag and plugged it into the docking station.

The doctor's office didn't open until 9:00, so until then he would get started on the backlog that accumulated during his two-week absence. While waiting for the laptop to boot up, he removed the files from his bag—the non-urgent projects he'd been working on that hadn't been reassigned—then moved the leather bag to the floor.

He fanned the folders out on his desk and started to refresh his memory. There were two new home designs for people with disposable incomes; an urban redevelopment concept for an investment group; a sports stadium remodel; and a 50's plus community of single-family homes and apartments, with a golf course, shopping center, and restaurants.

On the computer screen, he clicked the icon for his mailbox. When he logged out two weeks ago, thirty-two messages were in his inbox. While waiting for the server to load his unread messages, he leaned forward and rested his chin on his hand. First 60 new emails, then 100 ...

He scraped his thumbnail across the peeling epithelium on his bottom lip as the email count continued to climb—

150 ... 200 ... 250—

He rolled his bottom lip into his mouth and tasted the blood.

***

After deleting the junk mail and skimming the corporate updates, his email count ended up at 198. He promptly called his doctor's office at 9:01. The receptionist remembered him and was kind enough to squeeze him in today at 4p.m. He accepted, knowing he could leave work a little early.

In the meantime, he had the chaos of work to keep his mind from dwelling on *shades* and root cellars. Confined to his office, none of his coworkers had the opportunity to notice that he looked as if he'd been run over by a truck. He felt like it too—

Knock-knock.

Before he could look up from his monitor, the door opened, and a familiar bespectacled pale round face appeared.

"Jesus, Jimmy ... You look like shit."

"Thanks, Tom."

Not even a closed door could keep Tommy Mathes out. Without an invitation, he stepped inside and sat in one of the leather upholstered armchairs positioned on the visitor side of Jimmy's desk. "I guess home ownership doesn't agree with you."

"It's been a lot of work," Jimmy said, trying not to take his eyes away from the computer screen. "But nothing we can't handle."

"Good ... That's good to know."

Jimmy glanced across the table just long enough to see Tommy lean back in the chair as he looked around the room. He wanted something but Jimmy didn't dare ask what. Everyone in the office knew by now that if you offered to help Tom Mathes, you might as well clear your calendar.

"I don't want to be rude, Tom, but I've got a lot to catch up on."

"Sure, sure ... That's why I'm here. I wanted to let you know that if you need anything—"

"Jimmy," Greg said, peaking around the doorway. "I need you in the conference room."

Saved by the conference room trick. It was a pact Jimmy and the rest of his team had concocted years ago. A sort of 'get out of Tommy Mathes jail free card.' Whenever Tom cornered anyone on the team, everyone else was duty-bound to set them free. It was called the Mathes Rule.

Good ol' Greg.

"Be right there," Jimmy answered as he opened a drawer and pulled out a fat folder. It was meant to look like a project but really it was stuffed full of takeout menus and sale fliers. All the team members had one—everyone except Tom.

"Sorry, Tom. I gotta go." He engaged the screen lock on his computer, stood up and scurried around the corner of his desk. "Thanks for the offer. I'll let you know."

Not a chance in hell of that happening. He was out the door before Tom could respond.

***

Greg was already seated at the long mahogany table when Jimmy entered the conference room and closed the door. The windows along the far wall over-looked the same pond he could see from his office—just at a different angle. He sat beside his friend, facing the door and the row of windows with a view of the hallway and interior cubicles.

Tom would most certainly walk by—he always did—but he would never enter. Wouldn't even so much as knock. He didn't want to risk being roped into the project. That was the beauty of their pact. Jimmy spread open the folder and prepared to put on a show of two colleagues, busy at work. With their heads angled toward each other in conversation, they each kept an eye on the hallway.

"Thanks for the save," he said.

They bumped fists.

"Mathes Rule," Greg answered. "I've got you, brother. Welcome back, by the way. You must be swamped."

"I'm managing. Hey, do you want to get lunch after?"

"What did you have in mind?"

"I don't know ... I could really use a beer though."

"Oh ... You mean *lunch*." Greg answered with a wink. "You're on—Oh, here he comes."

They closed ranks around the folder, tapping their fingers to the desk and turning pages as they spoke in muffled voices until Tom was out of sight.

***

After securing the faux project file in his desk drawer, Jimmy grabbed his jacket then he and Greg made the short drive from PJM to *Meat and Potatoes*, their favorite hole-in-the-wall that serves made-to-order natural cut fries and half-pound burgers along with locally brewed craft beers.

A gum-chewing woman named Rhonda showed them to a table by the front windows. "Can I get you started with drinks?" she asked, slapping two menus onto the table.

"Two IPAs from the tap," Greg answered.

"You got it." Her pink ponytail whipped around as she hurried to the bar.

Jimmy removed his jacket then picked up the sticky laminated 8 ½ by 11 menu. It was the same as the last time they were here and the time before that. But still, he perused the offerings to avoid talking.

He met Greg when they both enrolled in the same college program straight out of high school and, having much in common, they quickly became friends. Before graduation, they applied to apprenticeships at all the major architecture firms around the country and, coincidently, were both accepted at PJM. So, when Jimmy asked his best friend to stand up with him when he married Roni, Greg accepted the honor and was likely planning a festive sendoff for his buddy.

He was on the back side of the menu when the beers arrived. "Thank you," he said.

"Are you ready to order?"

"Can I get the house half-pounder with caramelized onions, cheddar cheese, lettuce, and tomato on a toasted onion roll with a side of fries."

"Sure thing, hon," she said without writing anything down. Then she turned to Greg. "And for you?"

Jimmy downed a few swallows of pale ale while Greg ordered and wondered what mind trick Rhonda used. She was at least twice their age but had a memory like an elephant—or so the saying went. Whether she was serving a table of one or six, he never saw a pad in her hand.

"You got it," she said. Then she took the greasy menus and hustled off to the kitchen.

"You don't usually drink during lunch," Greg said as he sprinkled salt on the paper coaster. "What's going on?"

He shook his head. "I haven't been sleeping."

"Buyer's remorse or cold feet?"

He furrowed his brow. The suggestion he may be having second thoughts about the wedding was just part of the usual ribbing best friends gave each other and would generally have elicited a snarky comeback. However, Jimmy wasn't up to it.

After another drink, he answered, "It's the house."

"Fixer-uppers can be a bitch," Greg agreed.

"It's not that." Jimmy twirled the pilsner glass on the coaster as he contemplated telling his friend all about what he had heard and seen over the past week. He would sound crazy—he knew that. What other explanation was there? He'd have to be—

"That wouldn't happen if you'd salted your coaster," Greg said, pointing to the paper stuck to the bottom of Jimmy's glass.

"Forgot." Jimmy peeled the paper away and set it on the table. Then he sprinkled it with salt as Greg had done before taking another drink.

"Spit it out, Hobart. What's eating you?"

He let out a heavy sigh. "I'm having nightmares."

"Nightmares? What kind of nightmares?"

Jimmy shrugged and mustered a half-hearted laugh. "The kind that keep you awake at night."

"That bad, huh?" Greg sipped his beer then leaned back in his chair. "Has this ever happened before?"

Jimmy turned toward the window as a group of people walked by. He hated lying—and not just to Greg. But, in this case, he wasn't sure what would be worse: continuing with the nightmare lie or telling the truth—that a ghoulish creature was visiting him during the night. He would have a lot to explain if he said that out loud.

"Do you want to talk about this?" Greg asked.

"No, not really." Jimmy returned his attention to his half-empty pilsner glass and took another drink.

"New topic then ... So, when do I get a look at your house?"

"We're planning a housewarming party for this Friday."

"*This* Friday?"

"Yeah ... You don't have something better to do, do you?"

"Well, that depends ... Will your sister be there?"

For as long as he could remember, all of his single male friends have been interested in Bette. You'd think he'd be used to it by now. But he'd never stop being her overprotective big brother. "Yes, she'll be there."

"Here we are," Rhonda said, holding two plates as she arrived at their table. She set one plate in front of Jimmy. "The half-pounder with caramelized onions, cheddar cheese, lettuce, and tomato on a toasted onion roll with fries."

"Thank you," he said.

Then she set the other plate in front of Greg. "Half-pounder with bacon and Swiss cheese on a Kaiser roll with a side of fries. Anything else?"

"No, thank you," Greg said.

"Enjoy."

Then as the gum-chewing Rhonda spun around, Jimmy bit into the hamburger and let the sweet onions merge with the bitter cheese into a flavor explosion in his mouth. He dug into the fries while they were still hot, biting through the salty thin outer crust to the steamy soft insides. Then he wiped his mouth and looked across the table. "So, you'll be there, right?"

"Hm?"

"To the housewarming?"

"Oh, you mean to see Beth?"

"Ha, ha," Jimmy said, taking another bite of the burger.

"I wouldn't miss it."

Their conversation then turned to football, as it usually did. They recapped the highlights from yesterday's games until their bellies were full and the check had been paid. Rhonda thanked them for the tip as she cleared the plates from the table. Then they made the short drive back to PJM.

***

Later, at the doctor's office, the intake nurse noted Jimmy's blood pressure was a little high but nothing to worry about. "Lack of sleep will do that," she said, referring to his reason for the visit.

He wondered if it had more to do with his artery-clogging, two beer lunch—but he didn't say that out loud. That was twenty minutes ago. Now he was alone in the tiny exam room, waiting to be seen by the doctor.

He scanned through the fliers on the wall: *Do you have a cough? Have you had your flu shot?* A chart with emojis of various facial expressions asked, *How are you feeling today?* Another chart was a reminder of heart attack signs: *Chest pain or discomfort; Shortness of breath; Pain or discomfort in the jaw, neck, back, arm, or shoulder; Feeling nauseous, light-headed, or unusually tired.* If he was being honest, he was experiencing at least five of those symptoms right now.

He took a deep breath, removed his cell phone from his pocket then scrolled through the news headlines. As if his nightmares weren't bad enough: *Another Mass Shooting; Missile Strikes in the East; Nuclear Testing in the Sea of Japan;* and another reminder to get a flu shot.

He glanced at the time again: 4:17.

Why do they always want you here fifteen minutes early when they're always running at least fifteen minutes behind?

Finally, he heard a familiar muffled voice in the hall outside the exam room. He turned off the cell phone screen then double-checked that the ringer was off before sliding the phone into his back pocket.

Knock-knock-knock.

Dr. Palmer entered quickly, wearing gray slacks and a white collared shirt under his long white coat. He closed the door on his way to the wheeled stool in front of the computer workstation and took a seat. "Nice to see you, Jimmy," he said. "It's been a while."

"Couple years, I think."

"Sounds about right." He leaned his head back slightly to peer through the bifocal lenses he wore as he pulled Jimmy's chart up on the computer screen and began scrolling through the notes.

He was a bit grayer than the last time Jimmy had seen him and he'd grown a thick salt and pepper beard. He had an affinity for bow ties—but not the clip-on kind. Those were for shirkers and charlatans. And Dr. Jeffrey Palmer was neither of those.

"So, you're not sleeping?" he asked, the green paisley patterned bow tie around his neck wriggling up and down as he spoke.

Jimmy shook his head and rubbed his palms on his pant legs. "No."

"Tell me what's going on."

"Roni—my fiancé—and I bought a house."

"That's great. Congratulations. I didn't know you were engaged. When's the wedding?"

Jimmy sat a little straighter and said, "Few months from now."

"How are the plans coming?"

"Great ... We've had most everything in place for a while now. We just need to send our invitations—you should expect to receive one as well."

Dr. Palmer smiled. "Sounds like you've been involved in the planning."

"Yeah, I wanted to be."

"That's good. And the house?"

Jimmy's shoulders rounded as he sunk into the vinyl upholstery of the exam table. "It's in the middle of nowhere, adds thirty minutes to my commute, needs a lot of work ..."

"Uh-huh."

But Jimmy was just getting warmed up.

He'd been seeing Jeffrey Palmer, MD, since he was ten and came down with a stomach virus. They had just moved from the house that held his mother's memory, and being new to town, Jimmy's father asked their next-door neighbors for a recommendation. They were longtime residents and also presiding over a sick child. Dr. Palmer was kind and thorough. Jimmy liked him instantly.

Even back then he felt like he could tell Jeff anything—that's what he liked his patients to call him. He said it seemed to put them at ease to think of him as a friend. Jimmy agreed. But that didn't make explaining what was going on any easier. He decided only to tell Jeff what had been happening *lately*—no matter how strange or unbelievable. And he did so in great detail while not mentioning *the light* or *shades*.

As the tale unfolded, the doctor leaned forward and rested his elbows on his knees as a deep crease formed along his forehead. He was pregnant with questions but didn't dare to interrupt for fear the story would end.

Then, when his patient finished, the doctor straightened his back and rolled backward on his stool, folding his arms across his chest. His eyes drifted toward the wall then to the scrolling screensaver on the computer monitor. Then back to the wall.

Jimmy's knee bounced as he waited for a response. *Did I say too much? Am I crazy?* He rolled his bottom lip into his mouth and chewed on the raw wound he'd picked open while counting new email messages earlier that morning.

Finally, the crease along Dr. Palmer's forehead faded. He stood up and approached the exam table, his 6'6" frame now towering over his patient. He took Jimmy's hand from his trembling knee and pressed two fingers to the inside of his wrist. After a few moments he asked, "Your wedding's in ... What month?"

"April."

"What's the venue?"

Jimmy huffed. "Funny you should ask, Jeff."

"Oh?" he said, smiling through his thick beard.

"We wanted an outdoor wedding and looked at a lot of options, but nothing really clicked for us—"

Dr. Palmer finally released Jimmy's wrist and took the stethoscope from around his neck. He put the ear tubes in his ears and then pressed the metal diaphragm to Jimmy's chest. "What did you decide?"

"Remember that house in the middle of nowhere I've been telling you about?"

The doctor's eyes shifted toward Jimmy's. "Really? How do you feel about that?"

How do I feel about that? he repeated in his mind as his gaze returned to the wall, papered with fliers. *How do I feel about that?*

He wasn't sure. When they made the decision, it felt right. The property was beautiful, with ample space for a wedding party. And in the spring, the dogwoods would be in bloom, the forest would be green, and the air would be fragrant with pine, honeysuckle, and other wildflowers. But now ... *How* do *I feel—*

"Take some deep breaths for me."

The diaphragm was on Jimmy's back now. He did as the doctor asked, filling his lungs and then exhaling as Dr. Palmer repositioned the listening device. "How are things going between you and Roni?"

"Fine ... We had an argument the other day—not really an argument. I've been on a short fuse—because I'm not sleeping."

The doctor nodded, put the stethoscope away, removed the otoscope from his pocket and looked in Jimmy's right ear. "And how's work?" he asked, moving around to Jimmy's left ear.

"I took a couple weeks off for the move and now have a pile of work to catch up on. Nothing I can't manage ... My boss has been great. He let me shift a few projects off my desk to make room for the move and upcoming wedding."

"Wow ... That's great." He traded the otoscope for a tongue depressor and then said, "Open for me."

Jimmy did, and the doctor had a look in his throat.

Then Dr. Palmer returned to his stool and rolled backward, signaling the end of the exam. "Here's what I think ... You've got a lot going on: buying a new house, planning a wedding, work," he said, counting the stressors on his fingers. "It's logical to think all of this is disrupting your sleep pattern."

Jimmy nodded.

"And when your sleep is disrupted, sometimes this can cause variations of everything you described: sleep inertia, hypnagogic hallucinations, sleep paralysis, sleepwalking—"

"Hypno ... hallucinations?"

"Hypnagogic hallucinations—seeing images or shapes as you're falling asleep or the sensation of falling right before sleep—"

"It's not the same, Jeff," he interrupted, frustrated. He couldn't tell him *the shade* was real—at least, he thought it was. He was beginning to question why he was at the doctor's office at all. What could Dr. Palmer possibly do for him if *the shade* was real?

"What about alcohol? Drugs? Anything I should know about?"

"I don't use drugs, and I only have a few beers here and there." Jimmy swallowed out of pure reflex but there was no saliva in his mouth, so it felt like razor blades in his throat. He slumped over in the chair. "I feel like I'm going crazy," he muttered for the second time today.

"You're not crazy—and as a medical professional, we don't use that term."

"Is it a tumor?"

"Let's not jump to conclusions ... Hypnagogic hallucinations are common and nothing to worry about. Since they occur while you're on the cusp of sleep, this could explain why it's difficult for you to discern illusion from reality. And, given the frequency of the events and escalation, it's reasonable to conclude you're suffering from sleep anxiety."

"So, I'm doing this to myself."

"I wouldn't say that. But sleep anxiety and lack of sleep or stress can cause night terrors. How you describe waking distressed or in a terrified state and crying out ... It sounds like you may already be there."

"You mentioned sleep paralysis ... What's that?"

"It's when you're awake and aware of your surroundings, but unable to move—again, something that can be caused by increased stress or lack of sleep. I'm going to prescribe something to help you sleep—something stronger than Melatonin. Are you still running a few miles in the morning?"

"Not really. Not since we bought the house. My schedule has been screwed up with moving and everything."

"Make the time—it'll do you good."

Jimmy nodded and thought about the trails in the woods on their property. They should make for exciting morning runs.

"Between the exercise, sticking to a sleep routine, and Zolpidem, you should be able to get some rest and the hallucinations should go away in time. But I also want to do a full exam and order some scans—just to be sure."

Jimmy took a deep breath and slumped into his chair again.

"Nothing to be worried about," Dr. Palmer said, patting him on his knee. "I want to see you back in two weeks to see how you're doing. If nothing is better, or if things are worse, the next step is a sleep specialist."

The doctor clattered away on the computer keyboard, typing notes, ordering labs and a prescription for Zolpidem. At the same time, Jimmy sat quietly, envisioning what it would look like if things were any worse. His eyes found the chart taped to the wall that listed the heart attack signs and he focused on the familiar symptoms: *Chest pain or discomfort, shortness of breath, and unusually tired.* He closed his eyes and rubbed his forehead as he considered his options.

It was all starting to make sense. What started as an encounter with *a shade* somehow turned into a waking nightmare ... And it wasn't real.

But if Jeff is right and the night creature is a manifestation of my own anxiety, when will my nightmare end?

Or worse ... What if he's wrong?

***

Later that night, Jimmy and Roni watched the first half of Monday Night Football then he said he wanted to go to bed. She didn't think it was strange after he told her that his doctor had prescribed rest and exercise—he left out the part about the bottle of yellow pills he hid on the top shelf in the kitchen cabinet over the range hood.

He told himself it was because of guilt that he kept that from her. Guilt because the Melatonin she suggested didn't seem to be helping but rather making things worse. Guilt because he refused to take it anymore. Guilt because she was going through this just as much as he was.

Really it was out of embarrassment that he kept it from her. Embarrassment because he might be causing this himself. Embarrassment because maybe he was the reason the Melatonin wasn't working. Embarrassment because maybe this wouldn't have happened if he'd been honest with her from the beginning.

When she went upstairs, he snuck into the kitchen, poured a glass of water, then swallowed the Zolpidem pills. It was the beginning of a new routine.

Then he completed his ritualistic security sweep of the downstairs and checked to see if Coal was tucked into his igloo bed, the same as the night before and the night before that ...

How's the saying go? Insanity is doing the same thing over and over while expecting a different result.

As he lumbered up the staircase, he hoped that was wrong.

Chapter 21

Beep-beep-beep, beep-beep-beep, beep-beep-beep—

Jimmy slapped aimlessly at the bedside table, hoping to get lucky and hit the button that stopped the shrill cry of the alarm and—

Peace.

He lay there on his side, body torqued in an awkward pose, his hand on the electronic noisemaker—too heavy to lift away. His eyelids closed, immune to his request to open. He hadn't the strength to rise or reposition. He wanted only to drift ... float ... sleep—

Beep-beep—

With his hand already in place, he silenced the alarm faster this time but for how long? Apparently, he'd only found the snooze button before. He slowly pulled his arm toward his body and peeled open his eyelids.

6:07 a.m.

There'd been no nightmares or spectral visits during the night. No hypnagogic hallucinations, sleep paralysis, or sleepwalking. With one added ingredient to his sleep routine, he'd broken the cycle. He managed a slight smile as he pushed his body upright and swung his legs over the edge of the bed.

While Roni slept, he stretched and yawned, then finally convinced his body to stand. He blinked lazily as he shuffled along the hardwood. Enough grayish light was peeking through the curtains to show the way to the walk-in closet where he'd laid out his running clothes the night before.

In his periphery, something ducked into the murk, untouched by the morning hue. He stopped; his eyes suddenly wide as he searched. His grogginess quickly faded, but he found nothing hiding in the shadows. No creatures lurking in the darkness.

And by the time he was dressed, he'd convinced himself the movement was nothing more than a speck of protein floating across his cornea. He trotted down the steps and through the dining room. As he pushed open the butler door, a skittering fluff ball squeezed through the opening, mewing and bawling. He filled a 16-ounce glass with water and drank while refilling Coal's food and water dishes and scooping the litter box.

Then Jimmy donned a knit cap and made his way onto the back porch, down the four steps and into the side yard. The sun was just warming the frost that had formed overnight, melting it into a violet mist above the distant treetops. Eagles, just beginning their breakfast hunt, circled overhead while hawks cried in the distance. Other than that, it was quiet. No road noises. No wind. No neighbors yelling at each other.

He breathed in the possibilities and released his insecurities in a thin cloud that quickly dissipated in the morning chill. He popped an earbud into each ear and then started the running track on his smartphone, a combination of classic rock and fast-paced heavy metal. He started running as the squeal of electric guitars and pounding drumbeats entered his ears. His heart sped up as his breath moved in and out of his lungs.

At the bottom of the hill, beyond the dogwood trees, he dodged a tangle of bare vines and cut right, his feet pounding against the frozen ground. He was quickly learning that running on natural trails was different than the paved trails at the apartment complex he'd grown accustomed to. He had to focus on where his feet landed and what might be strung across the path. Ducking or dodging something every few steps. But he didn't mind. It seemed to be lending to the fun of it all, making it more of a challenge.

Jimmy loved the solitude of running. Not knowing where he would go or for how long. The freedom to leave everything and everyone behind while listening to music and thinking. Sometimes about nothing at all. But other times, when he was having a problem at work or at home, this was usually where he solved it. Alone, in the open air, just him, nature, and music.

Fifteen minutes into his run, he saw what looked like a small pile of trash ahead on the path. He thought about running around it, but this was his property and he felt obligated to clean it up.

A few more steps and the stench clued him in that it wasn't a pile of trash at all. He plucked the earbuds from his ears and then scanned his surroundings. Finding nothing but dormant trees waiting for the first thaw, he returned his attention to the trail.

He grabbed a nearby stick and poked at the mound of speckled brown fur. The rabbit's hind leg had been severed, and its belly slit open. Steam above the warm blood that leaked onto the ground as it met the cool air suggested it had been killed recently—

But not eaten ... How strange, he thought. *What sort of animal would do such a thing? Kill its prey in such a grisly fashion and then leave it, posed on the trail to rot? Even if I had interrupted it, wouldn't it have taken its meal with it?*

Suddenly, the forest felt different, like it had lost its innocence somehow. As he stood over the dead thing, staring into the spaces between the bare trees around him, he searched for a hint of the creature that did this. And wondered if the predator was out there, watching him.

He used the stick to push the carcass off the path and buried it under a pile of dried leaves so he wouldn't have to see it when he came through here the next time. Then he pushed the earbuds into his ears and pressed play on his smartphone.

A few minutes later, he'd lapsed back into a zone and forgot all about the mangled rabbit and what might be watching him from the trees.

***

Forty minutes later, Jimmy was at the back porch, refreshingly out of breath and sweaty. He removed the knit cap from his damp head and then pressed two fingers to his carotid while taking deep breaths. According to his phone, he logged 3.1 miles. That was less than his usual 5 miles—and it took longer than his best time of 30 minutes. But all things considered, he'd take it.

After a few stretches, he rechecked his pulse and then entered the kitchen, welcomed by the aroma of vanilla and maple. On the center island were the makings of a sandwich in progress. He closed the door, retrieved his glass from the drainboard, and filled it from the refrigerator's water dispenser.

A noise from around the corner startled him. He peered around the side of the hulking stainless steel as Roni appeared from the pantry, already dressed for work, kitten heels thumping on the steps.

"There you are," she said, returning to her half-made lunch. "I was hoping to catch you before I left. Have you eaten?"

He shook his head while guzzling from the glass.

"I made extra," she said, pointing at the stack of pancakes on the counter.

"Thanks." He grabbed one of the room-temperature flapjacks from the top of the stack and began eating it dry.

"What are you, an animal? Get a plate."

Jimmy laughed. "No time." He gave her a kiss while palming another pancake. "I'll see you tonight," he said on his way through the butler door.

Coal scampered in front of him without so much as a howdy-do.

When his feet landed on the first step, Jimmy was stuffing the last of the breakfast into his mouth. As he climbed, he removed his sweatshirt, pulling his sweaty T-shirt off along with it. In the bathroom, he dropped the lump of clothing into the hamper and then started the shower.

Downstairs, the front door opened, followed by a slam as Roni left.

In the shower steam, Jimmy couldn't help but wonder if a distance was growing between them. Subtle, like a tiny crack that forms at the edge of your windshield. Barely noticeable at first until you mistake it for something splashed or spilled. You spray it and scrub, scratch and pick. But it persists ... And grows. Longer and thicker, spreading its tentacles in all directions, distorting your line of sight so that you can't see what's right in front of you.

It's probably the exhaustion talking, he told himself.

He turned off the water and shook his head, spraying droplets around the shower stall like a wet dog. Then he stepped out and dried off. After securing the towel around his waist, he wiped the fog from the mirror and rubbed the scruff on his cheeks. As he tried to decide whether or not to shave, he pictured Dr. Palmer's thick beard.

I could pull off a beard ... Maybe I'll just trim it up.

He reached for the medicine cabinet door and noticed a dark smudge on the lower corner, where he was about to place his thumb. He touched the stain with his index finger and then tapped the tacky blot to his thumb. A metallic aroma wafted in the air.

He held his finger and thumb under a stream of water until the reddish stain circling the drain was gone, then he turned the faucet.

He rummaged through the basket of cleaning supplies under the basin and found the tube of pine-scented cleansing wipes. He tore off one sheet, scrubbed the spot on the mirror, and wiped down the sink, in and around the bowl. Satisfied he'd captured all traces of the blood, he leaned over to drop the cloth into the trash bin—

"What the hell?"

It was difficult to see in the shadow of the sink, so he reached down and picked up the bin, letting it rest in the bowl. He reached in with the cleansing wipe, plucked the strange mound from the plastic lining at the bottom of the can, and then held it under the light.

It was a tuft of brown speckled fur.

***

During the commute to work, Jimmy's subconscious mind took over as he endeavored to solve the mystery of the clump of fur, the bloody print, and the recently slaughtered rabbit. He navigated traffic signals, highway gridlock, and exit ramps from muscle memory while picking away at his bottom lip, unable to get the gruesome image of the recently slaughtered rabbit out of his mind—

Flesh slashed and splayed. Bones snapped and splintered. Muddled fur. Fresh blood. Flesh torn. Bones fractured.

He'd seen his fair share of gore in horror flicks, but as realistic as the effects seemed, they weren't real. It was theater. Meant to make you squirm and look away. Meant to make you squeamish and scream. And at the end of the film, you slept soundly in your bed, impressed with the realism while knowing that it wasn't real—

Slaughtered rabbit. Bloody print. Clump of fur—

Not being a hunter, it was an incredibly shocking sight to see. And now that he thought of it, it was nothing like the fictional depictions on the small or big screen. Filmmakers couldn't capture the smell of death, the taste of blood in the air, the texture of the fur—

Was it a coincidence? Finding the blood and the fur in the house on the same morning I found a mangled rabbit on the trail? And on the same morning I started running again? Are they connected?

By the time he pulled into the parking lot, his lip was raw and swollen and yet he was no closer to answering his questions. If he was a hunter or knew anything about hunting, he might know what sort of animal would leave its fresh kill to rot. A bear, a fox—

Or a cat? Could Coal have—of course he could have ... But would he?

Jimmy grabbed his backpack and thermos and exited the truck. He used the key fob to lock the doors as he walked, barely noticing the honk of the truck horn confirming the locks had been engaged. He walked quickly across the blacktop to the sidewalk—

The clump of fur in the waste basket. The bloody print on the mirrored cabinet door. The recently slaughtered rabbit on the trail. Flesh slashed and splayed. Bones snapped and splintered—

He shook the image away as he entered the building. He crossed the lobby to the elevator vestibule and pressed the call button—

Muddled fur. Blood smeared. Flesh torn. Bones fractured. Victim, posed like an offering or a message—

Or an omen.

He pressed and pressed and pressed the button until the doors finally opened, and he stepped inside. He pushed number 3 and heard someone running toward the elevator as the doors began to close. But he didn't want company. He pressed the 'close door' button—

Fur. Blood. Flesh. Bone. Blood.

Hunting, stalking, tracking.

Blood.

Claws cutting, ripping, tearing.

Blood.

Teeth biting through fur, skin, and bone.

Blood.

Blood.

BLOOD!

Jimmy rubbed his eyes and breathed as the car jerked and started climbing up, up, up. His leg shook until the doors opened on PJM's floor. He stepped out of the elevator and turned left, wiping the sweat from his brow. He used his badge to open the double glass doors and walked past the reception desk and toward his office.

Victim. Murder. Death. Predator. Prey—

Sweat gathered in the skin folds of his armpits and seeped through the button-down poly-cotton blend as one thought was beginning to rise above all of his internal ramblings. A thought he'd been pushing down. A thought he couldn't bear to indulge but one that was clawing its way to the surface despite his best efforts to smother it.

He closed his office door then just stood there, staring at the wood grain as his heart thumped in his throat and ears. He swallowed as he turned, then stepped toward his desk, where his trembling hand deposited the thermos. He dropped his laptop bag into one of the guest chairs and then brought his hands to his face, pressing his fingers into his eyelids before spreading his fingers and peering through the gaps—

What if the creature ... is me?

***

After several minutes of deep breathing exercises, Jimmy put his invasive thoughts aside and logged in to his computer. He pulled up an internet search engine and typed in a query for Zolpidem side effects, then scrolled through the results on the page, reading the headlines:

Jun 10, 2023 – Common side effects of Zolpidem may include vertigo and lethargy as well as muscle aches or pain, hallucinations, ...

Aug 14, 2022 – Symptoms or side effects of Ambien may include nausea or vomiting, labored or difficulty breathing, confusion, muscle cramps, nervousness ...

Jul 13, 2021 – Side effects of Zolpidem, commonly known as Ambien, may include tiredness, light-headedness, headache, diarrhea ...

Aug 29, 2020 – Studies have shown that rare but serious injuries may occur when taking the insomnia medicine Zolpidem, also known as Ambien ...

The last result caught his attention, so he clicked the link and rubbed his forehead as he skimmed the article detailing the results of the 2020 study:

... Less than 1% of patients taking Zolpidem (Ambien) reported sleepwalking, driving while asleep, or engaging in other activities while not fully awake. In rare cases, serious injuries or death has been reported in patients exhibiting complex sleep behaviors, even when taking the lowest recommended doses of the drug or after just one dose. Patients who engage in activities while not fully awake or are unable to remember activities engaged in while taking Zolpidem (Ambien) should stop taking the drug immediately and contact their health care professional.

"Jesus," he muttered. *Would I even know if I was sleepwalking?*

***

He didn't recount all of the morning's gory details while on the phone with his doctor. Only that he'd found some things out of place that he didn't remember moving or using—although 'out of place' was an oversimplification for what he'd found. He also admitted to self-diagnosing based on internet search results, something Jeff Palmer was strongly against.

"It's possible, Jimmy, but I'm not inclined to think it's the Zolpidem," Dr. Palmer said. *"In fact, I would bet that after a week, you're no longer experiencing parasomnia—if that's what this was."*

"Parasomnia?" The search engine didn't show him *that* term.

"Yes, another term for complex sleep behaviors which includes some of the abnormal disruptions of sleep you were already experiencing—like nightmares. Parasomnia can also include sleepwalking or talking, nighttime seizures, sleep apnea—"

"Sleep apnea?"

"A condition where you stop breathing during—"

"Yeah, I know what it is," Jimmy said, recalling what happened to him as a boy and then again more recently. *Do two incidents equal a condition?* "How would I know if I suffered from sleep apnea?"

"Well, we already know you feel tired after sleeping, but with the other patterns of sleep disruption you've described, it's hard to say. There's a test called nocturnal polysomnography—basically, a machine monitors your breathing, blood oxygen, heart, lung, and brain activity all while you sleep."

"At a sleep clinic?"

"Actually, it's a test you can do at home, but it may be easier just to ask Roni if she's noticed whether or not your snore at night."

If he was snoring, Roni would already have let him know with an elbow to the ribs and some choice words. He was pretty sure he could rule that out. *But what about the other symptoms? Sleepwalking? Sleep talking?* He clicked the back button on the monitor and scrolled up to the first search result: *Other side effects include: myalgia, visual hallucination, ...*

"Jimmy? Are you still there?"

"Yeah, I'm here. So, you don't think I'm sleepwalking?" Jimmy said into the phone.

"You have no history of it. Besides, don't you think that by now, Roni would have noticed?"

Jimmy raised his eyebrows and nodded his agreement to the doctor's point. "So, I should continue to take the Zolpidem?"

"I think you should give it a few days. Then, if you're still concerned, there's always the sleep specialist I mentioned."

"Okay," he sighed.

"And Jimmy?"

"Yeah, Jeff?"

"Stay off the internet."

Chapter 22

For the rest of the week, Jimmy continued to follow his doctor's advice. Every night, he popped the magic yellow pill and was in bed by ten o'clock so he could rise by 6:00 a.m. for a run before work.

Friday was no different. After changing into his running clothes, Jimmy trotted down the steps, through the dining room, and into the kitchen, where he filled a 16-ounce glass with water, drank while refilling Coal's food and water dishes and then scooped the litter box.

When he was finished, he donned a knit cap and made his way out the kitchen door to the side yard. The sky was thick with clouds like rows of cotton balls that masked the sun. There were no birds of prey on the hunt this morning. No wind. It was quiet. Maybe more so than usual—but maybe that was his imagination. He zipped his jacket a little higher on his neck to keep out the chill, then pressed the earbuds into his ears and welcomed the soundtrack that drowned out the eerie silence.

Somewhere between moving, unpacking, household projects, returning to work, and managing a possible sleep disorder, Jimmy had managed to help Roni plan for the housewarming party scheduled for tonight. It would be an intimate dinner with drinks and a few games. Of course, Bette was coming, and Greg—to whom he'd made no promises about whether his sister had any interest. Four others rounded out the guest list for a total of eight including the hosts. And now that the day had arrived, he found he was actually looking forward to it.

But not for the reasons he should've been.

He hoped the party would be a much-needed distraction. Sure, he was glad to have his sister and friends over for a few laughs. And it had been days since he'd last been awakened by *the shade* in the middle of the night. Yet he felt no more rested—and no less anxious—than he did before.

He was becoming increasingly more alarmed by the number of dead, mutilated animals he continued to find along the path in the woods, each missing a limb—the calling card of some deranged forest serial killer. And it wasn't always rabbits.

As he ran, he wondered why he continued to take the same path morning after morning. Was it morbid curiosity? He hoped not. He was more inclined to think it was out of hope that the bloodshed would end, and he wanted to bear witness to that.

He had convinced himself that Coal was doing it—cats were known to earn their keep, so to speak, by killing rodents and dropping the bodies where you could find them. And while rabbits and foxes weren't exactly rodents, Coal was no ordinary cat—he was a Maine Coon.

If Jimmy could catch Coal in the act, he might put his conscience to rest. And then that fissure he sensed forming between him and Roni (the crack that was starting to feel more like the San Andreas fault) could be repaired as well.

Up ahead, he saw something on the trail that caused him to break stride: fifty feet away, a grayish-brown mound blending in with the winter earth and dry fallen leaves. He stopped, cut off the music, and removed the earbuds from his ears as he scanned the trees for movement.

At thirty feet, the mound began to take shape: the curve of the rib cage, the long neck, and the thick, rounded ears. At twenty feet, the foul odor of decay hung heavy in the air. He grimaced and turned to the side, gulping one untainted breath before moving on. At ten feet, he pulled the collar of his jacket up over his nose and mouth while veering to the left and circling around to the front of the animal.

Weighing over twenty pounds, Coal was larger than most of the forest creatures Jimmy had seen scurrying about the property. He was also agile and quick, so it was easy—and logical—to think he could be responsible for the carnage on the trail. But this ...

This was no four-pound rabbit or thirty-pound red fox.

The deer's throat had a large bite wound and deep scratches on its shoulder. Like all the other victims, the belly was slit open—a clean cut like he imagined a hunter would make. The innards had spilled out on the ground but were otherwise intact.

He wanted to look away, but he had to know if a trophy had been taken like with all the others. His eyes searched the body, avoiding the wounds and focusing instead on the limbs until he found it. The deer's left front leg had been severed just below the knee—the bone snapped, judging by the splintering.

Coal didn't do this. It was something ... bigger.

Jimmy pulled the jacket away from his mouth as he spun around and arched his back, retching on the ground. He rested his hands on his knees, gasping and coughing until his stomach contracted again. And when he tasted bile in the back of his throat, he spat it out.

He wiped his lips with the back of his arm and slowly straightened his body. He looked at his trembling hands, at his fingernails, at the puke on the ground, and again he wondered—

What if the killer ... is me?

***

Back at the house, he searched for clues about what he'd done—blood stains, fur, the missing hoof—opening cabinet doors, rooting through trash bins, emptying the clothes hampers. If Roni was still home, he'd have to explain the mess he created, but she was already gone. He was alone in the house ... just him and Coal ... And *the shade*.

He could feel it lurking in the shadows, hiding just out of sight, always watching, waiting for an opportunity to pounce. Sometimes, he thought he glimpsed its dark silhouette in the periphery, slithering toward him, reaching out one spindly finger—

But it was always nothing. Just normal shadows ...

At least, that's what he told himself.

An exhaustive search of the house didn't turn up any evidence. Either he'd become more careful, or it wasn't him after all. After cleaning up his mess, it was already 7:45 a.m.

By the time he showered and dressed, he'd be stuck in rush hour traffic on the interstate and wouldn't arrive at the office until nine o'clock—if he was lucky. It was as good an excuse as any to work from home.

He found his cell phone in the kitchen next to the crock pot. After a quick peek under the lid at the chili Roni had prepared for the party before leaving for work, he sent a message to his boss on his way back up the steps. In the bathroom, he slid the shower curtain aside. He turned the faucet then stripped away his sweaty running clothes while the water warmed up.

As he stepped under the spray, he noticed the swirl of red circling the drain. He gasped and returned his feet to the bathmat. His skin tingled, and his heart pumped faster. A tremor spread over his body, and for a moment he was paralyzed to react.

Finally, his hypothalamus sent a signal to release a short burst of adrenaline and he turned off the water. Then he found a scrub brush and a bottle of all-purpose bathroom cleanser with bleach. Still naked, he dropped to his knees and scoured the acrylic shower pan. He gritted his teeth and grunted with each stroke, sweat dripping from his forehead and glistening on his back until he was sure he'd removed all traces of blood.

Chapter 23

After showering away all traces of bleach and exertion from his skin, Jimmy was too keyed up to focus on work. He spent the rest of the day in a haze, managing only to concoct a cover story to explain to Roni why he didn't go into the office. Although it appeared he wouldn't need it after all.

The crock pot of chili had been brewing on low heat for twelve hours when she finally arrived at 6:15, complaining that a last-minute project at work and an accident on the freeway made her late. And in her frenzy to prepare for the housewarming party, she hadn't noticed that he'd worked from home.

"And now I only have forty-five minutes to prepare for our guests."

"They'll probably be late anyway."

"Yeah, right," she scoffed, slamming around the kitchen.

The house smelled like a Mexican cantina, masking the stench of secrets and lies. He lifted the crock pot lid and stirred. Hints of garlic and spicey peppers wafted in a warm cloud of steam against his cheeks. "At least the chili's ready ... How can I help?"

"You can set the table."

"On it," he said. He needed to keep busy to avoid finding a corner and curling up into the fetal position. Breaking down wasn't an option. After setting the table, he moved the fire pit around the backyard to make room for their guests' vehicles on the parking pad. Then he gathered some kindling and logs and started a fire in the cast iron belly.

Contrary to Jimmy's prediction, no one was late.

Roni's college roommate Cara and her husband Jack arrived first. They met after graduation and had been married for five years now. Cara, planning to be Jack's designated driver, drove her car. Bette arrived next, sans Corvette, as she planned to do enough drinking for herself and Cara.

While Jimmy showed Jack to the beer cooler in the pantry, Chase and Libby arrived. Chase and Jimmy had been friends since high school, while Libby was a friend of Roni's from work that joined their group six years ago. Chase and Libby lived near each other, so they decided to share a ride to the party.

Greg was the last to arrive at 6:55. "You weren't kidding," he said as he walked past his host and into the foyer. "You're way out in the sticks ... No one would hear you scream out here."

He swallowed and then cleared his throat. "Yeah, I guess not."

"I was just kidding."

He nodded, lowering his eyes as an image of himself screaming under the shower stream after cleaning away the blood flashed through his mind.

"I was a little worried when I didn't see you at work today. Everything okay?"

"Yeah, I was just running late, so I worked from home—"

"What are you boys whispering about?" Roni said, sneaking up behind Jimmy and wrapping her arms around his waist.

"Nothing," he said. "Just work."

"Well, everyone's here now." Then to Greg, she said, "Let's get you a drink so we can start the tour."

***

After showing their friends around the house, Jimmy led the gathering to the backyard, where the fire pit was ablaze with warmth, while Roni stayed inside to finish dinner preparations. On Bluetooth speakers, selections from Jimmy's playlist provided the perfect background music. And while his friends caught up with each other, he nursed a bottle of beer and stared into the dark woods, so lost in thought that he hadn't noticed Greg walk up beside him.

"Where are you at, my friend?"

"Just thinking," he said.

"You've been awfully quiet."

"Hey, you're a hunter, right?"

"Yeah ... You know that."

"What kind of animals do you think live out there?" he asked, pointing toward the trees.

"I'm guessing ... foxes, deer—"

"Bear?"

"Here?" he said, jerking his head back. "Doubtful ... Why?"

Before he could answer, a sudden darkness appeared in the corner of his eye, and the house music fell silent. From the kitchen, Roni yelled out a few choice words that would make a sailor blush.

"Damn," Jimmy said. "Guess we're eating by candlelight."

***

It had been a couple of weeks since that night when the temperamental wiring gave way to their first—and until now only—power outage. Jimmy found it curious though that there was no storm bearing down on them tonight, unlike last time. It was only by a stroke of luck that it waited until the food was ready this time.

In the dining room, Roni scooped chili into individual serving bowls. "Smudge, can you help me pass these out?"

"Okay, so I'm relatively new to the group," Jack said. "What's the story behind 'Smudge'?"

Jimmy smiled, passing around the chili bowls, "I'll let Roni tell that story."

"Why me?" she asked.

"Because you started it."

She groaned as she placed the crock pot on the sideboard. "It actually started the night we met ... He had this cute little smudge of dirt on his cheek—"

"From handling dusty bottles of Mad Dog 20/20 at the liquor store," Jimmy explained.

"Anyway, I wiped it away and for the rest of the night ... He was my Smudge."

"Aww," the group cooed while butter melted into the nooks and crannies of their cornbread, and they garnished their chili with cheese, sour cream, and chives.

"But that's not even the best story from that night," Cara said. "Tell them what happened later."

Roni and Jimmy locked eyes, then she said, "Oh, you mean the birthdate?"

"Yes, that's the one. Tell them."

"Have I heard this story?" Bette asked her brother.

Jimmy shook his head.

"You remember how it is when you first meet someone," Roni began. "Your heart is racing; your stomach is a-flutter—"

"Isn't that indigestion?" Chase joked.

"That's when you're old," Greg laughed.

"Anyway," Roni said. "We spent the evening asking each other all the usual questions: what's your favorite movie, where did you grow up. Then Jimmy asked what my birthday was. Well, I decided to be coy and tell him to guess—"

"Uh-oh," Greg said. "I smell a trap."

Libby and Cara shushed him.

"Sorry," he responded with his hands raised. Then he made the gesture of locking his lips and tossing the key over his shoulder before scooping a spoonful of chili into his mouth.

Roni continued. "So he said October. And without letting on to whether he was right or wrong, I asked, 'what day?' And Jimmy guessed the tenth. So then I said, 'what year?'—"

"This is where it got tricky," Jimmy chimed in. "Because she'd already told me her age. But I didn't know if she'd rounded up or not. I mean, if I was guessing right, her birthday was right around the corner."

"It was September when you met, right?" Cara said.

Jimmy nodded. "Labor Day weekend."

"So, what happened?" Bette asked.

"He guessed 1993," Roni answered. "October 10th, 1993."

The table fell silent.

"Were you right?" Chase finally asked.

Jimmy let them wait a few more seconds before finally answering, "Yep."

The friends erupted in a mixture of gasps and laughter as silverware scraped against ceramic bowls. While across the table, Bette regarded her brother with curiosity.

"No way," Greg said, shaking his head. "That's amazing."

Jimmy shrugged as he enjoyed a bite of cornbread, refusing to reveal that it was *the light* that guided him that night.

Tink, tink, tink.

He turned toward the sound and saw Libby had raised her wine glass and was waiting for the others to end their conversations.

"I, for one, think your new house is charming," she finally said. Then, with a snicker, she added, "Even with the shitty wiring. To Jimmy and Roni."

"To Jimmy and Roni," the others repeated, followed by the sound of glasses *clinking* together.

The candle in front of Jimmy flickered as his glass touched his lips and in the low light, he noticed the merlot had taken on the appearance of blood. He shook away the image, tipped the glass and savored the earthy blend of dark fruits and vanilla.

"I believe I've had a little too much wine," Libby said as she pushed away from the table. "I need to use the little girl's room."

"Do you remember where it is?" Roni asked, pointing up to the second floor.

"Oh yes, don't you worry about me ... I'll find it." She enabled her cell phone flashlight as she walked away, disappearing into the shadows until she was only an orb of white light.

"I need another beer," Jack said.

"I'll get it for you," Jimmy offered, wiping his mouth as he prepared to stand up.

But Jack was already on his feet. "Nope, I got it ... Just point me in the right direction."

"They're in the pantry—the little room around the corner from the fridge—in a cooler on the floor. Just be careful on the steps."

"Oh right," he laughed, holding his smartphone beneath his chin so the flashlight lit up his face like a kid telling a ghost story during a pre-teen sleepover. "The creepy room."

Greg and Chase made ghostly noises while Cara and Bette laughed.

"Anyone else need a beer while I'm at it?"

Several voices answered at once:

"Yes."

"Me."

"I'll take another."

"Me too."

"Maybe I should go help," Jimmy muttered with a sideways grin as his friend disappeared through the door and into the kitchen. Then he stood up and slipped his smartphone from his back pocket. But before he engaged the flashlight, there were two loud *thuds* from the next room, followed by the *crash* of breaking glass and several curse words.

He pushed through the butler door and found Jack lying on his back on the tile, surrounded by chips of amber and green glass, glinting like gemstones as they floated in an aura of foam. "Jesus, don't move," Jimmy said. "There's glass everywhere."

Jack lifted his head. "Why the hell couldn't you have served *cans* rather than *bottles*?"

The door opened and Cara entered. "Babe, are you okay?"

"Yep. But I'm gonna feel this tomorrow."

"I'll get some towels," Roni said from the doorway as Greg and Bette squeezed past her and into the kitchen.

While they waited for her to return, Bette and Cara shined some light on the accident scene and Jimmy and Greg helped their friend to his feet. Then using kitchen towels, they gently wiped shards of glass from his clothing. "Bette, can you grab the broom? It's in the pantry—"

"Jimmy, come quick!"

Roni's panicked voice sent a chill through him. He dropped the towel on the floor and hurried to the dining room, where she stood behind Chase, trying to lift him from his chair.

"He's choking," she screamed, stepping aside.

Chase turned toward Jimmy, his face contorted in pain and eyes bulging as he struggled to breathe, only managing a pitiful wheezing sound.

Upstairs, a loud *bang* followed by a series of *thumps* provided a soundtrack to the horrific scene before him. Jimmy grabbed his friend around the torso and positioned his fist between Chase's ribcage and belly button. Then, as a flurry of footfalls fell like a drum solo in the stairwell, he squeezed. Once ... then again, lifting his friend's feet off the floor—

"Who did it?" Libby shouted as she stumbled into the dining room.

—a third thrust and Chase spit a glob of food onto the dining room table. Then after a couple of coughs he began breathing normally again.

"You okay?" Jimmy asked, still supporting his friend's weight as he helped him sit down.

The candlelight reflected on tears that had pooled around his eyes. "Better ... now," he answered in a raspy voice.

"What happened?" Roni asked, forgetting all about the broken glass and spilled beer in the other room.

"I dunno ... I think I ... stood up too fast—"

"I said, who did it?" Libby repeated.

Suddenly everyone's attention was on her. She was disheveled, her chest heaving. The light clenched in her trembling hand bounced on the floor around her feet.

"Did what?" Jimmy asked, unable to hide his frustration.

"Someone held the bathroom door closed and wouldn't let me out."

"That's crazy," Roni said. "We were all down here."

"Jack made a huge mess in the kitchen—or didn't you hear that?" Bette added.

"Not to mention Chase nearly choking to death," Jimmy said. "So excuse us if we don't move your crisis to the top of our list."

"Jimmy," Roni whispered while giving him a sideways glance.

"I'm not crazy," Libby said in a softer tone. "I heard someone in the hallway."

She had Jimmy's full attention now. "What do you mean you heard some-one? Heard what?"

Before she could elaborate, the butler door opened, and Cara appeared with a towel wrapped around her hand. "Guys, I need some help."

Judging by the dark blotches staining the yellow hand towel, it appeared to be a nasty cut. Stitches bad or bandage bad? The lighting was too dim to be sure.

"Are you okay?" Roni said.

"Fucking glass. We were cleaning up the mess and—wait, what's going on in here?"

"Let's get you cleaned up," Roni said as she wrapped her arm around Cara and led her to the downstairs bathroom where Coal's litter box was stowed. "I'll fill you in."

Without warning, the lights clicked on.

"Perfect timing," Greg said sarcastically. Then he and Bette dispersed to the kitchen to finish cleaning up the mess Jack was still standing in.

"I'll go help," Libby said. "It's the least I can do."

Jimmy flashed a half-hearted smile as she walked by.

"I should help too," Chase said.

Jimmy pressed down on his shoulders so he couldn't stand up. "No way. Just rest."

The haunting opening riff of Metallica's "Enter Sandman" oozed through the Bluetooth speakers as Jimmy gathered the dishes from the table. He carried glasses and plates through the butler door and into the kitchen, then returned to scoop up silverware and empty bowls. In the background, the guitars chugged as the lead singer growled out the lyrics.

The words cut through Jimmy like a dagger. He was suddenly paralyzed as the memory of the charred beast hiding under his bed flashed through his mind. The strange *swish-swish* as it slithered into view, its yellow eyes peering at him through the darkness as it raised one scraggly finger to its cracked lips and hissed, *"Shhhh."*

The stack of dishes slipped from his hands and *crashed* into the sink, the sound ripping him back to reality. He quickly began surveying the damage, hoping nothing broke, as he wondered what the songwriter might have seen to make him write such lyrics.

But even more curious was that "Enter Sandman" wasn't on Jimmy's playlist.

***

193

By 11:00 p.m., the dishes were done and the floor mopped. Outside, the ride-share drivers arrived, one by one, to shuttle his guests home. The evening was officially over.

Jimmy hugged Jack and then Cara before they walked through the door and into the night. The wound on her hand turned out to be superficial, so no stitches would be needed.

"Maybe we'll try this again when it warms up," he said to Greg.

"Sounds good—but with a little less excitement."

Jimmy smirked and nodded. "See you Monday."

"Goodnight, Jimmy," Libby said as she embraced him. "I really do like your house."

"Libs, I'm sorry about earlier. I shouldn't have—"

"I'm the one that should apologize—I feel so foolish. Let's just forget the whole thing."

Then he pulled her aside, away from the others. "Hey, when you were upstairs ... When you thought—"

"When I was stuck in your bathroom?" she said, rolling her eyes.

"Right ... What did you hear?"

"I dunno, Jimmy ... Maybe it was the wine."

"Just tell me."

She let out a heavy sigh and then leaned toward him. "I thought I heard someone say, *I see you ... I see you, Libby Suzanne Green.*" Then her body shook as if she were trying to shed the memory.

The hair on Jimmy's neck pricked up as he remembered the slithery voice that called out to him not so long ago. He'd hoped *the shade* had moved on, but now he wasn't so sure.

"It's silly, right," she said. "Just forget about it." Then she kissed him on the cheek. "I gotta go before Chase leaves me here."

He followed her to the door where Bette was waiting. They embraced, tighter and longer than usual.

"You okay?" she said into his ear.

"Yeah." He let her slip out of his arms. "Just ... disappointed. The night didn't go as planned."

She raised one eyebrow and cocked her head sideways as a flash of doubt glinted in her blue eyes. "Are you sure that's all it is?"

He broke from her stare and nodded. "I'll see you later."

Then he watched her walk across the porch and down the steps to the last remaining car. She opened the rear door, but before getting in, she paused to meet his gaze one last time. She raised her hand—a final 'goodnight' gesture—then slid onto the back seat and closed the door.

***

Later, lying in bed, Jimmy realized he'd forgotten to take his sleeping pills but was too exhausted to get up. He closed his eyes and waited to be carried off to never-never land.

And he wondered if *the shade* was lurking beneath his bed on this night.

Chapter 24

2:20 a.m.

Fuuuck, he thought to himself, lying on his side while staring at the red numbers on the bedside table. *I should have gotten up to take the damn pills*.

He closed his eyes, pulled his knees toward his chest and wrapped his arms around himself, shivering, before realizing he was uncovered. He reached for the stray blanket—relieved he hadn't been overtaken by sleep paralysis—and pulled it over his shoulder. Then he snuggled in deeper and tried to warm up.

The funny thing about wee hours mixed with alcohol compounded by the residual effects of Zolpidem was that it dulled the senses. That was why he didn't immediately feel the presence beside him. It snuck up on him the way the sun slowly creeps under your beach umbrella, first touching your toes, then the top of your foot, until suddenly your whole leg is exposed.

Jimmy's eyes sprung open as the bedcovers slid away, slowly exposing his neck, shoulder, and bicep. His heart sped up, his eyes darting left and right, his breaths coming in short puffs. He was in control of his body—he knew that—so he could have jumped from the bed. He *should* have escaped ... But his fear stopped him. *Fear* paralyzed him.

As a cold, scaly hand covered his nose and mouth, he tried to scream. He struggled to get away, but it was too late. He was already in the grip of *the shade*. Its paper-like lips touched his ear, and he smelled its warm, fowl breath.

And it whispered, "*Shhh.*"

Steely claws grated over his back as he wrenched from its grasp and spun around. He stood beside the bed, ready to face the creature that tormented him. But there was nothing ... Nothing but crumpled bedcovers and a wrinkled fitted sheet where he'd been lying.

In the muted light filtered through the curtains, he could see that Roni's side of the bed was empty, the covers tucked neatly under the pillow where she'd slept. He looked down at the clock on the side table: 7:03.

***

After his morning piss, he trudged downstairs, still wearing the T-shirt and boxer shorts he slept in, along with an air of confusion riding on his back. *Was I dreaming?* he wondered. *Or is it possible I woke up at two and then fell back asleep?* He rounded the corner at the landing, over the squeaky step, and then a few more steps until he reached the bottom.

"No run today?" Roni said. She was sitting at the dining room table, drinking coffee and reading the paper on her tablet.

Her voice was somewhere on the outer edges of reality, an apparition that didn't require a response like *the shade* from his nightmare.

It must have been a nightmare, he told himself as he continued past her and toward the kitchen. *Brought on by the beer and deviation from my sleep routine. Otherwise, how did I lose five hours—*

"Jimmy."

"Hm?" he answered.

"What's wrong with your shoulder?"

He stopped just outside the butler door, unaware he'd been massaging his shoulder. The same shoulder *the shade* cut into with its razor-sharp claws—

"Hello. Earth to Jimmy."

"Slept wrong, I guess. Hey, did you hear anything last night?"

"Like what?"

He was half hoping she would say that she heard him talking in his sleep or that he was restless. Maybe even that he was thrashing beside her and that she tried to wake him. But he wasn't that lucky. He shrugged, unwilling to elaborate. His smile was only a mask for the fear brewing within.

Either my night terrors are getting worse or—

He turned away and pushed through the doorway, unable to finish that terrifying thought.

"Hey, since you're not running this morning, let's go for a walk," she called out over the *slap* of the door swinging in the frame. "It's too nice to stay in."

He froze in front of the kitchen sink, picturing the slaughtered deer lying on the trail. It was too big for him to push aside with a stick and bury it like the other carcasses. And he couldn't bring himself to touch it. So, for all he knew, it was still there ... Rotting—

"Come on," she urged, suddenly standing behind him, her arms sliding around his waist. "You look like you could use the fresh air."

He trembled as déjà vu washed over him, but before he could grab onto the memory that brought it on, it had receded like the tide before a tsunami.

***

He relented like the coward he was. A coward that couldn't reveal the secret he'd been keeping since he was a scared eight-year-old boy. A coward that couldn't tell the truth about his nightmares. A coward that couldn't say, *"No, I don't want to go for a walk this morning."*

So here he was, carrying a tote bag filled with bottles of water, fruit, and trail mix. It was forty-five degrees outside, and probably a few degrees colder under the canopy of pines. Yet he was perspiring as he walked beside her, down the hill and beyond the dogwoods, his heart beating faster, his head swiveling as he scanned the tree line, his ears searching out for the slightest sound.

They ducked under the overgrowth to the path, but as she began to veer right toward some unspeakable horror, he pulled her to the left instead. For a moment, he wondered if this way might be worse. At least he knew what to expect on the other trail. But going left? Who knew? With each step, his eyes shifted left and then right. He glanced over his shoulder, searching for movement—any movement—in case they were being followed ... Or stalked.

Then he heard the gentle chorus of water tickling mossy banks as it snaked between rocks and made its way over pebbles and sticks. A distant song that grew louder as they continued northeast toward Woody Creek and the edge of their property line. And he began to forget about the deer and whatever might be spying on them from the trees.

He actually began to enjoy himself.

***

Hours later, the snacks had been eaten, the water bottles were empty, and it was time to return home. They climbed the rugged slope toward the trail, leaving the tranquility of the creek behind, and began hiking northwest, back in the direction they came from. It wasn't long before Jimmy began to feel the effects of two sixteen-ounce water bottles.

He handed Roni the much lighter tote bag that now carried only their trash. "I need to take a leak."

"I'm not standing around to watch. You can catch up."

"Ok."

He watched her sling the bag over her shoulder as she continued walking then he stepped off the path in the scant brush in search of privacy. After a few steps, he stopped and, with his hands out at his sides, he said, "I'm alone in the forest. Who am I hiding from?"

He rolled his eyes and shook his head. *Habit, I guess.* Then with his back to the trail, he unzipped his pants and aimed his cock at the nearest deciduous tree. The ridiculousness of it all made him smile as he waited for relief to come.

When he finished, he adjusted his boxers, fastened his pants, and turned around. The forest had grown quiet without the crunch of Roni's footfalls on dried leaves or the soft tap of his piss stream against tree bark.

And he was alone.

"Roni!"

In the short moments it took for him to relieve himself, he'd lost sight of her, and there was no answer but his own voice reverberating through the trees. A sudden sense of familiarity washed over him like a bucket of ice water had been dumped over his head. *Have I done this before? Been here before?* If he had, he couldn't recall. Yet still the feeling remained, resting on the tip of his tongue, unable to be spoken, like the name of a childhood friend he hadn't seen in ages. Except this didn't feel like a warm and cuddly memory from his past. There was something sinister about it … Like an omen.

He started walking, hoping to shake off the foreboding feeling, but he couldn't find the path through the blanket of leaves. "Jesus, how far off the trail am I?" he mumbled.

He turned in circles, kicking at the debris covering the earth, searching the landscape for something he recognized: a broken limb, a large rock, anything. But one tree looked like all the others, and there was no discernible path to be found. It was as if Roni had rolled it up like a carpet runner and took it with her.

"Roni!"

His voice traveled up the limbs of bare trees and disappeared into the thick clouds above where the sun had disappeared while they were enjoying the creek … Just like before—

No. Stop it. It's just déjà vu.

Despite his attempt to calm his nerves, the false memory hung over him like the thickening clouds overhead. It would rain soon—he didn't need intuition to tell him that. He reached around to his back pocket for his cell phone, but it wasn't there. It was in the tote bag with their trash.

He laid his head back and moaned a drawn-out, "Fuuuck."

He knew the house was west, but without the benefit of the sun or the compass on his phone to guide him—or the path—he didn't know which direction west was. Then he heard the trickle of the creek to his left. *The creek is east ... Which means*—he spun around 180 degrees and pointed—*the house is that way.*

"So, where's the damn path?"

Certain this was the direction they'd come from earlier, he started walking again, making no effort to mask his presence. Each heavy footfall sounded like a potato chip bag being smashed—or maybe he was just hungry. His stomach tightened and gurgled, and he rubbed his belly as he pushed branches aside, still hoping to stumble upon the path.

"Dammit, Roni," he snarled as panic began creeping in. "You'll be sorry—"

And there it was. The Easter Island-like boulder standing beside the mysterious trail. He ran to it, leaving behind the demons haunting him, and kept running until finally, he broke through the tree line, and the house was in sight. He guessed it to be about a hundred yards up the backyard hill. But before making the ascent, he stopped to catch his breath and noticed Roni was nowhere to be found.

He shook his head defiantly, then began the climb, taking long, measured strides as a thick gloom settled into the clearing and the clouds darkened. When he passed the row of dogwoods, the first drop of rain landed on top of his head ... Then another on his shoulder ... Then on his cheek. He started running to beat the storm, but it wasn't meant to be.

Lightning struck somewhere behind him then the rain began to fall in a steady shower of fat drops, stinging his face like a swarm of bees. He lost sight of the house, but he ran faster, up the sopping hill and toward the back porch where Roni was waiting with a towel.

"Jimmy! Where have you been?" She wrapped a towel around his shoulders and led him into the kitchen. "I thought you were right behind me."

"How l-long was I g-gone?"

While he stood there shivering, she draped the towel over his head before removing his wet jacket and muddy shoes. Then she wrapped another towel around him and led him through the butler door and toward the flickering glow in the sitting room.

She left him there only long enough to transfer a dining room chair so he could sit in front of the warmth of the hearth. He collapsed onto the seat, legs folding like a road map. Then she left him again, longer this time. And when she returned, she handed him a steaming mug of amber liquid.

"Drink this," she said.

His grip around the ceramic mug was so tight he thought it might shatter in his hands. Then he raised it toward his mouth and inhaled notes of ginger, cinnamon, and cloves that comforted his chilled bones. The first sip stung his tongue. He hissed then blew on the tea to cool it down before daring another taste.

"How is it?"

"Good ... Where did you go?"

"Home. I told you I wasn't waiting for you ... What took you so long?"

He took another slow sip as he thought that over. *How long was I out there? What was I doing? Where did I go? Do I really want to know?* He swallowed what was in his mouth and then lowered the mug to his lap. "I got lost," he finally answered.

"Lost? You run that trail every morning. How could you get lost?"

"I usually take the southern track, but we went north. It just turned me around I guess."

"Hm ... Finish your tea, then we'll get you out of those wet clothes."

He drank obediently as she hovered nearby.

Then when he finished, she sat the empty mug on the table and escorted him up the steps to the second-floor bathroom. She hung the damp towel over the shower rod then helped him remove his pants and sweatshirt. He could have managed himself, but somehow, he knew she wouldn't have allowed that.

After stripping off his socks, he slipped the T-shirt over his head, and she collected his discarded clothing from the floor. He pressed his body against the pedestal sink so she could slip out behind him, but instead, she stopped in the doorway. He looked up from the sink at her reflection in the mirror. She was staring at his back, mouth agape, forehead creased.

"What's wrong?"

"Your back," she whispered, reaching one hand toward him.

"What is it?" He turned his body and torqued his neck until the source of her concern came into view: three long and inflamed lacerations on the back of his shoulder—just where *the shade* scratched him that morning—

But that was a nightmare, he told himself as he reached around to touch them, believing—hoping—they weren't real. His fingers grazed over the welts, his skin stinging at his touch. *It's not possible. It was a dream—just a dream ... Wasn't it?*

He flinched at the feel of her hand on his side, and their eyes met in the mirror.

"How did it happen?" she asked.

What do I tell her? That I did this to myself during a nightmarish fit? Or that a shadowy demon visits me during the night and sometimes holds me down until I pass out? He continued to stare at the wound in the mirror as he weighed his options.

"Jimmy?"

Finding neither option to be very pleasant, he decided to go with door number three: lie. "It's nothing," he said, turning away from the mirror and pushing past her through the doorway. "It's just a rash or dry skin."

"That is *not* a rash."

He needed time to think, but she was on his heels as he went to the bedroom in search of fresh clothes. He walked past the bed and toward the closet with her a step behind.

"Let me look at it."

"I said it's nothing," he repeated as he reached for a T-shirt.

"It's not nothing."

She reached for his arm, but her fingernails scraped over the skin on his side instead. Suddenly *the shade* came to life in his mind. He pictured its yellow eyes with the oblong pupils; its blackened skin like the burnt husk of well-done meat; its sharp white teeth and saliva dripping through curled back lips; its razor-sharp claws—

He looked at her outstretched hands and noticed her long, manicured nails. He stepped back ... away from her, his chest heaving.

"Jimmy, what's wrong?"

He met her gaze, raised one quivering finger toward her, and said, "You did it ... Didn't you?"

"Did what?"

He turned his shoulder toward her. "This. It was you, wasn't it?"

"Jimmy ... No," she said, stepping toward him. "I would never hurt you."

He backed up another step and was against the wall. He grabbed his head and spread his fingers through his hair, his eyes pinballing around the closet ... Then to Roni ... Then beyond her to the bedroom ... The ceiling light—

What the fuck am I saying? Of course she wouldn't hurt me—

His gaze dropped to the floor ... Then the hanging clothes ... The light—

She gently slid her arm around him, careful not to touch the wound on his back. When he didn't pull away from her, she led him toward the bed.

She pulled the covers back and then helped him sit down. Then she stroked his forearms until he lowered his arms to his sides. As if in a trance, he eased his legs onto the mattress and laid his head on the pillow. He felt the covers pull up to his shoulders. It was only then that he heard her voice chanting the same phrase over and over.

"You're all right ... Everything will be all right."

He closed his eyes and hoped she was right.

Chapter 25

Jimmy opened his eyes with all the ease of a teenager that had slept 'til noon on the first day of summer break, with finals in the rearview mirror and nothing but afternoons of baseball, swimming pools, and puppy love in the future.

It was 2:20 a.m., but he wasn't stirred awake by a phantom presence, the obscene odor of rotting flesh, or the touch of papier-mâché fingers that cracked and flaked with each bending of the knuckles as they gripped his shoulder. It was the light that woke him.

The bedroom was cast in a bluish glow as if he were in a cruise ship cabin below sea level with porthole views of the ocean deep. He crooked his neck to peer over his shoulder and saw that the curtains were parted. The moon was staring back at him like some voyeur perched on a ladder and shining a spotlight on the emptiness beside him.

He flipped the covers aside and sat up. His T-shirt and boxers weren't enough to stave off the cold, and he shivered as the chill touched his skin. Arms wrapped around his body, he contemplated returning to the warmth of his cocoon, but—

Why are the curtains open? And where is Roni?

Reluctantly, he stood up and shuffled around the bed. The blankets on her side were still neatly tucked under her pillow, undisturbed as if she'd never come to bed. Understandable, given the events of the previous day. He cringed as he heard himself accusing her of hurting him. In the memory, it wasn't his voice he heard but rather that of a deranged imposter.

Reflexively, he began rubbing his shoulder. He couldn't feel the welts beneath the cotton, but he knew they were there.

At the window, he became trapped in the full moon's gaze, mesmerized by its mystery and wonder as it floated weightless in the abyss. Then his eyes lowered to the conifers lining the driveway like sentries, their tops worshiping the light before being swallowed up in the murk. The vehicles parked on the gravel reflected the scene like a still mountain lake. All was as it should be.

He grasped the curtain panels, eager to return the room to darkness in hopes of catching a few more hours of sleep, when a shadow at the base of the pines moved. A figure with long black hair flowing like raven wings stepped into the light with all the grace and stealth of a jungle cat.

"Roni?" he whispered.

It was her and not her. She was ... different. Her gait was that of purpose and trepidation, like a trespassing child collecting her ball after it wandered onto the lawn of the grumpy local geezer.

Then more movement in the shadows. A misshapen, lanky silhouette crept up behind her, placing its charred boney hands on her shoulders. Then it leaned forward and pressed its lips to her ear.

But she didn't scream or run or even flinch at its touch. She was enchanted. Almost as if—

"She was waiting for it."

Even at this distance, on the other side of the window glass, Jimmy could hear its silvery whisper, but what *the shade* was saying, he did not know. He only knew he had to stop it.

He banged his hands on the window and yelled, "Roni ... Roni!"

But she was under its hypnotic spell, and Jimmy's voice went unanswered. He tried to open the window, but it was locked. He twisted the knob and pulled up on the window sash, but it was painted shut and only rattled in the frame.

He slapped his hands against the glass again. "Hey! Get away from her ... Roni ... Run! Run away—"

The creature stopped speaking its susurrant spell and gazed toward the second-floor window.

Jimmy froze, overcome with the urge to step backward, out of the light, out of *the shade's* view, but it was too late to hide.

Staring up with its yellow eyes, it raised one hand and pointed its gnarled finger. Its lips curled back over its teeth, and in a voice as clear as if it were standing beside him, it said, "*I sssee you, Jamesss Massson.*"

He bolted upright in the bed, sweaty and shaking, chest heaving as if he'd just completed one of his early morning runs. But he hadn't been running or standing at the window. He was bundled under the covers, still in bed. The room aglow with morning light.

He whipped his head around to his left—the drapes were drawn shut. Roni's side of the bed was empty but slept in, rumpled covers pulled up to the pillow. He turned toward the bedside clock.

7:35.

As the brain fog lifted, he raised his hands to his head, then slumped over and took slow, deep breaths. It felt so real—the moon, the window, Roni ... *the shade.*

But as dreams often do, it was becoming fuzzy, and he began piecing together his last jumbled memories of the day before. Flashes really: the rain ... the creek ... the fire ... woods ... rain ... running—the scratches.

He reached over his shoulder and under the collar of his T-shirt until he felt the welts. They weren't a dream. He closed his eyes as he heard himself accusing Roni of hurting him, right before she helped him into bed.

Christ, she must be out of her mind, he thought. *If she's still here.* Then he furrowed his brow. *Was that yesterday or today? Is it morning? Or night?*

He swung his legs over the side of the bed and was welcomed by the aroma of coffee that had escaped the confines of the kitchen, wafted up the staircase and under the bedroom door. That was as sure a sign as any that it was morning.

He guessed he'd better quit stalling and go explain himself.

***

After getting dressed and emptying his bladder, he yawned and stretched his back, reaching his hands high above his head, then made his way to the staircase. The strange dream was but a distant memory by now as he prepared for what was likely going to be a tense discussion.

To his surprise, he also found his thoughts wandering to Coal. The feline who initially scared the bejeezus out of him, hissed, and wanted nothing to do with him had somehow managed to worm his way into Jimmy's heart. But he hadn't seen him since before the housewarming party and now feared he'd gotten out, was injured, or worse.

Then again, he could just be hiding ... He was a cat after all.

At the foot of the steps, he could see that the dining room was empty. So he peeked into the sitting room—Roni wasn't there either. Lured by the fresh brew, he steered into the dining room, where his eyes were drawn to the plastic bottle on the table in front of his chair.

She'd found the sleeping pills prescribed by Dr. Palmer.

He laid his head back and sighed, remembering the mug of warm tea he drank by the fire under the watchful eye of Dr. Roni.

She slipped me a couple of pills before putting me to bed.

As he stepped toward the swinging door, he heard a hushed voice from the other side. She wasn't whispering, but it was clear she didn't want to be overheard either. So of course, he stood quietly and listened, but he could only pick out a few words: *worried ... anxious ... scared ...*

He lowered his eyes, feeling sorry for what he'd put her through. He should have been honest with her from the beginning. He should have confided in her instead of only Bette and Greg. He reached for the door but then pulled his hand back. Eavesdropping was bad enough. He didn't want to barge in and interrupt her private conversation.

Instead, he went to the living room, flopped onto the sofa, and picked up the remote. She'd hear the television and would eventually come out to find him. He'd play dumb like he hadn't heard her on the phone. He'd explain what happened yesterday and answer her questions about the sleeping pills ... He'd have to tell her everything.

He wasn't ready for that.

He put the remote down, scooped up his truck key fob from the table in the entrance foyer, then left through the front door. He jogged down the porch steps, opened the truck door then slid into the driver's seat. After starting the engine, he reversed past her SUV, cutting the wheel to the right. Then slipped the truck into drive, turning left as he pressed the gas.

He was halfway down the driveway when he looked in the rearview mirror and saw her step onto the front porch with her phone to her ear.

He kept driving.

***

Three hours later, after two cups of coffee and one order of pancakes with sausage, one would think Jimmy knew what he was going to say to Roni when he returned home—but one would be incorrect. He needed time to think. Roni had probably been calling and texting, so he was grateful he'd left his cell phone on the bedside table.

On the drive home, he scraped his fingernails over his raw bottom lip and hoped for an epiphany. His father would say, "*Start from the beginning, and the rest will fall into place.*" You couldn't argue with fatherly wisdom. He wished his father were here now. He always knew what to say to make everything make sense. God knew he could use that right now because *nothing* made sense.

Earlier, before driving away, he'd considered telling her everything, but what did that mean? Everything since moving into the house on Woody Creek Lane? That wasn't really the beginning, though. If he followed his father's advice, the beginning would mean starting with that eight-year-old boy in Georgia that just learned he was 'special' and was unaware he was about to lose his mother. Was he brave enough to go back that far? To finally do the one thing his mother warned him against—

He winced at the sting of skin tearing away from his lip as the taste of blood landed on his tongue. Whatever his decision, he was out of time. The driveway was just ahead.

His stomach flip-flopped as he turned onto the gravel under the canopy of conifers. He took a deep breath and chewed on his bottom lip like a wad of bubble gum as the truck bobbed up and down, slowly approaching the house. As the Nassau Blue Corvette Stingray parked next to Roni's SUV came into view, his brow furrowed.

Did I forget Bette was coming over? He didn't think so, but it was possible with everything that had been going on. Still, he didn't think she mentioned it when she was here Friday.

He parked next to her car and then cut the engine. While his mind was distracted, the butterflies previously trapped in his belly had fluttered away, leaving him instead feeling suspicious. With his sister inside, his chances of being forced into making a heartfelt confession were dwindling. Likewise, the possibility of a much-anticipated knock-down-drag-out had also gone the way of the butterfly. This again begged the question—

Why is Bette here?

He took his time exiting the truck and then climbed the porch steps. The front door was unlocked. He dropped the truck key fob into the drawer of the entry table, closed the front door then proceeded toward the voices coming from the back of the house.

"That you, Smudge?" Roni called out.

"The one and only," he muttered under his breath. But before he could respond properly, his sister appeared from the parlor with her hands propped on her hips. "Hey, Bette," he said.

"You're in a heap of trouble."

"I know ... How is she?"

"How do you think?" she said, wrapping her arms around him. "I'm just glad you're okay ... You *are* okay, right?"

"Mm-hmm," he grunted as he hugged her back. And then it hit him like a sports highlight reel. "If you're in here ... Who's in the kitchen talking to Roni?"

"I have to tell you something," Bette said quickly as the butler door swung open.

"Too late," Jimmy muttered out of the corner of his mouth as Roni came into view with an unexpected guest in tow. "Did I forget we were having company today?" Then sarcastically to his guest, "Hey Greg ... What are you doing here?"

"I invited your sister," Roni said as she hugged her fiancé. Then she whispered into his ear. "Apparently, they spent the night together."

"I figured that out," he whispered while winking at his sister.

Bette rolled her eyes.

"Are you okay?" Roni asked.

"Yeah ... I'm sorry ... About yesterday and for not telling you about the pills—"

"It's okay. We don't have to talk about that right now. Let's sit down at the table."

He nodded and followed her to the dining room, where her tablet was propped up, and images of a beach, restaurants, and nightlife were scrolling in three-second intervals. "What's this," he said, picking up the tablet for a closer look. It was a website for an oceanside bed and breakfast down south. "Planning a vacation, Bette?"

When she didn't respond, he looked up—they were looking at him like he'd just told them he was dying. He set the tablet on the table and said, "Okay. What's going on?"

"It's not for Beth," Roni answered. "It's for us."

"What is this ... Some kind of intervention?"

"More like a rescue mission," Bette said. "We're all worried about you."

Then Greg said, "Maybe a quiet weekend at the beach will do you good."

"You too?" Jimmy said, glaring at his friend. Then he walked around the back of the table, away from them, and toward the kitchen. Toward solitude.

Roni started to follow him. "Jimmy—"

"I'm thirsty. Can I have a minute to get a drink? Please?" Once he was sure she wouldn't follow, he pushed through the door.

He wasn't thirsty, but he felt obligated to go to the fridge after his outburst. He removed a can of soda, popped the top then took a gulp. On the floor, uneaten pieces of kibble were scattered around Coal's dish, but the bowl was empty. He slumped over the center island, relieved that the cat was around somewhere. After a minute, the butler door opened.

"What the hell happened yesterday?" Bette asked.

"Was that you on the phone with Roni at 7:30?"

"Yes. She said you freaked out."

"Jesus," he whispered. He couldn't argue with that description. He also couldn't deny that he felt a little embarrassed. Maybe a lot embarrassed. "How much did she tell you?"

"Enough to get me out of bed and make the drive to your house."

"Speaking of getting out of bed," he said with a smirk.

She smiled and playfully slapped his arm. "You don't get to change the subject."

"I know, I know ... Greg's a good guy, though."

She nodded but didn't offer more, and he knew better than to push her. She'd had her heart broken more than once—she'd also done her fair share of the breaking. Jimmy hoped this time would be different for Bette's sake. He also knew she was a big girl who tended to ignore her older brother, so he would stay out of it. Even so, he thought it would be cool if his best friend became his brother.

"What are you smiling about?"

"Nothing," he said with a heavy sigh. He wasn't thrilled about being ambushed, but he also understood what it said about their level of concern. "So, tell me about the Chateau Primrose." Then he raised one eyebrow and added, "Why does that name sound familiar?"

"So you'll go?"

"Do I have a choice?"

"Probably not. Besides, what can it hurt?"

Bette hooked her arm around her brother's and then led him back to the dining room. Roni sat tall and straight as if frozen that way and the slightest movement would snap her bones. Only her eyes shifted slightly to meet Jimmy's. Still hiding from the truth, he looked away and noticed two bulging suitcases standing against the wall between the foyer and the sitting room. Apparently, the idea was to leave today.

"He said yes," Bette announced.

Roni exhaled and slumped in her chair like a deflated balloon.

"What about work?" Jimmy asked his friend.

"You're sick, and you're going to be out a couple of days."

"Was this your idea?"

Greg shrugged.

How would he even know about this place? Jimmy wondered as he held his friend's gaze. *Has he been there before? Or was he* planning *to go there—*

THE HOUSE ON WOODY CREEK LANE

Greg quickly glanced at Bette—she was looking at the tablet. When he returned his gaze to his friend, his cheeks had reddened as if he'd been in the sun too long. His eyes were wide as he slowly shook his head back and forth.

Jimmy nodded that he understood and wouldn't say anything.

Then Roni stood up from the table. "If we leave now, we'll make it in time for dinner."

***

Cachunk-cachunk-cachunk.

Jimmy's head jerked up as the pickup's tires ran over the highway rumble strips then he felt the sensation of weaving as the vehicle was redirected. "What happened?" he asked, stretching his arms and legs as he watched the scenery blur out the side window.

"Look who's awake," Roni said.

"How long was I out?"

"Couple of hours."

In the twilight, the glow of taillights ahead of them looked like an airport runway. "Are we lost?" he snickered as he squeezed her knee.

"Ha-ha. I'll have you know we're ahead of schedule."

He rolled the window down and smelled the salty air, then looked up at a flock of geese flying overhead, honking at one another to stay in formation. "You ever notice how geese look like flying bowling pins?"

She laughed, then became quiet. "It's nice to see a glimmer of the old Smudge," she finally remarked, glancing over at him before returning her attention to the highway. "It's been a while."

Was it the salty air or the short nap? He didn't know, but he was already starting to feel like himself too. And he wasn't missing the house or the forest at all. "So ... Bette and Greg?"

"I know," she gasped. "When did *that* happen?"

"Greg's always had a thing for Bette. I guess he finally wore her down at the housewarming party," he laughed.

"So you don't mind?"

"I've been secretly rooting for him."

"Oh, five more miles," she said, pointing at the green highway sign on the right shoulder.

Jimmy turned just in time to read it as they passed by: *Callaway 5 Miles*

Callaway Chrome Soft Truvis USA Golf Balls, he thought as he gazed into the distance. *Why do I know that? I don't play golf.* But something about it felt familiar to him, just like the name of the bed and breakfast: *Primrose.* "Have we ever been here before?" he asked her.

"No. Why do you ask?"

He shook his head. He couldn't explain the feeling, so he let it go. "I don't know about you, but I'm starving. What sounds good?"

"There's a steak restaurant I'd like to try. It's about a mile from the Inn."

"Wow. You really did your research."

"Not me—Greg. He told me about it. We can go after we check in."

"Sounds great," he said, smiling as he thought of his friend planning this getaway for himself and Bette. "The exit is coming up."

She flipped on the turn signal, glided into the right lane, and followed the exit ramp to a stoplight. While they waited to make a right turn, he spotted a sign directing drivers to The Chateau Primrose Bed and Breakfast, one mile east off the highway.

Primrose sweet and yummy candy. The thought rolled off his tongue as if he'd been reciting the tagline his entire life.

Chapter 26

Roni followed the winding driveway lit with pathway lights to resemble flickering flames reminiscent of a time before electricity, to a restored brick two-story, six-bedroom 1700s English Manor home. She parked on the cobblestone guest lot next to a red vintage Volkswagen Beetle and then cut the engine.

The Chateau sat on thirty acres of waterfront property and offered all the modern amenities, including satellite television and free Wi-Fi. The owners boasted the finest rose gardens the coastal town had to offer—dormant this time of year—a hedge maze, and an inground swimming pool.

After exiting on the passenger side, Jimmy hoisted their luggage from the back seat then followed the path through the white picket fence gate and up the brick steps to the white front door. Roni gripped the door handle and pressed the thumb latch, but the door wouldn't open.

Jimmy pointed to the door hanger that read, *Guests, Key-In Pin Code for Entry.* "We have a code, right?"

"I forgot." Then she dug her phone out of her purse and pulled up the confirmation email. When she entered a code into the keypad above the door handle, the lock disengaged, and they entered the foyer.

The flooring throughout the downstairs was wide pine planks. On the left was the great room with a fire burning in the hearth flanked by built-in cabinets holding rows of books. On the right was the dining room with a table and chairs for ten. A buffet table along the outer wall was topped with empty stainless steel warming trays, plates, and silverware. A sign indicated breakfast would be served starting at 7:00 a.m.

Ahead, a staircase led to the second floor. At the top, they looked left and right, where the hallway led to guest rooms and the communal bathroom. They found room number two and then entered the same pin code.

The door opened to a burgundy-painted room with floral window coverings and a Persian throw rug under a four-poster wooden bed made up with a white duvet and lace-trimmed pillows. And to Jimmy's surprise and relief, this room had a connecting *private* bathroom with a soaking tub.

A flyer on one of the bedside tables provided a reminder about breakfast and the Wi-Fi password. It also informed that cocktails would be served in the great room between 7 and 9 p.m.

"We have to make it back for cocktails," he said as he sat their bags on the luggage racks.

She nodded. Then, after freshening up, they were on their way to dinner.

***

The restaurant was open and lively with rustic seating, warm string lights, and classic rock in the background. A glass house that, during the daylight hours, would provide stunning views of the sandy beach and rolling waves to the east and the picturesque town of Callaway to the west. But on this night, the east-facing windows were as cold and black as the deepest part of the ocean.

The 1 ¼ inch thick ribeye Jimmy ordered was tender and flavorful, seasoned with garlic, onion, and salt and pepper. It melted in Jimmy's mouth like a pat of butter, and he devoured all ten ounces. They chatted about work, sports, Bette and Greg—anything but his 'episode.' Then they asked for the check and returned to the Inn.

It was just before eight o'clock. A few more cars were lined up on the cobblestone parking pad—five including the red Beetle, still in the same spot. The windows of the great room were brightly lit, covered only by sheer drapes that showed hazy shapes mingling about to a melancholy piano soundtrack.

Inside, it was standing room only as the piano played to a prestissimo finale in a cacophony of notes. The conversations were muted as the strangers seemed to keep to themselves for the most part, though an older couple was intent on changing that. They flitted from guest to guest, introducing themselves and the white Coton de Tuléar she carried in her arms.

Jimmy found the three-level bar cart positioned against the wall just inside the threshold. For the teetotalers, there was bottled water and assorted carbonated beverages on the bottom of the cart. White and red wines on the middle level with tulip-shaped stemware. A bucket of ice, tumbler glasses, and various distilled spirits on the top level. He poured a generous glass of red for Roni just as the social butterflies approached.

"You must be the couple in room two," the man said with his hand out. Wearing a tweed jacket and the fragrance of pipe tobacco, he was every bit the cliché college professor. He introduced himself and his wife as Robert and Constance Dwyer.

"You can call me Connie," she said with a sugary smile. "And this is Charlie." She turned her body so they could look into the malted milk ball eyes of the perfectly manicured pooch wearing a powder blue leather collar to match the color of his mistress' dress.

Charlie seemed to smile as he panted and welcomed a scratch on the head from Jimmy.

"He's adorable," Roni said, reaching toward him.

Charlie growled, baring four bright white incisors before she could stroke his soft fur.

"Oh, I'm so sorry," Connie said, squeezing the lapdog to her bosom. "He never does that." Then under her breath, she said, "Bad boy, Charlie."

"He must smell our cat," Roni said.

"Are you finding everything okay?" Robert asked Jimmy while his wife discussed dogs and cats with Roni.

"Yes, sir. I was just about to pour myself an after-dinner drink."

"Been to the steakhouse, have ya'?"

Jimmy placed his hand on his belly and nodded.

Robert Dwyer plucked a bottle of amber liquor from the cart and handed it to his guest. "Nothing beats this right here."

A chill spread over Jimmy as the blood rushed from his head to his abdomen and extremities. The room seemed to tilt to the left, and for a moment, he thought he might faint or throw up. From somewhere far away, he heard Robert say, *This is a fine Irish single malt.* Then he felt the pressure of a firm grip on his shoulder.

"Are you okay?"

Jimmy looked away from the bottle and into Robert's eyes as the queasy sensation passed.

"You look like you've seen a ghost."

"Jimmy?" Roni said. "Are you okay?"

"I'm fine ... Just a little tired."

"Shall I pour you a glass?" Robert asked, still holding the bottle.

Jimmy shook his head. "I think I'll stick with water."

"Suit yourself."

Jimmy's eyes followed Mr. Dwyer as he set the bottle on the cart. Then, an image flashed in his mind as the couple excused themselves. Just for a second. Just quick enough for him to remember the weight of the bottle in his hands as he read the label.

Dead Rabbit—a golden blend of aged Irish single malt and grain whiskies.

He inhaled sharply as the memory faded, then grabbed a bottle of water from the bottom level of the cart. "I'm not feeling very well," he said to Roni. "I'm going up to the room."

"Okay. I'll be up after I finish my wine."

***

In the room, he tossed the water bottle on the bed, then went into the bathroom and splashed cold water on his face—

Dead Rabbit Irish Whisky. Muddled fur. Blood. Flesh torn. Blood.

Callaway Chrome Soft Truvis USA Golf Balls. Blood. Bones snapped and splintered. Blood.

Primrose Sweet and Yummy Candy. Blood. Flesh slashed and splayed. Yummy. Blood. Yummy.

Blood.

Blood.

BLOOD!

He turned off the faucet and stared at his pale reflection through the water droplets on the mirror. "What's happening to me?"

Think of something else, he told himself as he leaned on the counter, closed his eyes, and lowered his head.

He breathed and focused on the waves crashing ashore just steps from the Inn's property line. He felt the sand sink beneath his feet as he walked the shoreline in his mind's eye. Tasted the salt in the air. Heard the gulls flying overhead and the roar as rolling water rushed toward the beach until it reached a crescendo and crashed at his feet. He imagined the pull of water and sand rushing against his skin as the ocean receded and made ready for an encore.

Salt. Sand. Water. Repeat.

Breathe.

He opened his eyes and took the hand towel from the wall-mounted wooden ring. After drying his face, he wiped up the water splashed onto the sink counter. In the bedroom, he found his toiletry bag in one of the suitcases

Roni had packed. He brushed his teeth, undressed, and stuffed his dirty clothes beneath the luggage rack.

It was 8:45 p.m. by then. He knew Roni would be up soon, but still, he switched off the light then climbed into bed, lured by the scent of lavender and sandalwood. The mattress *squeaked* and *moaned* as he settled in. Then he closed his eyes.

Voices roamed the second-floor hallway.

Outside the bedroom window, Charlie *yipped* and *yapped* at some four-legged trespasser—or perhaps at the wind—before urinating on the topiary.

Then Jimmy drifted, lulled by the vibrations permeating the house and the waves thrashing the imaginary shoreline in his mind.

***

In the morning, Jimmy woke with the sunrise beaming through the east-facing window of their rented room. Beside him, the bed was empty, the bedcovers in a rumpled heap. He lifted his head from the pillow and heard the soft spray of water against a plastic shower curtain coming from the bathroom.

He let his head fall back onto the pillow but then felt the ache of his bladder. He slipped out of bed and then hurried to the bathroom—

It's locked. He knocked. "Hon, let me in."

"Be out in a minute," she called back.

"I gotta pee. Open up."

"Use the communal bathroom, Smudge."

Just what he was hoping to avoid. He sighed as he turned away from the door, contemplating his options. He could wait for her to finish—who knew how long that might be. In the meantime, his bladder would continue to inflate like a water balloon. Or he could get dressed and hope the communal bathroom was unoccupied.

He decided on option two since he remembered there was also a guest bathroom on the first floor, which increased his odds. He carefully zipped his jeans over his bulging bladder, put on a clean T-shirt, then hurried into the hall. As he feared, the second-floor bathroom was in use, so he went downstairs, where he was immediately cornered by Mrs. Dwyer.

"Oh, James," she said, out of breath. "Have you seen my Charlie?"

"Actually, no. I just got up and—"

"He got away from me last night, and I haven't been able to find him anywhere. Oh, I'm so worried about him."

Jimmy looked over her shoulder at the open powder room door just steps away. Then his gaze returned to Connie. Her bleached blonde hair was out of place, and her pale blue eyes were red and swollen. Then he noticed her hands cupped tight to her chest where Charlie should be. And his thoughts strayed to Coal.

He placed his hand on her shoulder. "I'll be happy to help you look for him."

Her lip quivered as she met his gaze. "I wouldn't want to trouble you."

"It's no trouble. Just let me hit the little boy's room first."

"Of course. You're so kind, James. I don't know where Charlie could've gotten off to. He's never run away before."

"I'm sure he'll turn up." Then Jimmy scooted past Connie Dwyer and into the bathroom, where relief couldn't come fast enough.

After washing his hands, Jimmy sent a message to Roni's phone: *Helping Connie look for Charlie. Text when you're done. I'll find you.*

When he opened the door, Mrs. Dwyer was waiting for him in the hallway. In her distraught state, she resembled a little girl.

"I'm all yours," he said, taking her arm and leading her toward the front door.

"Are you sure you don't mind? What about your fiancé?"

"She's getting dressed and will help us when she comes down." He opened the door for Connie, stepped onto the brick porch, and closed the door. "Where should we start?"

"I think it would be better if we split up, don't you? I'll search the garden. Would you mind searching in the topiary maze? It's around that way."

Jimmy nodded and turned in the direction she was pointing. Fifty yards to the south stood a white octagonal gazebo where he imagined weddings being performed. And behind it was a boxwood hedge wall.

As he drew nearer, he found a slate paver path that led to the steps of the gazebo before resuming on the other side. A trellis arch was the entrance to the labyrinth. He imagined the spring and summer months, the brittle, bare vines wrapped around the wood like brown yarn sprouting colorful roses or some other flower to perfume the salty air.

Standing in front of the maze, he guessed the hedge walls were most likely seven or eight feet tall—tall enough for most to become lost. Private enough for a small dog to fall victim to a much larger predator.

As he stepped under the arch, his heart thumped faster. He pictured himself running in the woods behind his house. His feet pounding the earth. Arms pumping at his sides. Suddenly he was breathing faster and sweating as his mental run continued, further along the path, through the fallen leaves as broken rays of light peered through the bare trees. Heart beating faster and faster. Breaths shorter and shorter—

Fur. Blood. Flesh.

Bone. Blood. Skin.

Blood.

Blood.

BLOOD!

It had gone silent except for the *whoosh-whoosh* of blood pumping in his veins. A piercing whine filled his ears as the world around him became unsteady, warm, and bright. And in an instant, he was on the ground looking up at the blue sky as cotton candy clouds passed overhead. His limbs were heavy—too heavy to move. Not *wanting* to move.

And he closed his eyes.

***

"Jimmy."

A voice, hollow and empty, called out to him in the darkness.

"Jimmy, wake up."

The earth was moving all around him. Gyrating. Shaking ... Jostling. He opened his eyes.

"Jimmy." Roni was leaning over him, her hands around his shoulders.

"What," he answered, blinking to bring her face into focus.

"He's back ... Jimmy, you're back."

Connie and Robert were huddled together, looming over him like a pair of giants. With Roni's help, he sat up. He was on the grass beneath the trellis, just outside the topiary maze. "What happened?"

"I saw your message, but when you didn't respond to my text, I came looking for you. Connie said I'd find you in the maze, but I found you here ... out cold."

"How long?"

She looked up at Connie. "I don't know."

"We weren't apart more than a few minutes before you came down," Connie told her.

"No," Jimmy said. "It must have been longer than that ... I was in the maze—"

"I don't think so, dear."

He looked at the older woman like she'd sprouted a third eye in the middle of her forehead and it just winked at him. "Are—Are you sure?"

She nodded. "Let's get some breakfast in you. Robert, help the boy up."

With the help of Mr. Dwyer and Roni, Jimmy was on his feet. He was a little wobbly at first, but he was up. He leaned on Roni, unsure if he could trust his own legs, then the four of them returned to the house.

When they reached the porch, Robert opened the door and invited Roni to step in ahead of him. Connie started to fall in behind her, but then Jimmy raised his trembling hand and touched her on the arm. "Did you find Charlie?"

She sighed. "No, dear. Not yet." Then she stepped over the threshold.

Jimmy turned to the south, toward the maze, for one final look. Then he staggered past Robert and heard the door close behind him.

In the dining room, Jimmy took the nearest seat at the rectangular table, anxious to get off his unsteady legs. At the same time, Roni filled a plate at the buffet. A couple he recognized from the night before was seated at the opposite end—she fed him pancakes while he fondled her knee. After a minute or two, Roni returned with a plate of muffins, pancakes, and a glass of orange juice.

"Sorry, this is all that's left," she said.

The juice was chunky and tart and the best he'd ever had—or maybe it was just that he was parched, and his blood sugar was on empty. Either way, he gulped it down and asked for a refill. The antique clock on the wall began to chime. Once ... twice ... He moved the food around his plate, trying to decide if he was hungry or not.

He wasn't.

Roni returned with the second glass of juice on the ninth chime. He guzzled it then placed the empty glass on the table. His hands stopped shaking, and his head cleared. He pushed the plate of untouched food aside and stood up.

"Where are you going?" Roni asked.

"Upstairs."

"But you didn't eat anything."

"I'm not hungry."

Now feeling at full strength, he walked purposefully into the hall and up the staircase while Roni followed close behind, muttering for him to slow down.

But he didn't listen. He just kept moving, past the other guests milling around the second-floor hallway, until he reached the door to their room. Then he keyed in their code and went inside.

She entered behind him and closed the door. "Didn't you hear me asking you to wait for me?"

He was already in the bathroom, gathering his toiletries and repacking them into the organizer and didn't respond. He didn't want to engage with her, fearing he'd change his mind.

Standing in the bathroom doorway, she asked, "What are you doing?"

"I'm packing."

"Why?"

"Because I'm leaving."

"We don't check out until tomorrow. We have the time off from work—"

"I'm leaving now ... Excuse me," he said, then waited for her to step aside. Once she did, he returned the toiletry kit to his suitcase, then picked up his dirty laundry from the floor and stuffed those in as well. Then without looking at her, he said, "You should start packing too."

"I thought we were having a good time ... I thought getting away was what you needed ... That maybe this would help with whatever is going on with you."

After zipping his bag, he turned toward her and shrugged. "It's not. It's not helping."

She reached out to him as she stepped closer. "Tell me what's going on."

He held up one hand to stop her from advancing.

"Not here," he said. "Let's just go home ... Then I'll tell you everything."

Chapter 27

S ix hours was a long time to sit in silence ...

In six hours, you could listen to 65 of the greatest hits of the last four decades—some more than once—and never hum a bar. In six hours, you could drive 311 miles, stop for bathroom breaks, refuel, and never make eye-contact with the person sitting beside you. In six hours, two people could consume three cups of coffee, four bottles of water, two soft drinks, and a pair of cheeseburgers with fries without so much as a belch or fart between them.

But in all that silence and mental reflection, Jimmy couldn't find the words to explain why he had to leave the chateau a day early. Why, if he didn't leave right when they did, he felt like his head or heart—or both—might explode. Why he couldn't shake the feeling that it all meant something—

Dead Rabbit Irish single malt whiskey ... Callaway Chrome Soft Truvis USA Golf Balls ... Primrose Sweet and Salty candy ... Charlie's Angels—

Charlie ... Oh, God, what have I done?

An image of the smiling pooch with the cottony white fur and champagne-tinted ears broke free from the compartment where Jimmy had locked it away. Now, he was forced to imagine what he might have done ... What he must have done ... The reason he couldn't enter the hedge maze ... The reason his mind stopped him before he could return to the scene of the crime—

He closed his eyes and shook it away, readjusting in his seat.

Six hours was enough time to mentally rehearse twenty, fifty, or one hundred mock conversations with Roni. And he played out every scenario to its inevitable conclusion. None of them ended well. And now, as he made the right turn off Woody Creek Lane and onto their gravel driveway, he realized he still had no idea where to begin. Nevertheless, he was out of time.

He brought the truck to a stop beside Roni's SUV and applied the parking brake. But before he could cut the engine, she had snapped off her seatbelt and was out the passenger door.

Slam!

Jimmy exhaled as he removed his seatbelt, then opened the door and stepped out. He inhaled a generous helping of musky pine and wilderness as his father's voice reminded him, "*Start from the beginning, and the rest will fall into place.*"

Then a commotion startled him, and he turned around. Roni was fighting with the suitcases in the back of the pickup. "Let me help," he said as he circled around the bed to the passenger side, where he tried to wedge himself between her and the side of the truck.

"I can manage," she grumbled, with a firm grip around the handle of her bag, refusing to move.

He touched her shoulder and gently encouraged her to step back. "My bag needs to come out first."

She gritted her teeth, more determined than ever, grunting with each jerky movement as she tried to drag her bag over his.

"Stop being childish," he said.

"*I'm* being childish?"

Her razor-sharp stare turned his blood cold.

"You're the one keeping secrets," she snarled. "Lying ... And now *I'm* being childish?"

She was right, of course. "*Start from the beginning, and the rest will fall into place.*" But what was the beginning? The day of the open house when he first heard the susurrus voice ... Or should he go all the way back to that eight-year-old boy that saw his first *shade*—

"Well?" she said. "Say something."

He said nothing. After 311 miles, 65 top 40 songs, two pitstops, one crappy fast-food meal, and over a decade of secrecy, he still couldn't form the words.

She threw up her hands, turned, and walked around the front of the truck. But instead of climbing the steps to the porch, she went to the driver's side of her SUV and opened the door.

"Where are you going?" he asked.

"I need to be alone."

He watched her get in and close the door. Then she started the engine and backed up and around the bed of his truck until the front of the SUV was facing the driveway.

As the car accelerated, he yelled, "I'm sorry!"

But she was too far away to hear him.

Or didn't want to.

＊＊＊

He carried the suitcases inside and stood them against the wall in the foyer. The house was as they'd left it. Quiet.

He peeked into the igloo-shaped cat bed in the sitting room, but no emerald eyes stared back. In the kitchen, an empty ceramic bowl provided no evidence one way or the other that Coal was still around. Perhaps he'd eaten all the kibble, or perhaps Bette hadn't been over to feed him yet. But a clump in the center of the otherwise clean kitty litter was a sign of hope.

He stepped on the foot pedal of the small stainless-steel can beside the toilet, then scooped the clump and dropped it in. After washing his hands, he removed his phone from his back pocket and called Bette. She answered after three rings.

"You know," she said, her smile apparent in her tone. *"If I were on a romantic getaway at the beach, the last person I would want to call is you."*

"Yeah, about that ..."

"Oh, no. What happened?"

"I screwed up."

"Again?"

"Thanks," he said, leaning over the kitchen island. "Anyway, we're home so you don't have to come over tonight to feed the cat."

"You're home? I thought you weren't due back until tomorrow?"

It wasn't judgment or disappointment that he heard in her voice. It was worry.

"It's a long story. Hey, when were you last here?"

"This morning. Why?"

"Did you see Coal?"

"No. But the kibble I left out last night was gone, and the litter box had been used, so he's around."

He nodded as if she could see him, then stood straight, wondering where Coal could be hiding. He left the kitchen and started up the steps thinking he would start his search from the top and then work his way down—a good distraction while Roni was cooling off.

"Jimmy, you know you can talk to me, right?"

He knew that. And he wanted to tell her everything. Unburden himself of all of it, once and for all. To finally let someone in on what he'd been living through in this house and the secret he'd been keeping since he was a child. Maybe telling his sister would be good practice before he told Roni. Maybe Bette could come over and be his backup—

"Jimmy? Are you there?"

It's now or never. He was at the top of the steps when he took a deep breath and started at the beginning. "When we were kids, do you remember our trip with Mom? To Georgia?"

"Barely ... What was I ... Five or six years old?"

"Do you remember anything strange happening in that house?"

"Like what?"

He sighed into the phone. "Did you *see* anything?"

Now it was Bette's turn to be quiet. The only sound coming from the other line was the *tap-tap-tap* of her polished nail on the back of the phone. *"I remember you and Mom were being very secretive ... Sneaking away to talk about who knows what."* Another long pause. *"I was jealous—and curious. So I tried to eavesdrop a few times."*

He was standing in the master bedroom with his eyebrow raised. "What did you hear?"

"Not a lot, and what I did hear didn't make much sense."

"What? What did you hear?" he asked as he re-entered the hallway, searching for another feline hiding place.

"It was like a nursery rhyme but one I'd never heard before and never again since. I only remember two lines because they really creeped me out. It went, 'The light cried out, it's him, it's him. And the shade howled back, let me in, let me in.'"

He stood frozen in the hallway, his skin crawling as *the shade's* refrain snaked into his mind. *Let me in ... Let me in! Let me in!* And then a fuzzy memory began to come into focus. Something he'd stored away in the recesses of his mind for safe keeping. A treasured moment between a boy and his mother that, in the middle of growing up and growing older, had been forgotten.

We were on a bench overlooking a pond on the back side of the property. The others—uncles, cousins, Bette, and Grandma June—were occupied with games and enjoying lemonade in the Southern heat. Or so I thought. I had no idea Bette had snuck up on us. Then Mom told me something important ... Something she made me repeat back to her until we were reciting it together ... But what was it—

"Jimmy? What does it mean?"

—I can hear her voice, as clear now as on that day, but I can't make out her words. I can't remember the other lines—

"Jimmy?"

As he passed the attic door, he noticed it was standing ajar. He stopped and furrowed his brow. "Bette ... Did you go into the attic when you were here?"

"What? No ... Oh, wait ... I got the idea that maybe Coal had become trapped up there, so I left the door open, just in case."

"Shit."

"What's the matter?"

"We keep the door closed, so he probably wasn't up there before, but he might be now. I better go up and check."

"You're not s-s-s-scared, are you?" she laughed.

"You can be a real pain in the ass, you know that?"

"I know, but you love me. I'll keep you company ... Now march up those steps."

Each step *squeaked* and *squealed* more than the last as he climbed the ancient flight to the dusty, cobweb-infested chamber above. "Would you believe this is my first time up here?"

"Yes. But you've always been squeamish."

The attic was like a tomb, filled with left-behind treasures of a life once loved. An iron bed frame; a wire dress form wearing nothing but a wide-brimmed beach hat; yellowed boxes labeled 'X-Mas' that he guessed contained decorations; a rusty red tricycle; a card table with four folding chairs, and a steamer trunk that he hoped didn't contain the bones of the previous owner. And that was just the stuff he could see. Behind all that, were mounds and mounds of odds and ends, stacked in such a way to leave a path through the madness.

"Make some noise and flush him out," Bette suggested.

"Here, kitty-kitty-kitty," Jimmy called out as he weaved through the relics. Every few steps, he tapped or shook a box, hoping for a reaction.

Beep-beep-beep.

Jimmy recognized the call-waiting tone and held the phone away from his ear to see who was calling: *The Primrose Chateau ... Charlie.*

"Oh no," he said.

"What's wrong?"

"I got a call coming in ... Hang on a sec." He accepted the call while placing his sister on hold. After a hard swallow, he said, "Hello?"

"Is this James? James Hobart?"

He recognized Connie's voice. "Hello, Mrs. Dwyer. Yes, it's me. How are you?" He held his breath and braced himself for the terrible news.

"Oh, Jimmy. I'm wonderful. I just wanted to let you know that we found Charlie."

He nearly dropped the phone from his sweaty palm as his knees buckled. He lowered to a squat so he wouldn't fall over. "You did?"

"I wanted to call you sooner, but Mr. Dwyer thought I should wait since you were driving."

Jimmy pursed his lips and shook his head. *Good ol' Mr. Dwyer.* "So how is the little fella?"

"Charlie? He's fine. He was filthy but fine. Got a bath right after I fed him." Then in baby talk, she said, *"Isn't that right, Boo-Boo? Yes, it is. Yes, it is."*

He pictured her holding the Coton de Tuléar in her arms as she did when he first saw her and relished the smile that formed on his lips. While she continued cooing, he resumed his search for Coal. "So, where did you find him?"

"You know, it was the strangest thing. Not long after you and your fiancé left, he just wandered onto the porch and scratched at the door until someone opened it."

"Uh-huh," he said. As she talked, he shuffled between the stacks, jostling this, kicking that, hoping for two miracles in one day. Then he noticed a clean spot in the dust that coated the floor. "Uh-huh," he said again as he stepped closer. It appeared that a stack of boxes had been recently pulled from formation before being returned—odd since he didn't think anyone had been in the attic in a very long time.

Connie's voice became background noise as his curiosity was piqued. He unstacked the boxes one by one, setting each in the path, one on top of the other. When he finished, he found a void in the center of the clutter. And in that void, on the floor, was one more box.

It was brown with a hinged lid—the size of a shoebox.

His eyes grew wide, distorting his visual perception until he felt small and far away while the box grew impossibly larger and larger, consuming his field of vision. He closed his eyes—*Dead Rabbit Irish single malt whiskey ... Callaway Chrome Soft Truvis USA Golf Balls ... Primrose Sweet and Salty candy ... Charlie's Angels—*

He opened his eyes as finally, it all made sense.

It was my birthday—not really though. Because it was a dream. We had yellow cake with gooey chocolate buttercream icing with vanilla ice cream. Greg gave me a bottle of Dead Rabbit Irish single malt whiskey. Chase gave me a box of Callaway Chrome Soft Truvis USA Golf Balls—"I don't play golf," I said. Jack and Cara gave me assorted Primrose candies and popcorn. Then Libby gave me a DVD box set of the Charlie's Angels television series. "Now open my gift," Roni said. It was almost too beautifully wrapped to tear apart, but I did until I was holding a brown shoebox—

A layer of moisture had become trapped between the smartphone screen and his skin. As the dream faded, a scream formed within his gut. He took a step forward as he stared at the box on the floor before him. The lid was smeared with red stains but was free from dust, so it hadn't been here long. He knelt on the floor, heart pounding. He reached toward the box—

"Well, I've taken up enough of your time," Connie said.

"Huh?" He recoiled his hand and wiped it on his pants leg. "Nonsense. I'm just glad Charlie's okay."

"Maybe someday you'll come back to Primrose. Perhaps on your honeymoon?"

"That would be nice. You take care now, Mrs. Dwyer."

"You too, dear."

Jimmy lowered the phone to the floor as the call ended and returned his attention to the box. *It could be empty, right?* he told himself as he reached for the lid and flipped it up—

He gagged and fell backward onto his rear, then scooted along the filthy attic floor until his back slammed against another stack of artifacts. Images of the mutilated animal carcasses flashed through his mind as he imagined what he'd done—what he *must* have done.

But I couldn't have, he thought, shaking his head. *I wouldn't—*

"Do you like it?" Roni said.

The silvery words cut through him like molten steel, and for a moment, he wasn't sure if her voice was real or a memory from his dream. He turned around and saw her lurking just inside the attic doorway, smiling and blocking the only way out.

It was Roni, but she was ... different. Changed. A wild thing, uncomfortable in her clothing, unfamiliar with a hairbrush. Unafraid. Her posture stiffened like a cornered animal just before it pounced on the weaker prey.

And he was the prey.

He turned his gaze to the box—the box of bones. It was just feet away. And next to it, his unlocked phone ... *The line is open ... Bette!*

"I asked if you liked it?" Roni repeated, taking a step closer.

"Roni?"

"You shouldn't have been up here, Jimmy. It's not polite to snoop."

She took another step toward him. Her gate slow and deliberate ... Silent. Her fingers spread so she dragged her claws along the cardboard boxes that lined the path—

That's not claws ... She's holding something in her hands ... Two three-pronged garden tillers with steel tines sharpened to points. The injuries to the rabbit, the deer, and the other creatures ... The mutilation ... It wasn't me—

He slowly stood up, finally knowing the truth. "What did you do?"

"What needed to be done ... For him."

"Him? Who are you talking about?"

"Abaddon. He's been waiting far too long in the pit of darkness," she said, inching closer. "And with my help, he shall return."

Jimmy stepped backward. He had to stall her. Keep her talking while drawing her away from the door so he could make his escape. "How are you helping Abaddon, Roni?"

"The bones. The pit will open once the symbol is complete, and Abaddon will be free."

He remembered the bones in the root cellar. *They weren't just scattered in some random pattern ... It was a symbol. An incomplete symbol. But that was there before we moved in ... Before we bought the house.*

He swallowed away the image and refocused on her. "You're not the first to try and help him, are you?"

"Others failed ... They weren't strong enough."

"But *you* are, Roni. Is that right?"

She didn't answer except for what could only be described as a throaty growl as she prowled even closer.

"The root cellar—that's where you'll finish the symbol?"

She smiled and nodded, baring her teeth as she crouched lower, her tools scraping along the wooden floorboards.

Jimmy's heart was pumping at full speed. His skin tingled. He was unaware of his breathing but heard every raspy puff of air Roni inhaled. He smelled dust, rotting cardboard, and moth balls. Tasted mildew, copper, and sweat. His hands trembled. His legs twitched.

He was at the doorway, just feet away from her, when he said, "But I boarded up the root cellar."

In an inhuman voice, she replied, "I wish you hadn't done that."

Chapter 28

After a long lunch, Bette was back at her desk, entering data in a spreadsheet. She was somewhat of an Excel geek who searched out reasons to concatenate cells, insert vLookup formulas or pivot tables, and create macros. The more complex, the better. But today she was finding it difficult to focus. Her thoughts kept wandering to *him*.

She could smell him on her hands and clothes and in her hair. Her stomach fluttered as she remembered his kiss. Her heart thumped as she imagined his hands on her, unbuttoning her blouse. She closed her eyes and felt the warmth of his skin—

Ring-Ring. Ring-Ring.

Her dream was gone like a balloon pricked by a pin. She opened her desk drawer and fished her phone from her purse just as the second ring started. But it wasn't Greg calling. It was Jimmy. She furrowed her brow and let the phone ring once more before answering.

"You know," she said with a smirk as she leaned back in her chair. "If I were on a romantic getaway at the beach, the last person I would want to call is you."

She was glad for the distraction. She needed to clear her mind so she could focus on the looming work deadline. But even as she chatted about her brother's relationship troubles, his missing cat, and their mother, again her thoughts strayed to *him*.

She twirled her hair around one finger as she felt his tongue on her neck. She bit her bottom lip as she remembered the taste of his skin. She closed her eyes and felt his hands around her waist, pulling her close—

Beep-beep-beep.

"*Oh no,*" Jimmy gasped.

"What's wrong?"

"*I got a call coming in … Hang on a sec.*"

As the line fell silent, Bette straightened in her chair and returned her attention to the spreadsheet on the monitor in front of her. Balancing the cell phone between her shoulder and her ear, she began typing. Until another memory bored its way into her mind. But not of *him*. This time, it was *her*.

The thing about old forgotten memories was that sometimes, their roots become buried deep in your mind. And if you go digging around, accidentally uncovering one, you never know where it will lead. This root led to Moultrie, Georgia, her mother and brother, and that strange rhyme that she hadn't thought about in years but now couldn't get out of her head.

The light cried out, it's him, it's him. And the shade howled back, let me in, let me in.

She shivered as the memory washed over her. Before he could explain what the rhyme meant, Jimmy changed the subject to Coal and the open attic door. And the longer she waited for him to return on the line, the bigger her curiosity grew.

What were they whispering about, far away from where anyone could hear? What secret was she giving him? What's he been hiding from me all this time? What does he know about her that I don't—

After a few minutes, her neck was aching from holding the phone, and suddenly she had the urge to pee. She squirmed in her try and tried to work. But her leg began bobbing up and down as her stomach expanded against the fly of her trousers. She was losing her focus again.

"Come on, Jimmy," she whispered.

As if he heard her, the call reconnected. But he didn't say anything.

"Hello? Jimmy?"

No answer. She turned away from the sounds of the office trespassing into her cubicle, pressed the phone tighter to her ear, and listened harder. *A box, sliding on wood ... A gasp ... shuffling ...*

"Jimmy?"

Muffled voices, far away from the phone's mouthpiece ... Too far to make out any words, but she was certain there were two distinct voices: Jimmy and someone else. *Footsteps ... Something metallic, scraping against the floor ... Growling?*

"Jimmy," she whispered again.

Bette flinched as an explosion carried through the speaker of her cell phone. A chaos of sounds that she recognized as a struggle and pictured her brother in a fight for his life.

She grabbed her purse from the desk drawer, her work cell, and was on her feet. As she zig-zagged between cubicles and toward the stairwell to the first floor, she dialed 9-1-1 on her work phone.

"9-1-1. This is operator 5-7-9. What is the address of your emergency?"

"I'm on the phone with my brother ... Someone broke into his house." For all she knew, that was precisely what happened.

"Did you hear the break-in?"

"Yes ... He asked me to call the police." That wasn't true, but she had to tell the operator something that would make her send help now. "I heard them struggling."

She was out of the stairwell and running through the lobby. In her right ear, she heard the familiar *click-clack-click-clack* of keyboard keys as the operator logged her information. In her left ear, she heard silence. She held the phone away from her ear. The call had disconnected.

"What's your brother's address?"

"3845 Woody Creek Lane ... Please hurry."

***

In a sweeping move, Jimmy tumbled the nearest boxes into Roni's path, then practically slid down the attic steps. He knew the boxes wouldn't stop her from coming. He just needed to slow her down.

At the bottom of the stairs, he slammed the door closed, locked it, then hurled himself toward his office and reached around the corner for the vintage Jackie Robinson H&B Power Drive baseball bat leaning against the wall.

***

"All units—be advised, we have a 10-31 at 3845 Woody Creek Lane ... that's Woody: Whiskey, Oscar, Oscar, Delta, Yankee ... Creek: Charlie, Romeo, Echo, Echo, Kilo ... Lane: Lima, Alpha, November, Echo."

"We're not far," Officer Blake Elkins said to his partner as he typed the address into the cruiser's onboard computer.

"Repeat, 10-31 at 3845 ..."

Officer Deidre Denton clicked the talk button on her shoulder radio and leaned toward the mouthpiece. "Dispatch. Unit 284 is 10-77 in ..."

She paused while her partner pulled up the address.

"Less than five," Elkins said.

"Five minutes," she relayed as she started the Charger's engine.

"Copy 284. All other units are 10-12."

Officer Elkins fastened his seatbelt as the car jerked backward from the parking space at the Quick Stop before speeding forward. "You know what house that is, right?" he asked his partner.

"No," Denton answered, turning toward him. "Should I?"

"After tonight, I guarantee you won't forget it."

She grunted and diverted her attention back to the road as she switched on the lights and sirens.

***

Bette was at her car when the operator finally confirmed that officers were on their way and should arrive within five minutes. It would take her twenty-five minutes to reach her brother's house if she obeyed the speed limit.

But Bette wasn't much for following rules.

Out of the parking lot and racing toward the interstate onramp, Bette picked up her personal phone and enabled voice control. "Call Greg."

"Calling Greg," the virtual assistant answered.

She pressed "Speaker" on the phone's touchscreen, then set it on the center console as Greg's phone began ringing. Adrenaline coursing through her veins, white-knuckled grip on the leather steering wheel, she navigated end-of-day commuters like an Indie 500 driver, seeing two and three moves ahead.

"Come on, pick up, pick up," she grumbled through gritted teeth.

"Hey, Beth. Miss me al—"

"Greg. Something's happened to Jimmy."

"What? What's wrong?"

"I'm not sure ... I think he was attacked."

"At the beach?"

"No. They came home early. He's at the house."

"What about Roni? Is she okay?"

"I don't know ... I was on the phone with him, and I heard ..."

She swallowed back the tears that were fighting to come out. She couldn't lose control now—not yet.

"I called the police. Can you meet me there?"

"I'm on my way."

She nodded, took a deep breath, and then let it out slowly as she merged into highway traffic.

"Want me to stay on the phone?"

"No. I need to focus." The chances of the dam breaking were greater with him on the line. He made her feel safe, comforted, and vulnerable. Loved. "I'll see you there."

"All right ... Drive safe, Beth."

"You too."

In her rearview mirror, the sun was dropping below the distant horizon. Ahead of her, the sky was preparing for moonrise. It would be dark by the time she reached her brother.

She wiped her eyes and pressed the gas pedal.

***

His hand gripped around the handle of the bat, Jimmy ran toward the second-floor landing, shoes slipping on the wood floor just as the attic door splintered.

Roni tumbled into the hallway and slammed into the wall.

He flinched and turned away, dropping the bat while drawing his arms up to protect his head from shrapnel. If he had time to think, he would have wondered what happened to his sweet Roni. He would have wondered what or who Abaddon was. He would have wondered why his mother never warned him about the other creatures that were attracted to *the light*—his *light*. Creatures that are better left to the darkness.

But there wasn't time to think.

He lunged for the bat.

***

"According to the GPS, the driveway is in 100 feet," Elkins said, squinting through the windshield as he angled the spotlight on the blacktop in front of them. "I can't see a damn thing."

Deidre Denton slowed the cruiser and shut off the siren. Red and blue lights lit up the darkness like confetti falling on New Year's Eve. After fifteen years on the force, she still felt the flutter of anxiety in her gut when rolling up on a scene. And having a newbie beside her didn't help.

"There," she said, accelerating toward the entrance. She slowed enough to make the quick left turn. The engine revved but was quickly drowned out by the *crackle* and *pop* of tire rubber over gravel and dead branches.

"284, what's your status," the voice said through the radio.

"10-23," Denton answered, her voice shaking as the car bounced and bobbed.

"Copy that 284. Standing by."

"Looks quiet," Elkins said.

"Probably a false alarm." Other than the two vehicles in the driveway, it appeared no one was home. The house was dark except for a dim, yellow glow emanating from one of the second-floor windows. But her experience told her that not everything was always as it seemed. She brought the vehicle to a stop beside a dark-colored pickup and put the gear shift into park. "Let's get this over with."

They exited the vehicle and softly closed their doors as they listened for any signs of trouble or indication that anyone was inside the house. But there was no music or television noise. No voices either. Elkins approached the pickup and shined his light into the cab.

"Do you hear that?" Denton said as she swept her flashlight left and right along the north side of the property.

He turned toward her voice, eyes searching the darkness. "I don't hear anything."

"Exactly ... Not a damn thing."

He smirked and shook his head as he turned his attention back to the truck. "What's the matter? Don't like the woods?"

He was too young—too green—to know what could be waiting for them behind the door of a dark and quiet home. He would learn soon enough. Maybe not tonight or tomorrow. But in one horrible moment of terror, he would lose his innocence. Everyone that put on the uniform did.

Crash!

Reflexively, Officer Denton's dominant hand gripped the butt of the sidearm strapped to her waist as she turned and aimed her light at the house. "Guess there's someone home after all."

***

The bat was an arm's length out of reach.

Jimmy crawled toward it on his belly, gripped the handle, then rolled to his back as something that was no longer Roni pounced toward him.

She landed with a heavy thump, straddling his body, her weapons raised out to her sides as she prepared for the kill.

With a two-handed grip, he brought the bat down in a chopping motion onto the top of her head.

***

Tap, tap, tap.

Denton lowered her flashlight to her side after using it as a makeshift door-knocker. "Sheriff's office." She waited a few moments for a response, then said, "I don't hear anything, do you?"

Elkins had his head leaned toward the sidelight glass with his hands cupped around his eyes. "Nah ... I don't see anything either."

"Any sign of a struggle or break-in?"

"It's too dark to tell for sure."

She knocked again. "Police ... Anyone home?"

Still receiving no response, they slowly walked around the porch, she to the left, he to the right, carefully shining their flashlights along the wood in search of broken glass and peering through the windows while looking for movement or signs of disturbance.

A scream from within the house ripped through the silence, and Denton gripped her holstered Glock. Her body tensed as she shined her flashlight through the sitting room window and trained it on the base of the staircase just in time to see something long and thin fall from the second floor. It landed in a *clatter*, ends bouncing intermittently on the wood floor several times before finally settling. Then it rolled out of sight.

But not before she recognized it as a wooden baseball bat.

"That's good enough for me," she said as she hurried back to the front door, arriving at the same time as her partner. "We need to get in there."

***

Jimmy released the bat, rolled Roni's limp body off his, scooted out from under her, then sat against the wall, chest heaving. The grotesque *thunk* of the H&B making contact with her skull was still fresh and turning his stomach.

She lay in a heap, weapons still clutched in her hands, black hair spread over the floor like a Rorschach test as he watched over her. The woman he loved. The woman he planned to marry in a few short months. The woman he wanted to have children with. The woman he wanted to grow old with.

I've killed her, he thought, trembling as the scream he had been holding in fought to come out. But first, he had to be sure. He leaned forward and crawled silently toward her, only slightly aware of the red and blue flashing lights illuminating the otherwise dark hallway. When he was close enough, he reached out with one hand—

Her body jerked violently, and Jimmy fell backward. He reached for the bat and hopped to his feet. Standing with his feet wide, both hands gripping the H&B, he held the bat out to his side and prepared to swing for the nosebleeds.

She rose to her knees, swaying from the first blow to the head as she raised one weapon and swung it at the wall, grunting as the sharpened claws sunk into the wood. Then she used it to pull herself up. Maybe it was because he was slightly bent over, or maybe it was fear, but she seemed at least a foot taller than before she became this ... creature.

Jimmy firmed his stance.

She lurched the metal claw free from the wall, staggering backward. Then she turned to him—

"AHHH!"

He rushed toward her, hitting her in the gut with the first swing, pushing her backward as she wrapped her arms around him. He broke free, claws scraping his back, then cracked the bat across her shin. She doubled over, howling in pain. He swung and missed ... Swung again and hit her left ribs. She gripped the bat with her left arm and swung with her right. He hopped backward, losing his grip on the bat as she twisted her body.

The H&B soared into the stairwell in slow motion.

Jimmy was defenseless.

***

Elkins nodded and stepped back a few feet. Then with his back foot firmly planted, he swung his dominant leg forward. The wood fractured as his foot landed firmly just above the door handle, but it didn't open. So, he kicked again.

This time, the door gave way with a loud *crack,* and he stumbled through the doorway.

Denton slipped into the foyer behind him with her weapon drawn, flashlight resting on the barrel, while her partner armed himself and pressed his back against the opposite wall.

Quietly, they cleared the two front rooms, then the rookie made his way to the steps. With his flashlight resting over the top of his weapon, he quickly scanned up the first flight as his partner entered the dining room. Once she signaled it was clear, Elkins made his way to the landing and rounded the corner. He aimed his light up to the second-floor hallway and waited for his partner.

After clearing the kitchen, Officer Denton reappeared at the bottom of the steps and began to climb. They were together on the landing for only a few seconds when they heard the *swooshing* sound of something dragging over the wood floor, followed by primal grunts and moans.

Denton tapped her partner's shoulder and signaled for him to ascend to the second floor.

Elkins nodded, eyes trained on the yellow glow from an upstairs room. He took the steps one by one, back against the wall, ears ringing, pulse quickening, his partner a step behind. As he neared the top, he prepared to turn right toward the back of the house—his blind spot—but Denton signaled to hold.

She crossed to the wall opposite him and quickly poked her head around the wall. The light was coming from the front of the house—the southwest bedroom. She lowered her light to the hallway floor and the beam reflected on what appeared to be blood. She signaled to her partner to advance.

Elkins held his breath and scurried across the hall, stopping directly across from the room with the light source while his partner began a sweep of the back bedrooms.

This was the most excitement he'd seen in his few short months on the job. Their small town hadn't had a murder or so much as a bank robbery in years.

But Elkins had his sights set high on the law enforcement food chain. And a bust like this could go a long way toward getting him there.

His training told him to wait for his partner, but, the door in front of him was open, casting just enough light on this end of the hallway to confirm it was clear. So, he stepped forward, heart thumping, his light and weapon aimed at the floor as he made his move toward the room.

***

As the beast that used to be Roni lunged toward him, Jimmy dove out of the way. The sharpened tip of her weapon scraped his thigh, opening a gash in his skin. He hissed in pain as his body crashed onto the floor. But there was no time to tend his wound. He rolled to his back and scrambled to his feet. As she prepared for another attack, he ran into the master bedroom and dove onto the bed, sliding with the bedcovers and landing on the floor.

She stood in the doorway and snarled, "Abaddon will return when I cut out your heart and complete the symbol!"

Then, as if time stood still, he saw his mother sitting beside him on that bench, overlooking his grandmother's pond in Georgia. He heard her voice, reciting a poem or incantation. Repeating it over and over until Jimmy was saying it with her—

> *There's one way to break the spell,*
> *And send the creature back to hell.*
> *The light must see beyond the dark,*
> *And find the love within her heart.*

—He rolled onto his back in time to see Roni leap over the bed and land in front of him. Her eyes were black slits, brows furrowed in rage, clawed weapons ready to strike.

But all he saw was Roni. The woman he loved. The woman he planned to marry in a few short months. The woman he wanted to have children with. The woman he wanted to grow old with.

He only saw her.

As she reeled back, he didn't fight. He didn't try to escape or protect himself. He looked at her and said, "I see you, Veronica Marie Hobbs."

***

Just outside the bedroom, with his back against the wall, Officer Elkins poked his head around the corner so quickly that what he saw didn't make sense. But it appeared to be clear, so he turned his body and entered the room. And as he swept his weapon and light up to follow his line of sight, the scene slowly came into focus.

Blood smears on the wall ... Blood on the floor ... The mattress askew in its frame ... Bedcovers in disarray ... White sheets spattered with blood in an avant-garde pattern like a piece of macabre artwork you would hang on the wall ... A bedside lamp, missing the shade, bare bulb glowing as it lay on the floor ... Blood spray on the ceiling. Blood, everywhere. An enormous amount of blood. Too much for one person to lose and still be alive.

***

"Jimmy?"

It was Roni—the *real* Roni. She lowered her arms and looked at the weapons gripped in her bloody hands. In his wide eyes she saw the reflection of a madwoman she didn't recognize. And beneath her, squeezed between her thighs, the motionless body of her lover.

"I see you," he muttered.

"Jimmy!"

She dropped the claws and wrapped her arms around him, lifting his upper body against hers.

"I see you," he repeated. "I see you, Veronica Marie Hobbs—"

"Jimmy, don't go," she sobbed. "Don't go—"

***

Elkins heard voices mumbling incoherent words. He stepped further into the room, passed the foot of the king-sized bed, and toward the sound until his light cast upon a twisted beast with ragged black fur crouched over a body. In shock, he began to lower his weapon. "Christ, what the—"

"Don't shoot—"

The creature whipped around, hissing and baring its teeth as it peered back with black eyes.

Officer Elkins raised his weapon and fired two rounds—

BAM-BAM!

—A white cloud appeared where the bullets penetrated the drywall, and two shell casings bounced across the floor. The beast was nowhere in sight. The body on the floor—a man—was bloody but alive.

"Hang on, man," Elkins said. "We're gonna get you some help. Just hang on."

"What the hell happened in here?" Denton said as she entered the room behind her partner. "Talk to me, Blake."

"We've got a man down, Dee," he yelled over his shoulder as he swept the area in search of the creature. "Some kind of animal attack ... Call for a bus."

She pressed the button on her radio. "Dispatch, this is 284. Shots fired at 3845 Woody Creek Lane. Ambulance and backup requested."

"Copy that, 284. On the way."

"Where is it, Elkins?"

"I—I dunno ... I missed."

She stepped closer and saw the bloody victim on the floor. "Shit. Cover me." She knelt beside Jimmy as she began removing her belt. "Sir, can you tell me your name? Sir ... Don't close your eyes ... Sir ... "

***

Bette swerved from the middle lane and into the right lane, then veered onto the exit ramp for Woody Creek Lane, coming to a stop behind five other cars halted by the red traffic light. There was no shoulder between her and a steep six-foot drop into a gully, otherwise she would have gone around them.

Instead, she had no choice but to wait as she tapped her red nails against the steering wheel and grumbled, "Come on. Come on"

Finally, the light turned green, but the cars didn't move. For what seemed like forever, they just sat there. "Come on!" she yelled, pounding her palm against the steering wheel.

Out of patience, she was just about to lay into her car horn when an ambulance sped by, lights flashing and siren wailing.

"Jimmy!"

***

"Sir, open your eyes," Denton said as she patted the man's cheek.

As Jimmy opened his eyes, a brown-eyed woman with long lashes and chestnut hair pulled back in a tight bun came into focus.

"He's back," she said to her partner while keeping her eyes on the victim. "Sir, can you tell me your name?"

"James Hobart ... Jimmy."

"Jimmy, I'm Officer Denton, and that's my partner, Officer Elkins. An ambulance is on the way. Can you tell me who did this to you?"

"My fiancé."

"No way that thing is human," Elkins mumbled.

"Did you see where she went?" Denton asked Jimmy.

"Closet ... I think."

The walk-in closet was dark, untouched by the light from the bedroom.

"Elkins, check it out. I'll stay with him."

The rookie nodded as he stepped forward. Then, raising his weapon and flashlight together, he lit up the closet. Blouses, dresses, and slacks had been pulled down along with the hanging rod. Shelves had been swept free of whatever had been there. Drawers had been emptied into a rumpled pile littering the floor. It was moving ... Pulsating like a beating heart. And from somewhere deep within the pile, a susurrant chant.

"I got her," Elkins called out over his shoulder as he stepped closer, Glock trained on the target hidden beneath the clothing ... Closer ... *What is she saying,* he wondered, stepping closer still ... Leaning closer—

"I sssee you, Blake Jossseph Elkinsss."

It sprang up from the floor, scattering clothing around the closet.

Elkins froze.

BAM-BAM! BAM-BAM-BAM!

"Roni!"

Denton fired five shots in rapid succession over her partner's shoulder, striking the creature in the torso and sending it backward onto the floor, howling and writhing in pain.

Jimmy closed his eyes.

Chapter 29

The afternoon Georgia sun reflected on the pond like silver and gold glitter, twinkling and dancing on the soft ripples. The air was thick with honeysuckle and rose petals from his grandmother's garden ... And Noxzema and baby lotion from his mother.

She was beside him on the concrete bench. Her auburn hair swept up off her shoulders. Ruby-stained lips to match her nails. Brilliant blue eyes that made you believe you were swimming in the Maldives.

In the distance, his uncles' deep baritone was nearly overshadowed by the squeals and screams of his cousins playing lawn games. Birds chirped and chattered as they congregated in the pecan trees. But he wasn't a little boy. He was a grown man.

He turned to his mother. "Am I dead?"

"No, sweetheart."

"I've missed you, Mom."

"I've always been with you, Jimmy." Then she placed her hand on his chest. "Right here."

He placed his hand over hers and felt her warmth. "Will I ever see you again?"

"*The light* burns bright in our family tree, Jimmy. And many creatures are attracted to *the light*. You know that now."

He nodded.

"*Shades* are harmless. But others ... Some creatures are better left to the darkness."

Then she faded away, and Jimmy opened his eyes.

Through the fog, he heard *beeps* and *blips* ... Far away voices. Not his uncles or cousins or mother. He blinked and saw tubes and machines on the edge of the shadows. Greg was slumped in a chair in the corner. He turned his head and saw Bette sitting beside the bed, her head resting on his arm. He reached over and touched her curly red hair.

She raised her head. Her eyes were wet and puffy. "Jimmy!" She leaned over him and covered his cheeks and forehead in kisses until her lips were dry. Then she sat down. "I thought I'd lost you."

Greg was now standing at Bette's side with his hand on her shoulder, looking more uncertain than his new lover. "Good to have you back, buddy."

Jimmy's throat was raw. He grimaced as he swallowed, then accepted the straw from a cup of water as his sister held it to his lips. Then he leaned back against the pillow, images flashing through his mind as the pain medication waned. Finally, he lifted the thin hospital linens covering his body. His right leg was elevated and wrapped in bandages.

"You lost a lot of blood," Bette said. "Forty stitches ... Your femoral artery was nicked."

"If not for the quick thinking of Officer Denton," Greg added, dragging his fingertips across his neck.

Jimmy vaguely remembered her tightening a belt around his thigh before blacking out. He winced from the ache in his leg as he tried to scoot up in the bed.

Bette handed him a button attached to a long wire. "Press this for the pain."

He shook his head and waved her off as he settled on the mattress.

"If you won't take the Morphine, then maybe you'll take this," she said as she picked up her oversized handbag and lifted out the fluffy black Maine Coon.

"Mhr-aou."

"Coal," Jimmy gasped, taking the cat from her. "Where did you find him?"

"You were in surgery and then in a recovery room for a while, so Greg and I went back to the house to feed him, and there he was as soon as I opened the door. I didn't want to take the chance he'd hide again ... So, I took him."

He let the cat settle on his lap, then turned to her and said, "Roni?"

Bette squeezed his hand and shook her head. "I'm sorry, Jimmy."

A part of him already knew. He remembered the shooting right before he blacked out. But still, he hoped he was wrong. Now hope was lost. The scream pent up in his belly finally came out as tears. "It was my fault," he said through the sobs. "We shouldn't have bought that house ... I knew something was wrong ... I should have told her."

"You can't blame yourself—"

He buried his face in the cat's fur and listened to the rattle of his deep-throated purr as if it could make everything go back to the way it was.

"Jimmy," Bette said softly, caressing her brother's arm. "What happened?"

He closed his eyes. "*Start from the beginning, and the rest will fall into place.*" Finally, he decided to follow his father's advice.

While he cradled Coal, Jimmy told his sister and Greg a tale that started with that road trip to Georgia. He explained what Bette had overheard—what he now remembered and understood. What ultimately saved his life. "But I'll get back to that part." He continued, telling them about *the shades* he'd seen over the years. How he was never frightened by their presence. How he had kept all this secret from everyone, including Roni.

As he talked about the house on Woody Creek Lane, his pulse quickened, and he began to perspire. His voice quivered when he described the visitations from what he now understood was Abaddon.

"Abaddon?" Bette repeated.

"That's what Roni called him."

"Why is that familiar?"

"She was killing animals and stealing their bones to create a symbol that would free him from his prison."

"Not just a prison," Bette gasped. "A pit of darkness."

"Right—How did you know that?"

She gave a half smile and stared back at him with one brow raised.

He went wide-eyed and tilted his head back, remembering her obsession with dreams, mythology, and the occult. Then as Bette rummaged through her oversized bag, his thoughts returned to Roni ... The mutilated animals ... The bones ... The thing that attacked him. He shook away the memory and quietly said, "It wasn't her ... She wouldn't have. She must have been ... I don't know—"

"Beguiled," Bette said.

"Beguiled?"

"While imprisoned, Abaddon has no physical form," she said as she dropped her bag on the floor. Now she was holding a notepad on her lap and began drawing with a pen emblazoned with a logo from some insurance company. "He needed a host to harvest the bones and build the portal for him so he could emerge with his army and pass judgment on us."

"Do you believe that?" Greg asked.

She shrugged as she continued to draw. "I read a lot of things that sound insane ... Until they don't." She put the pen down and showed her brother the drawing. "Is this the symbol?"

He shook his head. "I don't know. It wasn't finished ... But the triangle is correct."

She nodded. "I've seen this in books and on Tarot cards ... It's probably what she was making. But you said she was trying to *finish* the symbol, right? That means there have been others—"

"And there will be more."

Jimmy sat quietly, contemplating the absurdity of it all. Myths, fairytales, ghost stories ... All meant to entertain or explain things we didn't understand. Fiction. Unless ... The possibility that Abaddon was real and still trying to escape his prison, no matter how farfetched it seemed, was a risk Jimmy didn't want to take. And he thought there may be a way to stop him.

Staring blankly, he said, "I should have bulldozed that root cellar when I had the chance ... When I'm out of here, I will."

"Actually, you can't."

He turned to her. "What do you mean? It's my property. I can do whatever the hell I want."

"I wanted to wait to tell you this," she sighed. Then she leaned over the chair, and when she sat up again, she held a yellow piece of paper with red lettering. "This was on your door when we returned to feed Coal this morning."

He took it from her and read it. "Eviction notice?" He furrowed his brow and reread the words. "But we *own* the house."

"Not according to the county. I did some checking since they wouldn't let me in to see you for hours ... The house is owned by Friends of Woody Creek, LLC—a land trust. As far as the county is concerned, you're a squatter."

"This is bullshit ... We signed mortgage documents ... We wrote a settlement check ... Did you contact our realtor? Millie—I can't remember her last name."

"Well, I tried."

"Let me guess—she wasn't a realtor?"

"Oh, she was," Bette said as she unlocked her cell phone. Then she turned it around so Jimmy could see the screen. "Is this her?"

He nodded.

"Mildred McCleery—Milly to her friends." Bette flipped the phone around, swiped the screen, then showed her brother another image. "Is this the root cellar on your property?"

He remembered the stone tomb just off the forest path and the haunting chant etched into the walls. "Yes. That's where—"

The words caught in his throat as he pictured Roni, the love of his life, enchanted by the demon called Abaddon. Tricked into doing the creature's bidding. *Did she know what she was doing?* he wondered as tears leaked from his eyes. *When she woke from the trance ... When she transformed into that* thing ... *Did she know what she'd done?*

"We don't have to talk about this," Bette said.

He swallowed down the lump and wiped his eyes. "The root cellar ... That's where Roni was making the symbol to release Abaddon. But what does that have to do with Millie?"

"She was found there, hanging from the rafters ... In 1989."

Some months later ...

A small metal sign comes into view at the end of a long conifer-lined gravel driveway. Tied to the sign are three helium-filled mylar balloons colored silver, red, and blue, flapping in the spring breeze.

You lift your foot from the gas pedal and as your vehicle decelerates, you read the sign:

OPEN HOUSE
12 – 4 P.M.

Curious, you turn off Woody Creek Lane and make your approach toward a dilapidated Queen Anne-style Victorian home. You notice the now empty 120 square foot wooden shed with a ten-foot ceiling, barn door opening, and plenty of windows to let in the natural light.

You park and wander around back where thorny rose bushes are displaying a kaleidoscope of yellow, deep red, coral, and pale pink. And beyond them, a row of dogwood trees are adorned in white as their leaves prepare to burst forth.

You climb the porch steps and peer through the windows, beyond the layer of grime and climbing ivy-coated clapboard siding. Inside the empty home, warm, yellow-painted walls seem to welcome you like a field of daffodils.

Then the silence is broken by a *clack* as the deadbolt turns on the front door and it swings open. On the other side stands an out-of-breath woman with round cheeks and wearing a Chanel suit. She pushes the oversized plastic-rimmed glasses up higher on the bridge of her nose, then reaches out her hand.

"I'm Millie," she says. "I was beginning to think those balloons had ripped my sign right out of the ground and carried it away, but here you are. Sometimes, a house waits for just the right buyer."

Maybe that's you ...

Acknowledgements

Thank you, David Jennings, for joining my small team of Beta Readers and providing valuable feedback. You helped make the book better.

I also want to thank my mother who, even though she claims not to like horror, stuck it out and read the entire manuscript ... twice. Mom, you are my litmus test.

Thanks to my awesome team of ARC readers who enthusiastically accept unformatted ebooks without complaint and always tell me what they think. I appreciate you all taking this journey with me.

And thank you, L.A. Dalton, for your editorial insight. You have a keen eye and a passion for what you do. You are talented in so many ways and I look forward to growing our collaboration.

Last but not least, thank you ...

I hope you enjoyed reading "The House on Woody Creek Lane" as much as I enjoyed writing it. Many of the visitations Jimmy Hobart experienced in the book are based on first-hand, true events. Others are completely made up. I'll leave it up to you to decide which is which. Please take a few moments to leave your comments on Amazon, GoodReads, Barnes & Noble, other retail sites, and your blog.

For more information about my books and to join my mailing list, please visit www.claudinemarcin.com. You may also contact me directly at mmadtales@gmail.com and follow me on any of the below platforms.

Happy Reading!

Facebook.com/mmadtales
Twitter.com/marcinclaudine
Instagram.com/claudinemarcin

Made in the USA
Middletown, DE
30 October 2023

41627412R00163